TELL
SOMEONE

KEVIN O'HARA

TELL SOMEONE

JOHN BLAKE

Published by John Blake Publishing Ltd,
3 Bramber Court, 2 Bramber Road,
London W14 9PB, England

www.blake.co.uk

First published in paperback in 2007

ISBN-13: 978-1-84454-347-2

British Library Cataloguing-in-Publication Data:

A catalogue record for this book is available from the British Library.

Design by www.envydesign.co.uk

Printed and bound in Great Britain by Bookmarque Ltd,
Croydon, Surrey

1 3 5 7 9 10 8 6 4 2

Papers used by John Blake Publishing are natural, recyclable products made from
wood grown in sustainable forests. The manufacturing processes conform to the
environmental regulations of the country of origin.

Every attempt has been made to contact the relevant copyright-holders, but some
were unobtainable. We would be grateful if the appropriate people could contact us.

'Be kind.
Everyone you meet is fighting a battle.'

About the author

Kevin O'Hara is from Chorley, Lancashire. He is 39.
With his wife Cathy and their baby daughter, Rose,
he spent just over a year in Spain's Costa del Sol. It was
there that he managed a fitness club during the day and
wrote this, his debut novel, by night. He now has
another beautiful daughter, Violet, and is currently
writing a novel set in the Costa del Sol.

Acknowledgements

To the four most important girls in my life:

To the most giving mum in the world.
I am truly sorry that I haven't been able to give you
back as much love as you have shown me.

To my very understanding wife.
Thanks for everything you have done for me
and thanks for being so patient (with the novel as well!).

To my beautiful daughters.
You don't know it yet, but you have made my life!

Many thanks goes to John Blake for seeing the
potential in this novel. Also to my editor Lucian
Randall, for taking out the rough edges

Contents

1 Love Mum... Hate Dad   1
2 All Grown Up   5
3 The Return of The White Horse   19
4 The Girl of His Dreams   31
5 Pre-Season Training   41
6 Army Bullshit   51
7 Sex Education   61
8 Germany 1 – England 5   65
9 The Pain Game   77
10 The Caribbean Disaster   87
11 Pub Politics   97
12 An Eye for an Eye   107
13 The Monday Blues   113
14 The 'Hot' Date   121
15 Will Things Ever Be the Same, Harry?   131
16 It's Not a Matter of Life and Death   139
17 Beckham the Saviour   147

18 She's the One 155
19 A Real Family 163
20 Respect 169
21 The Winter of Love 177
22 The Charge of the White Horse 191
23 Smackheads Rule 201
24 A Waste of a Life? 209
25 Like Father, Like Son? 217
26 Sorry 229
27 Wedding Bells 241
28 The Beautiful Game 249
29 Your Mum's a Loony 263
30 Nothing But a Lazy Bitch 269
31 Don't Be Dead, Dad 279
32 Love Her as in Childhood... 289
33 End of an Era 297
34 The Jolly Boys' Outing 305
35 Life Really Can Get Better 321
36 Thank You 337

1
Love Mum... Hate Dad
August 1976 (Liam aged 6)

The start of Liam's first ever holiday to Rhyl had been a complete nightmare. He had cried all the way back to the caravan after the incident. In between tears, his sisters had then told their mum that they thought their brother was going to drown before the man rescued him from the sea.

As she tucked him in the bunk bed, his mum promised that his dad would not be angry because of what had happened. However, before he had fallen asleep, Liam couldn't stop his body from shaking and knew that, even though it was his birthday, he would be in trouble again when his dad returned from the pub.

'You stupid little bastard. I heard your mum telling you this morning that you didn't need your coat on.'

For a few seconds, Liam panicked, unable to breathe again. The realisation that this time it was his father pushing down on his chest and he was not back in the sea

1

somehow made him feel safer, secure in the knowledge that his legs would soon be numb.

He still screamed as he felt the burning sensation as his father's free hand whipped down on his upper thighs.

'Jim, leave him alone will you... we nearly lost him, for God's sake!' Liam's mum was banging at the door trying to get into the tiny bedroom, but her husband had wedged his full body weight in the doorway.

'You can stay in the caravan for the rest of the day and don't think you're getting another coat, you spoiled little shit...'

Jim stopped the smacking, but loomed over Liam, swaying, pointing a finger inches from his son's eyes. Liam could see the hate in his dad's grimacing face and smell the alcohol on his breath. He could now also hear his two sisters shouting and screaming from behind the door.

Jim released his grip and staggered out. He wasn't finished yet, though. He pushed his protesting wife back out of the room.

'Leave him in there, Mary.'

'No, Jim, it's his bloody birthday.'

'I fuckin' well mean it... leave him.'

Liam heard more screams and then a thud. It felt like the caravan was going to turn over. As everything quietened down, he tried not to cry. There was only a whimper as he looked down at his reddened legs. He bit into his bottom lip as his body began to shake once more. He made sure his dad couldn't hear him crying by biting into the thick blanket. He didn't want his mum or his sisters to get into any more trouble.

He was woken up some time later by his mum. She

2

spoke very quietly. 'Are you all right, love?' She kissed his forehead before looking under the sheets. Mary could see the outlines of her husband's hand imprinted on Liam's thighs, but managed to stop herself from crying. As she felt round his legs, she realised the sheet was damp.

'Listen, love... your dad was mad because his work flask was in the rucksack with your coat, but he'll be all right after. When he goes back out tonight, we'll have a party for you.'

She changed the sheet and gave Liam another hug and kiss before telling him to go back to sleep. Liam always loved being cuddled by his mum, but he didn't like getting smacked by his dad. He knew his father didn't love him because he never gave him a cuddle.

Liam started drifting off back to sleep, wondering why his dad always hit him and said bad things. He couldn't really understand what had happened. It hadn't been his fault the sea had come in and surrounded him and his sisters. The man who rescued him said that if he had gone under again he would have been dead.

It was the first time he'd been away, but Liam hoped he'd never have to go on holiday with his dad again.

No wonder his older brother Michael hated their dad. Liam also hated him now. He hadn't even wished him happy birthday. He just hoped his mum would buy him another birthday coat.

2
All Grown Up
Sunday, 26 August 2001

Liam woke up and immediately felt round his bum to make sure he hadn't wet his bed again. He was still feeling guilty about the split with Natalie and he knew that the 'accident' he'd had while unconscious had been the final nail in their relationship. If only she hadn't stayed that night they may have still been together. Well, possibly not, because she had become less and less tolerant of his other antics long before that.

Some of the reasons she gave for finishing their two-year relationship he didn't agree with, but even Liam had to admit that he had been drinking more before the split. Perhaps if Natalie had taken more time to listen to him instead of mouthing off she might have realised that her boyfriend had problems, real problems. However, all of Natalie's efforts were apparently focused on ensuring that nobody else's voice could be heard above hers.

Liam had started drinking excessively to forget about

the past, but all she had wanted to hear about was the future, getting married and how good she looked.

Paddy, whom Liam had known since they were both in nappies, had told him that the split had been the best thing that could have happened to him. 'Sorry, mate, but you're better off without motormouth anyway,' he'd said.

Deep down, Liam knew his friend was right. Then again, if he couldn't tell friends whom he had known all his life how much he had started hurting inside lately, then who *could* he tell? Being one of the lads who never seemed to take anything seriously had made it impossible for him to talk to anybody without turning it into a joke. Unfortunately, he had therefore taken an alternative route to erase the bad childhood memories. A route that he had always hated his dad for taking – destination alcohol.

Following his latest bender, his bladder now felt like it was going to explode again. He quickly jumped out of bed and headed for the toilet, expertly managing to avoid the debris scattered over his bedroom floor. After peeing for what seemed like a good five minutes, he drank some tap water to breathe some life into his dry, cracked lips.

On examining his yellowing teeth and seeing the effects of his hangover reflected in the bathroom mirror, Liam knew he was at a crucial crossroads – go one way, and he might find salvation; he didn't even want to think about the other direction. He pressed a finger into the saggy swellings under his eyes and looked closer at the blemishes on his cheeks. He shook his head as he took some more of his dad's tablets out of the cabinet.

He then heard the television booming from downstairs and realised that his mum was already up and about as usual.

'Mum, make us a brew, will you?' he shouted from the landing. With the noise of the television, he didn't think she could have heard his request so he started to make his way downstairs. However, mid-step, before he could say or do anything else, Mrs Mitchell came out of the living room with two empty cups in her hands. She dropped them both on seeing Liam playing naked charades.

'Good morning, Margaret. I'm sorry, I didn't know you were here...' He quickly cupped his hairy bollocks and todger in both hands – fleetingly wishing he really needed to. 'I was just after me mum making us a brew.' With that, he darted back upstairs and into bed.

He could hear his mum at the bottom of the stairs laughing, telling her old friend as they cleaned up the cups that 'he was always messing around' and 'it's about time he grew up'.

It was weird. Liam had been really upset when Natalie had thrown him out of her flat, but now he somehow felt it was meant to be. He had dreaded having to move back home, but now it was great to see his mum back on form.

His dad hadn't been too pleased at the return of his youngest son, but Liam's sisters had said his mum seemed to have gained a new lease of life. Liam had soon become re-accustomed to the pampering.

'Would you like a cup of tea and some toast?'

'Lovely, Mum... you couldn't bring the paper up, too, could you? I am feeling a bit rough.'

'No problem, love. You stay in bed.'

Liam lay back under the warm quilt and did just that. He knew he had taken advantage of his mum since he moved back in, but it gave her something to do – her words. At least her state of mind had improved again.

Then it came, the usual morning urge. His mum would take a good ten minutes to make breakfast and it crossed his mind that he had plenty of time to carry out his favourite one-handed exercise. However, remembering Mad Al's recent embarrassment at being caught in the act by his new girlfriend, he decided against going for it. This was another reason Natalie had found somebody else. Liam knew he shouldn't have told her about his hobby, but his mum had taught him to be honest. Anyway, do women really not know that their boyfriends or husbands masturbate, no matter how good their sex life is? He laughed, remembering the count up in the pub when he told the lads he had been silly enough to tell Natalie about his relaxation technique. Liam had asked for a show of hands to find out how many fellow wankers were present. Out of 14 blokes of differing ages, everyone admitted to indulging in the five-knuckle shuffle, some far more regularly than others.

'There you are, love.'

'You're a star, Mum. I don't know what I'd do without you.'

'Don't be daft, love... if you want anything else just give me a shout.' As she attempted to leave the room without tripping over the clothes, books and shoes, she muttered, 'I'll give your room a clean after.'

She gave him a lovely smile but Liam couldn't stop the thoughts... about how wrinkled her face had become. It was as if she had aged ten years in the last two. He then felt the usual pang of guilt as he heard her making the slow descent of the stairs.

After finishing his toast, he gulped down the cup of tea and began to read the back of his dad's *News of the World* – half-decent football coverage, and tits and scandal on nearly every page. No wonder his dad had started having it delivered. Fair play to him, Liam thought. Then he started to recall the very drunken argument they'd had the previous night. He hoped his old fella had forgotten about the threat of putting his rent up. Cheeky sod, he'd be asking him to pay for the paper next.

He attempted to read, but his alcohol-induced blurred vision wasn't helping him. He was mad at himself for drinking so much again. He had only set out to have one or two beers the night before, but then the celebratory drinking session had kicked in. After years of continual harassment by his former teammates, Paddy's older brother Rob had finally decided to re-form The White Horse football team. Liam just hoped their celebrations weren't premature. Rob, after a quick phone call, had arranged to meet the League Secretary in St George's Club to discuss their chances of being re-elected. He had been rather drunk before going to meet him, so anything could have happened. Liam had always wanted to play one more season with all his proper mates and the lads had been talking about it for years. Bring a team together with a mixture of the older and younger lads now going into the pub and they could win the league and cup double they had won ten years previously, no problem. That was the theory anyway. It might not be the professional football Liam still fantasised about playing, but it was still important to him, even if the standard was pretty crap. His recent back injury, caused by playing 5-a-side, seemed to be better now, so he was raring to play again.

'Eh, Liam, there's a few policemen outside, what d'ya think is going on?' shouted his mum as she collected the milk bottles from the front doorstep.

Liam quickly jumped out of bed to peep out through the gap in his curtains.

'Jesus Christ, Mum, get back in the bloody house, will you?'

Armed police were positioned not 30 yards from their house in a neighbour's front garden further up the street. All of them were pointing their high-calibre rifles in the direction of James Mulligan's house – one of the local drug dealers.

'James, throw the shotgun in the front garden and come out with your hands on the back of your head,' bellowed one of the police officers.

Out came the shotgun, quickly followed by Mulligan, who was told to lie on the floor before being set upon by a number of officers.

'How the fuck did we end up down here?' Liam murmured to himself. He didn't need a reply. His now elderly parents had moved because all five of their children had left the four-bedroom council house they had grown up in. The lure of central heating, double-glazing and a smaller house had been too much for Mr and Mrs O'Sullivan. Unfortunately, Liam knew all about the Pincroft project. The 'new' estate had a notoriously bad reputation, even though it was only the local park that split it from the brilliant old Elsmere council estate he had grown up on. The local authority was making an effort to clean up the area, but new windows, doors, central heating and a change of street names were not having much of an effect on Chorley's version of Beirut. It just meant that the dealers, smackheads, alcoholics, petty criminals and the odd suspected paedophile who came and went were cosier at the taxpayers' expense.

The police vans and cars then screamed away to a hail of abuse from a number of residents, more concerned about their supplies than the welfare of Mulligan.

Liam couldn't believe his mum had ended up in such a place. He felt like crying knowing everything she had been through, and he really wanted to come good on the promises he had recently made her. For now, though, as he slid back into bed, he was starting to become more and more concerned about the pathetic thoughts that had been swirling around his head. If he wasn't going to be around soon, how could he get his mum out of this shit-hole of a place?

Before he could preoccupy himself with anything more depressing, he decided it was time to ring Rob to see if he had put the wheels in motion to get the old team re-formed. Talking football always managed to cheer Liam up.

After finding his tracksuit bottoms and T-shirt, he made his way downstairs. His mum and Mrs Mitchell had just sat back down and were discussing the police activity over another cup of tea.

'What are they picking on him for again? He's a lovely lad... he's always got friends coming to see him.'

Even Mrs Mitchell looked at Liam and smiled.

'Sorry about before, Margaret,' Liam said with a sheepish grin.

'No problem, Liam... I'm used to it with the grandsons.'

Liam didn't know whether to laugh or ask her if she was taking the piss knowing that her grandchildren were only six and seven years old.

'I was out with your Steve last night... we're on about getting the football team back together.'

'Oh, that's what he must have been mumbling on about when he came home. I babysat for him.'

Steve, Liam's new next-door neighbour, was the former Secretary of the football team in the glory years. Unfortunately, he had recently had his own house repossessed, but Liam was grateful he at least knew somebody from the estate.

Liam then heard his dad coughing his guts up in the bathroom and thought he'd better give Rob a call quickly before Mr Misery came downstairs.

He received the perfect answer from Rob and was soon buzzing with the news. 'It's on, Mum. Rob's putting in the application form tomorrow. You couldn't iron some clothes for me while I have a quick bath, could you? He's organising a meeting in the pub this afternoon.'

His mum looked at her friend and they both smiled and shook their heads.

As he climbed the stairs, his dad came out of the bathroom looking like the Grim Reaper.

'Have you been using the phone again, James... Michael... Liam?' his dad growled as they passed each other. Liam had grown up being called his older brothers' names before his dad remembered he had fathered a third son.

Liam grabbed the old man and pretended to throw him down the stairs. He was surprised how much weight his dad had lost in the last few months – he felt like a bag of bones. Was this really the hard man who had scared the hell out of him when he was a kid?

'Stop pissin' around... I'm sick of it, and don't think I've forgotten about last night. I got it out of your mum that you're still only paying £20-a-week board. You've treated this house like a bloody hotel since you moved back in, coming and going when you want.'

'All right, cool it, Dad. I'll be getting another pay rise soon and I'll give you some more board and pay something towards the phone then.'

'Yeah, yeah.'

'Anyway, if you don't chill out, I'm going to tell me mum why you keep taping those "good" films on Channel Five and then only watch them when she's at the bingo, you dirty old sod.'

'I mean it, Liam. And have you been at my tablets again?'

His mum, on overhearing the muffled exchange, took Liam's side as usual. 'Stop picking on Liam, Jim. That's all you do all the time – moan, moan, moan. It's no wonder the others left.'

Margaret passed Jim on her way out.

'Good mornin', Margaret, I didn't realise you were here. I was out with your hubby last night.'

'I believe so. Anyway, I'd better get back, Mary. He'll be wantin' his breakfast.'

Liam really liked Margaret; she had always tried to help

her best friend and the rest of the family, especially through the dark times of his mum's depression.

His dad was oblivious to what had just happened in the street, being partly deaf – particularly when it suited him – and, as normal, he settled down in his chair for the day. The remote control for the television and video, the television page from the *News of the World* magazine and his tobacco were all that he needed until around 9.00pm when he took his daily exercise to the pub. He trawled through the rack for his new Sunday paper and cursed the paper lad when he realised it hadn't arrived.

After opening the bathroom window to let out the terrible smell left by his dad, Liam started to run the bath. 'Bloody hell... 2001 and this house hasn't even got a shower. A long way we've come!' he laughed, thinking back to watching *Space 1999* when he was a kid.

Knowing that the bath would take a few minutes to fill to the top, he settled down on the toilet and attempted to read the paper again. Liam could never have a number two without reading something – anything. He would sometimes run round the house seconds from disaster in his quest to find reading material, preferably with some football news in it.

After reading about Sven-Göran Eriksson saying that England could still qualify for the World Cup, Liam grabbed for the bog roll to wipe his backside, only to find the empty cardboard roll. His dad had done him again. He ripped the back page from the paper and wiped his bottom with Mr Eriksson's face. That's what he thought of England's chances of qualifying. He flushed the toilet, watching the water drown the Swede before jumping into the red-hot bath.

He slumped back, closed his eyes and began to think about why he had been feeling so down lately. Even though she was never going to be his soul mate, the split with Natalie had hurt Liam much more than he had let on to his friends. The truth was that he didn't like being on his own because it gave him too much time to dwell on the past. In fact, everything was becoming an act lately because his job was now starting to get to him. His old army buddy and top shagger Harty had a lot to answer for. Not only had he got Liam working for a Bible basher with a number of personal problems, but also Harty had starting preaching more lately.

Liam opened his eyes, looked down at his stomach and love handles and thought about his current situation. If only he could lose the stone and a bit he had put on in the last year, he would at least start to feel better about himself. His mates slaughtered him for putting weight on while managing a fitness club, but he couldn't help it. He'd not been able to play football for the past six months because of his back and, as football was his life, he'd started to drink even more, eat more and exercise less – all the reasons he told prospective clients why they should join the fitness club.

It wasn't his fault, though. It hadn't helped that Natalie had finally ended their relationship after a reprieve because he wouldn't 'commit more'. She had also tried to stop him playing football – without success. Unfortunately, the split happened just before Liam hurt his back and, on realising that his injury was going to be long-term, he had rung her to try to patch things up. Natalie had then informed him that, after a three-week courtship, she was now engaged and she wouldn't ever consider giving their relationship another go. She finished the conversation by telling him that her new boyfriend had also thought it was disgusting that Liam admitted that he still 'played with himself' while he was in a relationship – the two-faced bastard. It was just like that quote Liam's mate Mad Al had found: 'There are only two types of men in the world – wankers and liars.'

That was it, Liam decided; this was going to be his life-changing season. The re-forming of The White Horse and, with that, the league title, cup, and a new girlfriend. The coveted treble – it was a long shot, but not impossible. He then heard his mum on the stairs.

'Mum, you couldn't bring us up me clothes, could you?'

'No problem, love.'

He jumped out of the bath and on to the scales. Liam was like the male Bridget Jones; he was always checking his weight and physique in the mirror. After breathing in, tensing his upper body muscles and striking a pose, he looked closer into the mirror to squeeze a few blackheads on his nose, and broke into 'It's Not Unusual' by Tom Jones.

'You're a lovely singer,' said his ever-supportive mother as she opened the door slightly and passed him his jeans and T-shirt.

'D'ya think so, Mum?'

'Yes definitely, love, you always have been.'

It was a pity his mum was the only one to think so. He had been dying to sing on the karaoke at The White Horse for ages, but had been musically scarred for life when he was younger. He still remembered, 15 years ago, spending hours singing Rick Astley songs into his own tape recorder before proudly presenting the finished cassette to his first love, Susan. She had taped the Top Forty over it the next day.

'Dad, will you give us a lift to The White Horse?'

'Jesus, Mary and Joseph,' growled Jim in his strong Irish accent – strong, even though he'd lived in Chorley since 1957. 'You better not have used all the hot water.'

Within minutes, they were in the car after the usual 'Look after yourself...' from Liam's mum.

'Bloody hell, Dad, watch where you're going, will you?'

His dad had braked sharply, nearly running over one of the many kids who took it in turns to run from between parked cars playing chicken. After some 'V' signs from a few kids, most of them looking about ten years old, they safely made their way out of the estate.

Liam was always wary when he was in the car with his dad. Jim had been a lorry driver for over 30 years before his firm had been forced to make him take a job in the factory after several accidents and mishaps. Jim had loved the long-distance lifestyle of being away four to five days a week and hated working in the factory. He had therefore recently taken redundancy and, in effect, early retirement, while also putting in a claim for a bad back.

Unfortunately, he still drove his new mobility car as if it was his lorry – grinding through the gears, sitting right on the back bumper of the car in front, and cursing anybody who didn't clearly indicate their gratitude if he let them in front of him.

'Right, Dad, thanks a lot, I'll be in about half-twelve.

Oh, you couldn't lend us 20 quid, could you?'

'Jesus Christ, you still *owe* me 20 quid.'

'Oh, forget it then, you tight old git.'

Liam smiled and waved as his dad pulled away, nearly taking the wing mirror from a parked car.

Handing over the crisp new £20 note at the bar and receiving his pint of Stella, Liam thought to himself how much his dad had changed for the better since he had retired, especially in how he treated his mum. Mind you, he couldn't have got any worse. Liam's own relationship with his father was still up and down. Some days he had a laugh with him and, on others, he still wanted to kill him for what he had put his mum through.

Liam looked over to the group of lads who'd already gathered expectantly – Rob, Mad Al, Paddy, Wolfman, Knobhead and Spanish Phil to name just a few. This was it, he thought, a fresh start, the beginning of his revival – definitely his season.

3
The Return of The White Horse
Sunday, 26 August 2001

'Mind your own bloody business, will you?'

The meeting was only a few minutes old and already there was discontent in the pub ranks. Rob had just started his Churchillian speech about how the pub could win the league and cup double again with the players in front of him when a shout of 'bollocks' had come from the games room. The fact that it was one of the group of girls who had taken over the pool table every Sunday afternoon hadn't gone down too well with a number of the lads. After some more sniggering as Rob had tried to continue, it was obvious that someone had had enough.

'Eh, shut it, you fuckin' lesbians.'

Yvonne was out of the games room quicker than Linford Christie on drugs. 'Which one of you tossers said that?'

Seventeen grown blokes sat in silence as she eyeballed them all, daring anyone to challenge her.

'You lot couldn't beat a friggin' egg, never mind win the League,' she growled, fists clenched, waiting to attack any misguided reply.

'Yvonne, don't let them bother you, come back in here,' a girl's voice called out.

'I'd love to shag that,' murmured Knobhead, with his hand over his mouth, looking over to Yvonne's girlfriend Stephanie, who was now trying to coax her away from teaching the gobby bastards a lesson.

However, Knobhead's attempt at a low voice was, as usual, about to get him into trouble. Yvonne charged at him and used her full 15-stone frame to catapult him from his stool, sending him to the floor. It took two of the lads to drag her off and she only calmed down when Stephanie pleaded with her to 'ignore the Neanderthals' and escorted her back into the other room.

Knobhead dusted himself down and looked round for some sympathy. 'What did I say... what did I say?'

'Phwoooar, what a shame,' whispered Mad Al much more discreetly, as he watched Stephanie's beautiful pert bottom disappear into the partially separated room. 'What a waste to mankind Stephanie is, now she's battin' for the other side. Bet I know who wears the strap-on...'

He was about to continue but Liam kicked him under the table. Al then glanced over to the back of the room, as he remembered Woody had started coming back in the pub. He hoped that he hadn't been overheard. Head down, Woody cut a forlorn figure sitting on his own in his usual place next to the cigarette machine. He had a right to feel upset and humiliated. Three months earlier, his fiancée Stephanie had told him she didn't want to get married and, in fact, had fallen for someone else. If this news hadn't been devastating enough, the second part of her admission had sent him into severe depression. She told him she had been keeping a secret for years. Stephanie had realised she found women more attractive and had fallen for Yvonne when he'd been away on the pub golf trip. The fact that her new lover bore more than a slight resemblance to him had also done his head in and he had vowed never to come in the pub again unless Jack the landlord banned the lesbians.

Of course, Jack had refused. 'It would cause a human rights outcry,' he said.

In reality, Jack was a shrewd businessman and knew that some of the girls could outdrink a number of the lads pint for pint, and two of his bar staff were part of their gang anyway.

Woody, who never really bothered with any of the lads and paraded his ex like a trophy, had only just started coming back into the pub. Liam had still tried to make sure that nobody gave him any stick, but even he couldn't believe that he had come back for more punishment.

'Can we get on with the meeting please?' The noise of Rob banging an ashtray on a table in his usual authoritarian way brought the lads back to attention.

Everyone listened to the manager, not because he was loud, but because he was the most sensible and articulate lad in the pub – until he'd downed four or five pints.

'As I was saying before, I am sure that the application will be accepted. In fact, I *know* the application will be accepted, because I got Derek Davis, the League Secretary, rather drunk in St George's Club last night and he agreed to the application even though the League starts in a week's time. Not only that, but, because of our background, he said he'd push for us to go into the First Division because the Second Division is really shit. I was going to try for the Premier but it would probably be pushing it a bit.'

'How can he do that, Rob? It's ten years since we had a team and half of us haven't played properly for a few years,' reasoned Kenny, keen to have some input, having been captain in the previous golden era.

'*You* know that, *I* know that, but do you think the old fart does? Does he 'eck. I told him I could get a superb squad together. It was also strippers' night there yesterday, so I bunged one of the girls a tenner to drag him on stage. I then reasoned with him that it would probably break his old girl's heart to find out what he'd been up to. I think that probably clinched it.'

'Nice one...'

Within 20 minutes, Rob had everything sorted. Manager – Rob again; Secretary – Steve again; Captain – Liam, probably due to him being one of the only original double winners still playing regularly. Kenny, on the other hand, hadn't played for years but, despite his recent admission that he'd joined the Weight Watchers sessions taking place in the pub, had vowed to make a comeback. The list continued right down to the bucket and sponge man and even fundraising events were arranged. Rob had always been a perpetual list-maker and Liam had never ceased to be amazed by his meticulous attention to detail. These organisational skills had probably helped him get his management position at work. During the week, Rob was a Procurements Manager for British Nuclear Fuels, in charge of buying and selling the raw materials needed for energy production throughout the world but, by night, and especially at weekends, he was definitely one of the lads. Since his recent divorce, he had put himself in charge of organising most of the pub piss-ups including stag parties, golf trips, horseracing days and anything else that would get the lads together.

He finished the meeting by explaining that he had already arranged a training session with daft Mark, an ex-army Physical Training Instructor. For the one and only day of pre-season training, this nutter would be putting the re-formed White Horse football team through their paces to get them in tip-top condition for their opening game in a week's time.

'Fixture and venues are being sorted by the committee and Derek's promised me one of the better pitches,' concluded Rob.

'Bollocks, Rob, we know the venue,' commented Giant, Rob's not-so-small other brother. The first-choice goalkeeper for the coming season knew the venue would be the park where they had all grown up playing together, which was conveniently situated behind the old pub.

'Have you seen those piles of shit lately?' he continued, referring to the 18 pitches which had suffered from an inadequate drainage system for years. The surface had also recently been relined differently to add more pitches. This meant they were now so close together that when you played away you could be ten yards away from your 'home' ground but, if you were really unlucky, you could end up on pitch 18, the furthest from the changing rooms. The walk back was a right bastard, especially in winter.

'The pitches aren't too bad, you know... the council lads do a good job,' interrupted Liam's older brother Mick, who worked for the council on general maintenance.

'Yeah, right, Mick, you won't be trying to judge the bounce from a dodgy back pass from Kenny in the next few weeks and then diving through the shit in December,' replied Giant.

'Neither will you. There hasn't been a game on Croft Park in December and January for three years with the crap weather and, if Kenny gets in the team now, well, there's hope for us all.'

'Hark at the silver fox,' retorted Kenny. 'I'm only 35, not fuckin' 55 like you, you grey old bastard.'

'Thirty-eight actually, and still White Horse's top scorer from the last season.'

'The last season being ten years ago. How many have you scored since then? You haven't been playing.'

'I've scored hundreds since then. I've been playing 7-a-side with the council lads, week in, week out, and I've been banging them in for fun.'

'You'll be counting the goals in the warm-up soon.'

'Anyway, when was the last time you played, Kenny? Probably the last time you saw your dick,' continued Mick.

Kenny's face was a picture as he realised his taking the piss out of his mate's grey hair had hit a nerve and, by the red glow on his face, it was clear that he was now embarrassed that some of the other lads had also started laughing.

'Don't worry, we'll see who's fitter on Tuesday. I may have put a stone or two on...'

'... Or three...'

'... but I'll still be one of the fittest there.'

Liam sat back listening to the banter from his brother and the rest of the lads. The enjoyment of this, his love for football and his other antics may have cost him his relationship with Natalie and it still upset him, but the craic was superb.

As he looked round the room, it felt like the clock had been turned back ten years. Yes, Mick's new nickname was the Silver Fox; Rob had started wearing slacks all the time; and Mad Al had got madder... but it was still the boys being boys.

Since his arrival, the landlord had also ensured the pub had kept its old worn-out look by keeping the same décor and furniture that had graced the interior for the last 20 years or so.

'As long as we pull a good pint and don't run out of beer, the punters don't mind too much,' Jack had recently told Liam.

'Yeah, but you could change the jukebox tracks more than once every five years, Jack.'

For all his well-hidden problems, Liam couldn't ask for a better set of friends. Some of them had lived away, but they all seemed to have made their way back to Chorley. Everyone had also always looked out for each other in the past, through the good times and the bad.

Over the years, one or two of them had gone off the rails – drugs, prison, broken relationships, divorces and the rest – but overall they all seemed to have got a grip and done well for themselves. In a lot of respects, it was better than that. The team would be made up of managers, businessmen and self-employed builders, but it didn't really matter what occupation any of the lads had aspired to or ended up in; there was still a definite bond.

However, Liam knew that everyone had different priorities now and, with the majority of the lads now ranging in age from late twenties to late thirties, it was bound to happen. Some of the group had been going round the same pubs in Chorley for the last 20 years or so, and this was undoubtedly taking its toll. He also knew that the women in the older lads' lives were starting to gain more and more influence over them. There were exceptions, of course – his brother Mick and Kenny – but nobody would ever tame Kenny. Two common-law wives and countless girlfriends spanning nearly 20 years had tried, but he was still dipping his wick all over the place.

Liam had also declared that having responsibilities was not for him. Or so he'd told the lads who were in relationships, but underneath he couldn't resist feeling jealous of what they had managed to achieve – their own homes, a wife or girlfriend, children... they had adult lives. What did he have? Apart from a mum he loved to death and a dad who had been a right bastard when all the kids were growing up but to some extent was better now... not a lot, he thought. He was 31 years old, still lived with his mummy and daddy, and was overweight and single – *very* single.

As the lads discussed the previous day's football, Liam sat back, contemplating again his situation compared to the majority of his apparently contented friends. He decided it was time to stop wallowing in the past, time to stop having the black thoughts and get a move on in life before it passed him by. He was even flirting with the idea of not having another pint and commencing his diet there and then before Mad Al brought him back to his senses.

'Right then, who's for getting hammered? Let's celebrate the re-forming of the team with an all-dayer before we get down to the pre-season training on Tuesday.' Al also knew that Man United were playing Villa and had already cleared it with his new girlfriend to stay out for the day.

'You might win today, Mad Man, but you'll only be above us for a day before we beat Liverpool tomorrow night.'

'Yeah, right.'

'White army... white army...'

All the Bolton lads couldn't believe the start their team had made to the season and were milking it before the inevitable relegation battle started. Liam always enjoyed the football chat and, with a pub full of supporters from other teams such as Man United, City, Blackburn, Everton, Preston, and even an Arsenal fan in the shape of Knobhead, the banter was relentless.

After some legitimate and some lame excuses for not staying out, it was clear that there were only a few of the usual suspects going to venture into the town centre. This was apart from some of the younger lads who had only just turned up and probably still hadn't been to bed.

Mick was always a definite for a Sunday all-dayer even though he was 'happily married' with two lovely kids. Liam didn't know how his brother managed it. He'd been staying out round the pubs for the last 18 years. That's how long he'd been seeing his wife Dawn. Sometimes, he would tell Dawn he was going to get his hair cut on a Friday afternoon and she wouldn't see him until Sunday night. His nickname down the council was Bob Geldof – 'I don't like Mondays' – and his illegal long weekends were legendary. He more or less worked a four-day week, but could get away with it working for the local authority. He always pointed out it wasn't a real job anyway. Although Liam had had a number of run-ins with him, reminding him how his dad treated their mum when they were younger, he'd reached the point where he just let him get on with it.

Rob, another all-day specialist, was different. He may have already been divorced but he now had a superb relationship with his girlfriend Karen – plus she was one of the straight girls who worked behind the bar at The White Horse on Sunday nights. So, if the lads made it back to the karaoke, she would be able to carry him home anyway.

Mad Al was a bit like Liam – still searching for somebody to put up with him and his crazy idiosyncrasies. His latest girlfriend Maria seemed really laidback about everything. She would have to be for the relationship to work. The 'Mad' had been added to his name as the lads had grown up because he was definitely a one-off. Some of the conversations and situations Al and Liam had shared over the years had been so off-the-wall it was ridiculous. However, he had recently told Liam that he was really hopeful that he'd found the 'right one' with Maria. To show that he was serious, he had even given away his legendary porn collection to a work colleague. Liam knew he must have wanted to give it a real go if he'd dispensed with *Debbie Does Dallas*. Maria had already forgiven him for his first indiscretion, so Liam was more hopeful than usual for his mate.

As the taxis arrived to take them to The White Bull, Liam was already feeling merry and was glad Big Rory had decided to join them. To say Rory, an ex-Marine, could handle himself was putting it mildly. However, the 'Big' nickname didn't arise just from his impressive frame, but from his huge dick. Rory was hung like a donkey and his party piece of getting his willy out and flopping it into a pint pot until it touched the bottom of the glass usually went down well with the slightly envious lads and, in certain situations, even impressed some of the ladies. Mind you, this was more likely to be in the less sophisticated places they had frequented.

Liam knew it was going to be a good night; with these lads, you couldn't go wrong.

4
The Girl of his Dreams
Monday, 27 August 2001

Liam woke up and immediately wished he hadn't. His head was throbbing and his mouth tasted like somebody had done something nasty in it. His lips were so dry again he started to whirl his tongue round and round on them to try and bring them back to life.

As he began to stretch, he realised his left hand was hurting like hell and, not only that, his double bed seemed more cramped than usual. Then he opened his eyes. Oh no, there was a girl in his bed... he tried hard to kick-start his brain into an explanation, but failed. She was presently crushed up against the wall and, for the moment anyway, still seemed to be asleep.

Liam moved away from her, lifted the quilt and realised that, although he was naked, she still seemed to have all her clothes on. This was becoming even more bizarre. He peered more closely to get a look at her face and instantly got a flashback from the previous night. It was the girl he'd been eyeing up earlier in the night in the Wine Lodge. He tried to think back, but couldn't remember a thing after coming out of the Tut 'n' Shive a few pubs later. As he continued to look at her, somewhat perplexed, he couldn't help thinking how gorgeous she still looked even while she slept. The beauty looked like an Egyptian goddess with her arms folded across her chest, opposite hands positioned on opposite shoulders. Her skin was very tanned, but not a Chorley bird sunbed tan. She also had a really dark, foreign look about her with natural jet-black hair. Her sleeveless top revealed she was slim as well, which Liam had remembered he had observed the night before. He was pleased his beer goggles hadn't let him down for once. There had been one or two occasions in the past when he had woken up with the monster at his side looking nothing like the supermodel he had met the previous night.

He started to think of what he could say when she woke up to try to find out what she was doing in his bed. The obvious signs were that, unfortunately, nothing intimate had taken place. He only hoped he hadn't embarrassed himself and, oh God, he didn't even have a clue what her name was.

He had just about plucked up enough courage to wake her up when the worst thing in the world happened. The one act he had unbelievably managed to avoid over a 15-year period of getting girls back to his parents' house happened. His dad got up to go to the toilet. Liam wished he could find some ear defenders to cover the goddess's ears. In fact, that's what he'd do; he would get something, *anything*, to block her ears to stop her hearing what was going to transpire in the next 15–20 minutes. He thought about putting a pillow over her head to reduce the noise, but what if she woke up at that point? Probably not a good idea. It hadn't bothered him when any of his mates stopped at his parents' house before. In fact, what was going to be heard very shortly had been a badge of honour in the pub with the lads. Some of his mates had thought Liam's dad was the best thing since sliced bread and the soon-to-be-heard performance was legendary in the pub. But not for this particular audience member, please God, no...

'Jesus, Mary and Joseph... is life worth livin'?' and so it began.

Liam's bedroom was only separated from the bathroom by a paper-thin dividing wall and you could hear everything that went on in there. His dad had risen in his usual hungover, self-pitying mood, no doubt forgetting that he'd been retired for the last two years and didn't really have a care in the world. Then it started. The coughing, farting and crapping in sequence. Jim seemed to have mastered this over the years; it was as if he was playing a tune. He would cough, although the word doesn't remotely do justice to the horror of the act; this was an explosion that had nearly 50 years of smoking written all over it. It came from the core of his stomach, through the length of his windpipe and then out in the form of gobs of mucus into the sink, expertly or luckily positioned next to the toilet so he could lean on it. Then he would fart copiously, and finish with a barrage of the contents of his bowels into the pan as he sprayed the toilet with the previous night's Guinness.

At the climax of his dad's symphony, Liam wanted to curl up and die but, as he looked at the vision lying next to him, she turned on her side and carried on sleeping. The coughing, farting and shitting seemed to go on for ages, as if Jim was emptying himself of the previous night's poisons to leave room for more self-abuse today. Liam always knew that his dad had finished when the smell of cigarette smoke wafted into the bedroom, confirming that his ablutions had been completed, and that he was rewarding his efforts with a congratulatory fag. He had survived another day. He would then remember that he didn't have to go to work and that he could go back to bed and stay there until his wife made him his breakfast.

When his parents' bedroom door closed, Liam knew he had approximately an hour or so to get rid of the goddess. Get rid of the goddess? He couldn't believe it. Since Natalie had kicked him into touch, he'd had a few dates and liaisons but none of them measured up to this. He was chuffed that his mum had tidied his bedroom and it did at least look decent. Liam had made it into a mini-flat since he had moved back in, and spent a great deal of his time in there with the intention of not inhaling the 60-plus cigarettes his parents consumed between them per day. Looking round the room, while wondering whether he had the bottle to wake the sleeping princess, he thought back to the women he had persuaded back to his shag palace over the years. He didn't have to think long and he wouldn't have had to use more than one hand to count. In fact, a great deal of his sex life had revolved around one hand. At least in the past he'd always made sure that the girls he did manage to get back were out of the house before his dad had surfaced and he'd also made sure that they didn't see the rest of the house.

Liam felt guilty that he was embarrassed about his parents and, in a way, about his council-house upbringing, too, because to a large extent he was really proud of his background and especially his mother. Bringing five kids up almost single-handedly, while her husband worked away during the week and then lived in the pub at the weekend, had taken its toll on his dear old mum.

For now, though, he just hoped he could sneak this exquisite creature out of the house without her noticing that she had somehow ended up down the roughest estate in Chorley.

What should he do? Wake her up and ask her what had happened? How should he act? Was it as good for you as it was for me? Maybe not, especially with the evidence that nothing seemed to have taken place.

He was about to tap her on the shoulder when she started to stretch, before letting out a small yawn. Liam used this as a cue to make contact with her, hoping she could speak English, such were her amazing Mediterranean looks. 'Excuse me, I'm sorry to bother you, but...'

She turned to face him and he nearly came on the spot. In fact, thinking back to when he was a young lad, he hoped at this moment that she would not require full sex. The dreaded premature ejaculation syndrome he had managed to train himself out of over the years seemed ready to raise its ugly head much too quickly in the next minute or so.

'Thanks for last night,' she said softly. 'I don't know

what would have happened if you and your friends hadn't stepped in.'

She looked Mediterranean, but she definitely had a Chorley accent – not as broad as usual, but there was definitely a bit of Chorley in her. Liam couldn't help thinking that he would have been pleased to give her a little more Chorley right there and then.

She explained she had been on the taxi rank alone after losing her friends when she had started to receive some unwanted attention from three or four youths.

'These young lads started saying things to me about going home with them. I wasn't really that bothered at first because I know what it's like on the rank. I must admit, though, I started to get scared when one of them started touching me and nobody seemed to want to intervene or say anything even though I was telling him to stop it. That was until you and your friends arrived. You were absolutely brilliant and I can't thank you enough.'

Liam was half-listening to her, but the other half was just mesmerised by her face, especially her gorgeous, big brown eyes. He let her do all the talking while he tried to look shocked. He hoped she hadn't spotted the odd glance he'd had at her breasts. Control yourself, control yourself, he repeated to himself as he also found himself falling in love with her voice.

She wasn't sure what had happened to the two lads who were with Liam, but along with him they had intervened when one of the youths had blatantly put his hand up her skirt. A fight had ensued with others also becoming involved. It turned out that Liam had been a hero by protecting the damsel in distress before ushering her into a taxi. They had both then escaped the mêlée that had broken out all along the queue. The usual Sunday-night Wild West show on the rank was legendary, as everybody tried to make their way back to their locals in the hope of a lock-in.

Kate – as Liam later discovered she was called – had tried to talk to Liam in the back of the taxi, but he had passed out. She was worried that he had taken a blow to the head, even though it seemed he had been luckier than his friends.

'When the taxi driver told me he knew you, I was really pleased when I realised you lived near me.'

'Why? Whereabouts do you live?' Liam felt embarrassed as his voice came out posher than usual. Live near him? She couldn't be the single diamond emerging from the rubble of Beirut, could she? Or an Elsmere girl who'd been hidden from all the lads for the last two decades? No, of course not. It turned out she was from the Collingswood Estate situated at the other end of the park, out of bounds to the riff-raff – middle-class suburbia.

'The taxi driver managed to lift you out of the car, but he was struggling so I gave him some help after you had fallen over and he couldn't get you back up.'

'Oh, I'm so sorry.' Liam could feel his face burning.

'No, don't worry about it. He then got a message on his radio and, as I was struggling with you to open your front door, he drove off. You just walked straight upstairs, but I was worried about you and, being a nurse, I thought I'd just make sure you were OK. I just lay next to you for a while thinking I would get a taxi, but I must have fallen asleep.'

A bloody nurse... Liam had visions of her in her nurse's outfit, but had to visualise an old matron with sussies on, otherwise Kate might start wondering what was poking into her side.

He decided that the best scenario would be to evacuate her before his mum and dad emerged from their bedroom and at least try to obtain her phone number. Liam realised that the skimpy outfit and high heels she was wearing weren't conducive to her current surroundings, and Kate gratefully accepted the lift he offered. He slipped on his boxer shorts and apologised for his former nakedness, but she didn't seem bothered.

Once dressed, it was Liam's intention to take Kate straight home, so, as he guided her out of his room, it was a shock to see his mother coming out of her bedroom with just her nightie on.

'Good mornin', love.' She then smiled in that motherly sort of way. She looked at Kate and repeated the pleasantries before adding, 'What a beautiful girl... much nicer than the last one...' and that was it; she headed for the loo.

Liam looked at Kate with an apologetic face and she stifled a giggle. He refrained from giving her a tour of the house and headed straight outside and to his car. Four or five young lads aged about 14 were already out playing football a little further down the road and, on seeing Kate, they all stopped and gawped.

'Eh up, Liam, she's gorgeous,' one of them shouted.

'Did you give her one?' shouted another.

At this stage, Liam wanted to jump on the bonnet of the car and tell the world he'd shagged the living daylights out of Kate, but he thought better of it. As he drove out of the estate, he felt like telling her to duck her head down if she didn't want to be seen, but the reality of it was that he was the one who felt humiliated. He started to feel even more subdued as his hangover kicked in. After Kate told him that she had just returned from working in Saudi Arabia, he managed to tell her that he had also lived abroad, having served three years in Germany in the Army. She seemed really interested but Liam, for once, felt overawed by the situation and thought she was out of his league.

'OK, I just live here on the right.'

She had told Liam she was back living with her parents after she had returned from abroad. However, she hadn't told him her parents owned a bloody mansion.

'Thanks once again.' Before Liam realised what was happening, she leaned towards him and gave him a kiss on the cheek. 'Might see you around then?'

'Yeah, no problem, I'll see you around.'

She waved as she headed off down the drive.

'No problem, no bloody problem, I'll see you around.'

Liam punched the steering wheel. He couldn't believe how pathetic he had just been. He knew he should have said more on the short journey and made an attempt to obtain her number, but his mind had been elsewhere. He couldn't believe the feelings he was already having for this girl. It felt like his head was going to explode.

Get real, he told himself, as he began the journey home. He didn't really think he had a chance with Kate. He felt even more ashamed of where he had ended up as he drove out of middle-class suburbia and back to his estate. At that point, he felt sure it was the only ride he would be getting with the goddess.

5
Pre-Season Training
Tuesday, 28 August 2001

Liam arrived late at the training session on the park due to the usual traffic jam on the M62. The lads were jogging round the outside of one of the pitches and there were already gaps all over the place as Daft Mark's jogging pace at the front was quicker than some of the lads' running pace at the back.

Turning to face everybody, the ex-PT instructor started to scream out his orders. 'Right, you shower of shit, when I say one, you go down and do press-ups; two and you do sit-ups; three you jump up and head the imaginary ball – no fuckin' slacking, it's only a warm-up.'

Liam joined the back of the rabble, but his timing couldn't have been worse. Kenny was the last man and, as Liam went to overtake him, he was met by projectile vomit as his team-mate got rid of the previous night's alcohol. He noticed Kenny's black eye straight away.

'You dirty bastard,' was met by a 'sorry', but Liam wasn't

really bothered and carried on jogging, laughing, looking down at his new boots covered in puke.

The banter was already flying about Kenny's fitness level but, by this time, he was walking so probably couldn't hear it anyway.

Even Daft Mark realised that most of the lads were completely knackered after a couple of laps of his 'warm-up pace' and the workout was toned down as people began to be lapped. Liam surveyed the scene and started to have second thoughts about the historic double chances. However, he was pleased to see Gazza, one of the young lads from the Pincroft Estate, running in front of him. His next-door neighbour, Steve, the man in the know, had told Liam that, although he had dabbled with hard drugs in the past, Gazza was a great footballer. Liam had been round to his house to persuade him to come to training, knowing that the older lads could do with some help. However, he had been surprised that the 18-year-old lived alone and, after talking to him, didn't think that he was going to turn up.

Apart from Gazza and four or five other under-twenties, most of the lads were anything from late twenties to thirty-something or above and it was showing.

The young lads weren't carrying an ounce of fat between them and the body shape differences were even more evident when the 8-a-side game started and went to skins against tops because the mad ex-PTI had forgotten the bibs. At the mere mention of skins, the young lads had quickly removed their tops so they could stay on the same side and also show everyone their six packs. Liam was instantly jealous of their physiques, and knew that he only had to adopt some of their lifestyle regimes to acquire this athletic look. However, theirs wasn't a training routine, more your four or five Ecstasy tablets and some cocaine every Friday and Saturday night, followed by up to six hours' dancing and no real food 'til Wednesday. This wasn't for Liam, as he liked his beer and food too much, couldn't dance and his one foray into drugs had ensured that he would never take any illegal substances ever again.

On seeing a couple of them comparing their abdominals, City Simon wasn't impressed and shouted, 'You skinny bastards, you look like Cambodians.'

The reply of 'What's a Cambodian?' showed either the difference in age or simple ignorance – or both.

Liam quickly moved over to the opposite side of the pitch so he didn't have to remove his top. He knew he was fitter than most of the lads but he was obsessed about his beer gut and love handles. Kenny, though, didn't give a toss. He was very astute and realised that the young lads would run around like whippets compared to the older lads, and his running would be done for him.

'Jesus, Kenny, when's it due?' and 'Who ate all the pies?' were the immediate taunts as he revealed his beer belly, man tits and workman's bum to everybody.

As the game got under way, it looked like it was going to be a mismatch, but Liam and Riggers, one of the hardest players he had ever played with, had other ideas. Liam was still quite a decent player and a leader on the pitch, so, while the young lads ran round like headless chickens, he had organised his side so they were playing as a team.

Riggers was just trying to kick the shit out of anything

that moved. He was not only built like a brick shithouse but had the even scarier feature of having a false eye. He had mellowed in the last few years after getting married and he now had a daughter, but he had told Liam recently that he couldn't wait to get playing again. He growled as he ran towards any of the opposition and the ball was quickly released before he tackled or assaulted the player. The Everton fanatic was a superb laugh away from the pitch, but on it he had always been an animal. Ten years previously, he had received a long ban after a horrible tackle had left the opposition's centre forward and best player with a broken leg. The lads had gone on to win the crucial game and, in turn, the League. However, Riggers had then been upset with Liam after the match when it was revealed that the player he'd maimed hadn't, in fact, called him a blind bastard, but had actually told another player to knock it to him on his blind side. The new captain was not only a decent organiser, but had always been a motivator on the pitch with his ability to wind the players up.

The game calmed down after a while, as everybody including the youngsters became increasingly tired. It was great to be playing again and it was even better for Liam that he'd been able to bring a number of the lads out of their various stages of retirement to have another go. He'd continued playing for the last ten years, injuries permitting, but at 31 even he realised that he may have to give up on his constant fantasy of playing for England. He would now even consider his dad's team. He still remembered the argument with his old man when he was 11 years old. His dad had shown a smidgen of interest in him, telling his mates in the pub his youngest lad was going to play for Ireland. Crying his eyes out, Liam got a smack for his troubles when he stubbornly pledged his allegiance to England and his boyhood hero Kevin Keegan with an 'I'll never play for Ireland' rant.

After a good hour-and-a-half of jogging, sprints and 8-a-side, the first and last training session before the season began had finished. As everybody sat round gulping the water down, at least half of them lit up cigarettes, sucking on them as if they were sticks of Lucozade, not a potential killer.

'That's better,' gasped Liam's brother Mick as he lay back and inhaled a roll-up.

Most of the lads were also smoking roll-ups as Mick's illegal business was flourishing.

'Anybody need any more tobacco, wine or beer? I'm going over to France this weekend. Oh, I've also started the trips to Spain. If any of you know anybody who can fly out midweek, let me know, I'll pay for the flights. I already have strips of two hundred Lambert and Butler priced 25 quid and Regal King Size priced 27 quid and some baccy.'

He began to take his orders as Rob arrived, still suited up, fresh from Manchester Airport and his business meeting in Germany.

'All right, lads, how's it going?'

A few groans and nods of heads confirmed to Rob that the lads had been put through it as required by Daft Mark.

'Right, before you go, I just want to go through a few things.' Rob opened his briefcase and took out his notebook.

'Here we go again,' whispered Kenny. 'The tactics have been sorted out on the plane.'

Rob began his lecture. 'It's all changed now, lads. I want you all to have a look at what you're eating, cut down on the alcohol intake if you can, and go easier on the fags.'

'You're taking the piss, aren't you, Rob? What you trying to do, put me out of business?' Mick blurted out.

He was probably serious, too, as he seemed to be doing all right out of being a tobacconist, his new car a testament to his shrewd workings.

Rob continued, 'You need to do more stretching before and after matches and even in the mornings and at work when you've got time.'

Sniggering broke out among the foot soldiers.

'Look at the older lads in the Premiership... some of them are even older than you lot and they're still going strong. You've got to get a grip, work hard and look after yourselves more. Sentiment won't come into it this season.' He shot a glance at Kenny who was now lying flat on his back, belly sticking over his shorts, eyes closed, with his face beetroot red from his exertions. 'I'll be picking people on merit, not how good they were ten years ago and I'm still hoping to bring in one or two new faces before the weekend to up the competition.'

The lads all looked at each other, wondering who he could mean. They didn't want any fancy dans coming in and upsetting the status quo and they definitely didn't want anybody who was going to turn up and play and then not go back to the pub for a few beers.

Rob pulled some more paperwork out of his briefcase. 'Right, everybody, sign these forms so I can get them back to the League Secretary before Thursday. If anybody you know wants to play but isn't here, sign one for them. Knobhead, remember, sign *their* name, not yours. You'll be pleased to know we are at home against the Caribbean Club.'

'Those black bas—' Knobhead was going to continue before a poke in the back from a corner flag winded him. 'Only joking, Phil, some of my best mates are black...' He'd forgotten that Spanish Phil's wife was black and one of her brothers played for the Caribbean Club.

Liam was now seriously worried. The Caribbean Club had not only been The White Horse's main rivals ten years ago, but had continued playing when the Horse had disbanded. He'd been down watching them at the end of the previous season and still recognised a number of the lads he used to have the odd rough and tumble with. The really worrying thing was that, although they had obviously aged and dropped down a division, they still looked very fit compared to most of the pot-bellied lads in front of him. Even more worrying was that some of their sons were now playing and they were lightning fast.

Rob could sense the apprehension. 'Look, lads, it's better to get the hard games out of the way first. We'll catch them cold and have a right go at them. Oh, I nearly forgot... Jack's putting a karaoke night on Saturday as well this week and it starts straight after the Germany–England game. There will be raffles on and everything.'

'The money-grabbing bastard. It's only because the pub will be packed. He'll be pissed off when we all do one when we get hammered... we haven't got a friggin' chance.' Jack was definitely not going to be on Kenny's

Christmas card list after they had fallen out over a bet, but he did have a point. Nobody was giving England a chance and everybody was just hoping they could sneak in through the back door of the play-offs.

Liam couldn't believe what he was now hearing. Rob had just been harping on about cutting down on the booze and was now inviting everybody to get bladdered the night before the start of the season.

Giant, who at 6 foot 5 and 20 stone would hopefully take some beating, started rubbing his rather large hands. 'John Smith's Smooth, £1.10 a pint... I'm gonna get leathered.'

'Right, that's it for tonight, anybody fancy a pint?' Rob was ready for a bar meal and a few scoops.

You could hear the groans as some of the lads struggled to their feet.

'Same time next week then, Mark,' shouted Rob, as the fitness freak prepared to run the five miles back to his house.

'No problem, Rob, but they'd better be up for it next week or they're in the shit.'

Within seconds, Mark had his Bergen on his back and away he went. Liam laughed as he quickly disappeared from sight. He was glad that he had only spent a relatively short time in the Army compared to the nutter's 12 years. He had no doubts that the ex-Para would be fully institutionalised and was probably still as green as ever. Everybody he knew who had been in for a long period in the forces seemed to struggle to adjust back in Civvy Street and he presumed that, even though he didn't really know him, Mark would now be in one of the uniformed services.

'Where's he work, Rob?' asked the ex-Marine Rory.

'Oh, he's a prison officer at Strangeways and he's on nights.'

Rory looked over to Liam and they both smiled. He was another who only did a three-year stint and had managed to stay out of uniform once he'd left. Out of all the lads, Browny had been in one of the services the longest – ten years in the Navy. However, Rory and Liam constantly took the mickey out of him and said that the Navy didn't really count because they were all arse bandits.

As the lads jumped into their company cars, work vans and clapped-out old bangers, Liam heard the shout of 'We're goin' to win the League'. He presumed it was Mad Al and his younger brother Tony, both Man United fans, because, after the training session they'd just had, he was having grave doubts about The White Horse's title ambitions.

Kenny made his way across the car park to Liam. 'What happened to that bird on Sunday night? Did yer give her one?'

'You wouldn't believe me if I told you what happened, Kenny.'

'You did, didn't you? Go on, tell me it was worth me black eye and Rory nearly getting arrested.'

Liam looked over to Rory who was shaking his head, smiling his normal Cheshire Cat grin.

'I wish I had, she was absolutely stunning.'

'I know she stayed at yours. Dave the taxi driver dropped you both at your house and he said he did one to give you a chance.'

'Well, I'll buy him a pint this weekend... but I didn't get anywhere.'

'Yeah, right.' Kenny wasn't having any of it.

Liam felt a familiar stiffening just thinking about Kate. He hadn't been able to get her out of his mind.

6
Army Bullshit
Friday, 31 August 2001

Work had been boring all week. The training session had been a welcome release from the monotony and, even though Liam had felt like an old man climbing out of bed the previous couple of days, he felt great for being back playing.

The job situation had to be sorted, though. As he arrived at the fitness club, all he could think was 'not another day'. The long hours and the 40-mile round trip to Bury had finally started taking its toll. It had been exciting helping set up the club and meeting new people for the first year or so, but now he was completely bored talking to the same old faces about the weather, their jobs and their personal lives. Ian, his boss, was also becoming more and more erratic. Liam was always sympathetic when Ian had talked about his problems, especially those concerning his father, but lately Liam had felt like he was just banging his head against a brick wall.

TELL SOMEONE

As he sat at his office desk, he picked up a pen and scribbled in his diary: 'Need a new job!'

At least the process would be simpler than leaving the Army. Realising on the first day of your new 'career' that you had made a mistake and then only being able to rectify that mistake three-and-a-half years later had taught Liam a harsh lesson, one of many the Army had taught him. For a start, being one of the main lads at his school had not prepared him well for basic training. It was a shock meeting blokes from the big cities for the first time. Being the youngest recruit in his intake had also proved very challenging.

Liam had only really been out of Chorley on family holidays and the odd school trip. He had never even been on a long rail journey before and he still vividly remembered arriving at London's Euston Station to go to Woolwich Arsenal, home of the Royal Artillery, as if it was yesterday. He'd cried on the train, as the homesickness and trepidation of what was about to happen kicked in. It had started only as a few tears, but the initial thoughts of missing his mates and not being able to watch Bolton play had turned towards thinking about his mum and this had changed the tears to sobs as he buried his head into the sleeve of his jumper.

When he had left the house an hour or two earlier that morning, he'd hugged and kissed his mum and looked into her eyes, but they had been empty. It was as if she wasn't really there taking it all in. He felt terrible. Was he running away from all his problems, or was he just a young lad chasing a dream after one of his mates had told him how good it was in the forces? At 17 years old, he didn't really know himself at the time.

On the train, an old lady had asked if he was OK after

she saw the tears rolling down his face as the conductor stamped his ticket.

'Yeah, yeah, thank you,' he'd said.

It was always the older people who showed concern. He had become a blubbering boy who, the night before in front of his mates, had been a man bragging about how he was ready to take on the world.

No, this rough, tough kid would be OK once his hangover had disappeared. It must have been the alcohol making him all teary and depressed, he had thought.

The officer waiting at the pick-up point outside the station convinced Liam straight away that the Army wasn't for him. This bastard would be the one who would help to make his life hell for the next 16 weeks and turn his thoughts towards suicide for the first time.

'What's your fuckin' name?'

Liam looked at this monster of a man, in his shining brown uniform and red beret, and couldn't get a word out.

'What's your fuckin' name?'

Liam still couldn't speak as the fear set in.

'Are you deaf or what?'

'Err... Liam O'Sullivan.'

'Oh, you're the Irish bastard, are you? Get on the coach. I'll deal with you later.'

Irish bastard? He must have got mixed up. Liam was from Chorley in Lancashire. Yeah, his dad may have been Irish, but Liam was proud to be Chorley born and bred.

He had then sat near the back of the coach for the journey to the training depot. Within minutes, he felt even more intimidated as men who looked much older than him talked to each other in voices he'd never really heard before, except on the television – Scousers, Geordies, Jocks, Cockneys and accents he couldn't even make out all made the bus come alive. They all seemed to be competing to see who could be the loudest as they tried to hide their own insecurities. Liam just sat and listened, but didn't say a word as he was too scared. He nodded and shook his head, hopefully in the right places, but couldn't really understand most of what was being said as two Geordies and a Scouser spoke to each other at machine-gun speed.

As the coach arrived at the main gates, the new recruits were ordered out and told to collect their bags. They were then lined up inside the main gates. Other officers now screamed their demands, telling people by name where to go.

Liam lined up with a group of men in a pre-designated area. He didn't have a clue what was going on. He hadn't known what to expect, what was going to happen, and, until that moment, he hadn't even given it a thought, the naive little sod.

Then the worst thing possible happened. It was clear that the tosser who had already picked on him was going to be one of the staff in charge of his section. As he stood in front of the assembled group, which had already been put into rows, the gorilla seemed to look at Liam and then go berserk.

'What the fuck is going on? I am not having that little bastard in my section.'

Liam felt like crying again.

'Somebody's taking the piss out of me.' He was now smashing his drill stick into the ground. He looked over to one of the staff standing in front of another group of blokes. 'Bombardier Hollins, you know my dislike of black bastards. I am not having him in my section... *you* are.'

Liam couldn't believe it. Not only was he an Irish bastard, he was also now a *black* Irish bastard. What was going on?

'Pick up your stuff and get over there now, you fuckin' banana eater.'

Liam picked up his bags.

'Not you, you fuckin' Paddy idiot.'

Liam then realised there had been a black lad standing behind him who was now making his way over to the other section. However, Sergeant Marsden was over to Liam before he could move another muscle. The sergeant stood an inch away from Liam's face and positioned the drill stick about a centimetre under the new recruit's nose.

'I bet your fuckin' daddy used to throw stones at the soldiers, didn't he?'

Liam didn't have a clue what he was going on about. 'Sir, I'm from Lancashire.'

'Do I look like a fuckin' idiot?' Spittle was landing on Liam's face.

'No, sir.'

'Well, don't call me fuckin' "sir", I work for a livin'. You're not going to get through this, you little shit. You will be home to your mummy and your Irish bastard daddy in the next couple of weeks.'

Liam wished he could have gone home there and then, but what would he tell everyone? What would he tell his brothers and sisters, his girlfriend and all the lads who had turned up for his leaving do? What would he tell his mum and his proud grandma and even his dad whom he had seen cry for the first time in a long time the night before. No, he wasn't going to be a failure.

Over the following 16 weeks, Marsden tried everything to get rid of him and he came close to succeeding. There had been many times when Liam had wanted to pack it all in, a time when he had nearly gone AWOL and, yes, a time when he was close to committing suicide.

He could laugh now as he thought of how young and naive he had been in joining the Army. Was it his fault, though? Nobody at home had mentioned that it probably wasn't a good idea to join when you were from an Irish Catholic background. Liam had only signed up so he could play sports all the time.

Looking back, he still didn't know how he had managed to pass through basic training. In the first week, he had been summoned to an office and quizzed on where his dad was from and also his reasons for joining the Army.

'He's from 'Derry, isn't he?' asked a senior-looking officer.

'No, I think he's from Londonderry, sir.'

In hindsight, even Liam couldn't believe how stupid he had been. He'd actually thought they were separate places – Londonderry being in Northern Ireland and the former being in the south. The army hierarchy must have realised at this point that this soldier was no threat to National Security.

It was only in the last week that Liam found out why Marsden hated him so much. How was he to know that the Sergeant was on a transfer from the Parachute Regiment and his brother had served in Derry at the time of the Bloody Sunday outrage?

All the bigotry was completely new to Liam. Religion

had never been a problem in Chorley and nor was the colour of your skin. One of Liam's best friends was black – Black Wayne. He thought about his mate as he saw the lad racially abused every day. Sergeant Marsden took it on himself to make all the soldiers in his section, including Liam, who didn't dare not to, make monkey noises as they marched past him. The other section officers just laughed at the poor bastard. He never passed out.

However, the squaddie humour and the fear of failure got Liam through. He subsequently experienced many humorous and treasured moments throughout his time in the Army and he at least had met a superb friend in Harty. His fellow recruit was a right handsome bastard but, being from the Lancashire town of Bacup, he talked even slower than Liam. This had never stopped him, though, from pulling plenty of women when they were both posted to Dortmund, Germany. Liam started to laugh to himself as he thought of the many escapades that he had been involved in with the Tom Cruise look-a-like.

'Glad you keep smiling, Liam, because the sales figures are not looking good. We might have to let one of the staff go.' Ian had walked into the office and sat down while Liam had been daydreaming.

Here we go again, he thought. 'No, don't worry, Ian, the dark nights will soon be here and they'll be flocking back in to join.'

Liam couldn't help noticing how stressed his boss looked, but he was becoming bored stiff with the same old crap... 'Get the members in or heads will roll...' He knew the theory of customer care and employee management taught at degree level was not as easy in real life, but Ian's way was definitely beginning to bore him. The only thing keeping Liam going at the moment was the thought of the football games coming up on Saturday and Sunday, and the hope that he would meet Kate again one day. This thought, though, had more to do with his dick than anything else.

Before the bulge in his tracksuit bottoms started to become visible, and to move the subject away from membership sales, he attempted to engage Ian in some conversation. 'Are you watching the game on Saturday?'

Ian looked at him with the overanxious, scary eyes he got when he was really stressed. 'What game... what sport are you on about?' he spluttered, shuffling some paperwork in his habitual, over-authoritative manner.

Liam felt like having a go at him, but realised Ian really didn't know that England were playing Germany. He started to explain about the game, but knew that Ian wasn't listening as he continued to read through the stats he had just picked up.

'Oh, sorry about that, Liam, I've just realised that the membership sales figures and all-round profits are *up*. Sorry for jumping down your throat.'

He scooted his chair along closer to Liam. A touch too close, as usual. He may have been married with two kids, but Ian was very touchy-feely and he sometimes made Liam feel uncomfortable when he became very intense.

'The doctors put me on some more tablets. I haven't been coping very well lately with the stress.'

Liam did feel sorry for Ian and wished he could help him more. Ian was always talking about how his dad had never given him any attention when he was a boy and had always criticised him when he was growing up. He also told Liam how he, in turn, was now finding it difficult to show affection to his wife and children. Liam had tried to help him with some different solutions. He felt OK being the psychologist in an attempt to solve somebody else's problems. However, in reality, he had many troubles of his own. Problems that he never showed outwardly to his family, friends and work colleagues. On the contrary, everybody was forever asking Liam, 'Why're you always smiling? Why're you always so happy?' and it was true, to a large extent, that he always appeared to be light-hearted, always up for the craic and seeing the funny side in every situation.

Deep down, though, there were problems. Things he couldn't talk about to anyone. It wasn't wholly to do with his father and how he'd treated him, because he had got used to that. His dad was from the old brigade of working-class fathers who worked hard, and drank hard. Most of his mates had been in the same boat as they grew up and this was probably why they were all still close now. In some respects, Liam had been lucky being the youngest son. His older brothers had been treated far worse than him. James, the eldest, just seemed to be totally ignored by their father, but it was Mick who bore the brunt of his dad's alcohol-fuelled behaviour.

Liam had been close to Mick as they grew up, even though there was a big age gap. He remembered jumping down behind the settee and crying – no, howling – after finding out his brother had been sent to Borstal. His mum and auntie had tried to console Liam as well as themselves as they all cried.

Poor Mum, Liam thought. He may have started feeling sorry for himself more and more lately, but she'd suffered a hundred times worse. His dad's reaction when he had arrived home from work to find out the news of his son's imprisonment hadn't eased his mum's anguish.

'The thievin' little shite deserves all he gets... he's no son of mine.' Then he said those fateful words that, at the time, had cheered Liam up. 'Anyway, our Seamus can sleep in his bed. He's coming across from Ireland again to stay with us for the summer.'

Ian was trying to talk to him, but all Liam could think about was why everything was starting to get him down. Why did he keep thinking about the past? Why should what his uncle had done over 20 years ago be affecting him now? Move forward, move forward, he kept telling Ian, let it go... but he couldn't let it go himself.

He didn't have a clue what Ian had been going on about, so, thankfully, before he had to reply to him, the phone rang.

'I bet you've got your hand down your boxers.'

It was Paddy. For once, Liam hadn't, but the amount of times he'd been pulled up for playing with his package was a standing joke.

'Be in the Horse early tomorrow night for the game and, oh, who's this fit bird Kenny was telling me about. Did you give her one?'

'Yes, no problem, I'll book you in for 7.00pm, Mr Hampson, that'll be fine.'

'See you, tugger.'

'Another member... you're the man, Liam.' His boss unknowingly smiled before walking off, probably to rant at one of the staff.

At the end of the night, Liam picked up his things, end of another shift, another groundhog day, roll on the weekend.

7
Sex Education
August 1977 (Liam aged 7)

Liam couldn't wait for the arrival of his uncle Seamus. His dad's brother was everything his dad wasn't. When he had stayed the previous summer holidays, he had looked after Liam, Jean and Fiona like they were his own. He'd taken them for days out everywhere – Blackpool, Southport and even a trip to the Lake District – and it had meant that Liam had had the best summer of his life. Coinciding with one of the hottest summers on record meant that he had also spent a large amount of time camping out down the woods with all his mates from the estate, so it had been a brilliant time. Liam was hoping this summer would be just the same.

He had missed his brother over the last few weeks, but this had been overtaken with the anticipation of his uncle's arrival.

'Uncle Seamus is here.'

The taxi had pulled up and Fiona and Liam were

already jumping up and down waving through the front window. There was only a year between Jim and his younger brother, but Seamus was totally different in personality. He didn't drink or smoke and still played football. He enjoyed all sports, being a Head of Physical Education. Liam's dad had never taken any interest in his son but, within minutes of his arrival, Seamus was kicking a ball about.

'I'll be Kevin Keegan,' said Liam as he started doing keepy-uppies.

'No, you'll have to be Kenny Dalglish now he's at Liverpool.'

The first week of the holidays went superbly as Liam's dad was working away and Uncle Seamus took him and his two sisters everywhere. Liam was getting the love and attention he had never received from his dad. Day trips out, presents including a Liverpool top, and one night he was nearly sick from the sweets his uncle bought for the children to stay up and watch the Hammer House of Horror film. His mum also seemed to be so much happier when his dad was on long-distance deliveries. With Uncle Seamus in the house playing the fool, Liam wished sometimes that his dad didn't have to come back. He was also chuffed with his uncle sharing his room with him because he felt lonely without Michael at night-time.

He also looked forward to the nights because, when Seamus came to bed, he would put the radio on and listen to music. Liam and his brother only listened to the radio at night to follow Liverpool in Europe.

It was only in the second week that things changed. Things that Liam didn't really understand. He worshipped his uncle, so, when he said one night, 'Would you like to get in my bed with me and talk about how much you're missing your brother?' Liam jumped at the chance.

He didn't really know what to do when his uncle asked him to do the 'things' to him, but Seamus encouraged him, telling him he was a good boy. It was only when his uncle did the same to him that Liam would get scared, but Seamus would say he was sorry and made sure he didn't hurt him again.

'Don't tell anybody what we've been up to because they wouldn't understand and your mum and dad wouldn't let me come over and see you ever again.'

Liam hated the thought of not seeing his uncle again and, although he was hurt some nights by what Seamus did to him, he was always quiet and a 'brave and wonderful little boy', as his uncle called him.

Liam had another fantastic summer as he and his sisters were taken all over the place and treated to sweets and ice cream most days. His mates were really jealous. His biggest treat was the day before Seamus went back to Ireland when he took Liam to watch Liverpool playing Crystal Palace. The young boy had never been to a proper football match and was amazed by everything.

He had cried on the day that Seamus had gone back to Ireland and, as he helped his uncle pack, he promised to keep 'our little secret' until he came back, hopefully at Christmas time.

It was only a few weeks later that his dad received a call from one of his sisters in Ireland and he had burst into tears. Liam had never seen his dad upset before, but now he was crying, 'Jesus, Mary and Joseph... Jesus, Mary and

Joseph...' over and over as he gathered some clothes together and, without really saying goodbye, he went.

It was Liam's mum who sat him and his two sisters down and told them that Uncle Seamus had been killed in a car accident and their dad was going across for the funeral.

'Do you mean he won't be coming back, Mum?'

On the shake of her head, Liam had run up to his room and sobbed his heart out. He would make sure that he wouldn't tell anybody his and Seamus's secret, not even his brother Michael when he came back from prison.

8
Germany 1 – England 5
Saturday, 1 September 2001

L iam was usually nervous before an England game, but he had long given up on their chances of automatic qualification and wasn't even confident they'd qualify through the play-offs this time.

He looked round as he headed for the bar. The same old faces had gathered in the usual over-anticipation of an England win. The lads had religiously met in The White Horse to watch the big England games, but it had always ended in tears.

Liam remembered the tears shared with Gazza in Italia '90, and the explosion of joy when he scored that brilliant goal against Scotland in Euro '96. He smiled to himself and shook his head as he closed his eyes and visualised Gazza sliding in at the back post, just failing to score the winner against Germany in the semi-final. The loss on penalties had cost Liam £400, but he still wasn't mad at Gascoigne, one of his all-time favourite players. He was just gutted that England missed out on their best ever chance since 1966 to win a major competition.

In France '98, he may not have wanted Beckham lynched when he was sent off against Argentina but, as he was leaving the pitch, Liam had shouted to the big screen that he had cost England the World Cup. Maybe a touch harsh, as England only went out on penalties after a heroic display. Even then, the deficiencies in England's preparations were shown up. David Batty, who hadn't taken a spot kick since leaving school, missed the vital penalty – preparation and planning and all that.

No, tonight was different, no pressure – England were crap and would be lucky to get a positive result against the boxheads. The pub was packed so at least Jack would have a smile on his face.

Liam made his way over to the lads.

'Come on, England,' roared Giant as he outstretched his palm to shake his mate's hand. The customary pint of John Smith's in his other was dwarfed to look like a half.

'I don't believe it, Liam. You're not drinking orange, are you?' Mad Al had sussed Liam out straight away.

'You soft bastard, you soft bastard...'

The chant lasted for a minute or so but Liam didn't care. He couldn't be bothered spending money on Jack's inflated Stella prices, which he knew would, in turn, give him a depressive hangover. No, he was really up for the first Sunday League game of the season the next day.

He started having the craic with a few of the lads as the game kicked off and, within a few minutes, it was obvious that England were as bad as he'd expected.

Rob edged his way over to him and they started to discuss the team for the following morning.

'The keeper picks himself with our Giant between the sticks and, of course, you're in as captain.'

'Cheers, boss.'

'But I'm not too sure about the rest of them. We'd better wait and see who turns up in the morning, but hopefully everybody will be keen and, if England don't win, they won't be that pissed anyway.'

Rob was right. The saving grace was that England getting beaten or drawing would result in only a semi-pissed team. Welcome back to Sunday League, Liam thought.

The orange juice was going straight through his system and he decided that, after he'd been to the toilet, he would just have one pint, but no more than two as he had sensibly driven to the pub so he wouldn't get drunk. While shaking his todger to avoid leaving a stain on his light-coloured trousers, having gone commando, he heard the telltale noises of a German goal.

'We're fuckin' shit' and 'You're not fit to wear the shirt' were being screamed at the screen as he made his way back to the lads.

'How did they let that big pillock score?' screamed Kenny, referring to Jancker, the big German donkey, as the replays showed him sliding the ball past Seaman.

'He's worse than you, Mick.'

'Piss off, Kenny, Campbell looked like you then – a fuckin' statue at the back.'

The banter flew from all sides and, unfortunately, England were similarly all over the place.

Liam looked round the pub and sensed that the mood was already turning black. People couldn't bear the thought of another defeat to the Germans. Punters were shaking their heads, shouting at the screen. One regular called Eriksson 'a foreign tosser' as the cameras homed in on the England manager. Seaman managed to pull off a magnificent save, but it was looking bad.

Liam started shaking his head, the depression setting in. He was already losing hope and turned round, looking to see if there were any decent women knocking about. He knew the chances were as slim as England's of winning now. The White Horse was a proper drinking-man's pub. This was great for the lads who wanted to escape from their wives or girlfriends, but not so good if you were on the hunt for the love of your life. Not that he was really interested in any of the usual slappers that frequented his local. Liam had driven past Kate's house a few times hoping to catch a glimpse of her. Since their meeting, he had felt like he had a schoolboy crush again. He couldn't stop thinking about her and had struggled to concentrate on anything.

Then, suddenly, the roar went up and he turned back to see Michael Owen wheeling away after scoring. There may have been no goddesses in the bar that night, but things were definitely looking up. Beer was being spilled everywhere as everybody celebrated, but Jack wouldn't be bothered. The more beer spilled the better, as the lads would be dipping in their pockets again. The carpet would last another year or two anyway. It might get even stickier and claim someone's shoes again, but it would last.

Liam didn't join in the celebrations as he still thought there would only be Jack laughing at the end of the night.

'We can do it, Liam.'

Liam turned to see Wolfman with his usual beaming face. He loved Wolfman's attitude. Liam just hoped he wouldn't be too disappointed if he was named as one of the subs in the morning. His mate loved his football and was really looking forward to playing again, but he hadn't played competitively since his team Liverpool had last won the League.

'Pint of Stella, Jack.' Liam edged his way to the bar. The place was packed, but Bainesy, the man mountain, was sat in his usual swivel chair at the bar taking up about three spaces. He stared at the optics, not once looking at the mayhem going on behind him. ''Scuse me, Stevie.' Liam was always wary of Bainesy. The guy was a total prick, but at 20 stone you had to tread lightly, even though nobody could stand him.

'Fuckin' bunch of pussies,' he grunted, still not moving a muscle.

Liam knew about his dislike for football, and wasn't surprised that he was still in his seat moaning about anything and everything.

He had to wait ages for his pint but, just as he received it from the barmaid's outstretched hand, the place erupted again as Steven Gerrard smashed a 25-yarder into the bottom corner. Somebody bounced into Liam and his pint went all over Bainesy, but the dickhead didn't even move, didn't even turn round, just carried on looking at the bar.

'That'll be another for me and one for Stevie.'

Jack looked like he had won the lottery.

Half-time came and people were now shoulder to shoulder. Even more came in from the other pubs. Liam noticed a few surprisingly half-decent women knocking about, and Wolfman and Rory were already sniffing about as Liam started talking to Mad Al's brother Tony.

'What do you reckon, Tiger?'

'Can't believe two Scousers have scored. Not happy...' he said with a wry smile on his face.

'We'll be lucky to hang on to this. I reckon we could still get beat.' As Liam said the words, he felt like the prophet of doom. Euro 2000 had definitely got to him.

'4–1 we'll win.'

It could only be Simon. Seventeen years as a Man City season-ticket holder had finally taken its toll on him, Liam thought. His prediction was mocked as usual, especially by the red half of Manchester, but the eternal City optimist was at it again.

'If we win 4–1, Simon, I'll go swimming in the lake after.' Mad Al knew all about Simon's daft predictions and had won plenty of money from him in the past, especially when United had played City.

'So will I,' said Liam, joining in the camaraderie.

The banter died down as the game resumed with Germany looking the more likely to score. The Stella had started to go down well and Liam abandoned the idea of driving home, but consoled himself with the belief that he had the willpower only to have around five pints even if England won. He would have a couple of pints of water when he arrived home and be fit as a fiddle in the morning.

The game started to get better and better, but Liam thought it was best to carry on his anti-damping control and headed for the toilets. He had just about started peeing when the place erupted again. He was out of the toilets as quick as a flash so he could join in the celebrations. The place was going absolutely bananas. He jumped in front of the big screen as if he was on a pogo stick. Germany 1 – England 3. He hadn't seen any of the goals and it didn't mean England would still qualify, but it was great anyway.

'Liam, you loony, you've pissed yourself,' pointed out Paddy.

Liam looked down, arms still raised, fists clenched. It was true, he had forgotten to shake his willy and there was a telltale damp patch. The rather good-looking women who had been jumping about near the lads were now laughing along with them as a chant of 'Pissy Pants... Pissy Pants... Pissy Pants' broke out.

Time for another pint, thought Liam. He couldn't get near the bar so he made a few hand signals and a three-quarter-full pint eventually arrived. He noticed that the fat knacker Bainesy was still facing the bar, probably oblivious to the score. The Stella was taking over now. Bainesy had turned from a man mountain to a fat bastard who was probably too slow to fight – oh, Stella, how brave it made you.

The chants of 'In-ger-land... Ing-er-land... Ing-er-land...' were echoing round the pub with both men and women joining in. The atmosphere was absolutely fantastic. The St George's flags, which had earlier been discarded, were now draped around their proud owners as everybody hugged each other, giving the nods and winks of 'I told you we'd beat them'.

Liam started to feel the urge to carry out his second favourite exercise, bouncing about naked, as the alcohol started to take over. He felt he couldn't miss his chance. If England scored again, he would strip for a laugh. It didn't matter that the pub was packed, it just made it better. How many times did England beat Germany 4–1? How many times did England beat Germany full stop?

He looked round. All the lads were up for it now. All together, this was what it was about. The pub was absolutely packed, but most of the lads were in the same place as usual, bang in the centre of the room, in front of the screen. The scene was set up brilliantly. He caught his usual double-act partner Paddy's attention and gave him the 'go on, if you do it, I'll do it' raised-eyebrows look back. They didn't even get the chance to plan anything as Owen went through and smashed in the fourth. The whole place now went completely berserk.

As everyone started bouncing about, Liam and Paddy whipped off their clothes and hid them under different tables before joining in the celebrations. The lads didn't even bat an eyelid as their friends bounced up and down bollock naked again and again. The rest of the pub also seemed to find it hilarious. The good-looking women who had started to look strangely familiar moved out of the way as the celebrations to the goal died down. A chant of 'Doggy Bollocks... Doggy Bollocks... Doggy Bollocks...' started and only receded when Paddy jumped in front of the screen and bent over showing his arse to the audience. A big cheer went up as he swayed from side to side revealing his massive pair of balls swinging through his legs, bouncing against the inside of his thighs.

Liam jumped about near the classy women, trying to breathe in, still feeling self-conscious even at this stage. As he leaped about, he looked at the girls, but nearly stopped in mid-air as he realised where he had seen them before. They were the other stunners he'd seen with Kate in the Wine Lodge. Even more embarrassing was that Kate, in all her goddess-like glory, had now joined them. What was she doing in this shit-hole? Kate was now looking straight at him, laughing, shaking her head. It could only happen to Liam.

Jack screamed at them to get dressed and they went to retrieve their clothes. Luckily for Liam, the lads had only spotted and stolen Paddy's kit from under one of the tables. Paddy had no chance of getting his stuff back and was forced to remain naked.

As the euphoria died down, Liam quickly dressed and made his way over to Kate, not really knowing what to expect. However, he wasn't going to miss his chance this time. The sixth or so pint of Stella was making him braver and braver. The other beauties giggled as he spoke to Kate.

'Hello... what's a nice girl like you doing in a place like this?'

Above the din, he managed to get her telephone number and the promise of a date when he rang her. He couldn't believe it. England winning 4–1, party piece already out of the way and now a proposed night out with the girl of his dreams. He'd be checking his lottery tickets when he got in at this rate.

'Who was that darlin'?' bellowed Mad Al, nearly popping Liam's eardrum.

'I'll tell you who it is. That's what got me a black eye, saving her on the taxi rank, and that bastard gets the telephone number.' Kenny had spotted the telephone number handover, but then received a kick from behind from his girlfriend.

'Piss off, will you?' was his instant reply before the blonde disappeared in tears.

Liam was just about to explain what had happened to Al when the fifth goal went in. The pub was now in uproar as a conga broke out.

'Five—one to the Ing-er-land... Five—one to the Ing-er-land...' reverberated round the place.

When the shout of 'One Emile Heskey... there's only one Emile Heskey...' went up, Liam knew he was in dreamland.

He turned to the bar to see a still naked Doggy Bollocks jumping on Bainesy's back – bad idea. Bainesy got Paddy in a headlock but, before he could do much damage, Giant ran over, swung them both round on the bar stool and cracked him straight in the face. Twenty-one stone of prime beef hitting twenty stone of fat. There was only one consequence as Bainesy nearly went through the bar before sliding from the stool with Paddy still under his arm. The fat pudding had deserved it but, as Giant stepped back, there was no doubting he had done some damage to his fist. He stood shaking his hand, grimacing.

As people tried to remove their mate's head from the headlock, Rory couldn't resist slapping Paddy's arse as hard as he could. He was brought to his feet and it was difficult to tell which had hurt most, the headlock or the slap, which was now looking like it had drawn blood.

Liam inspected Giant's hand, but it was already coming up like a balloon. He had no chance of playing in the morning.

As the match finished, Jack asked for calm before the karaoke was set up. Things couldn't get any better. Liam loved watching all the different characters getting up and having the bottle to have a go on the karaoke. Maybe some of the others would be better off not bothering, but some were superb and it all added to the fun. Rob singing 'American Pie', Kenny singing 'Mack the Knife' and Mad Al singing 'Brown-Eyed Girl'. Liam even thought about singing a Tom Jones number... but then again, he was been pissed, but not that pissed.

Kate touched Liam on the shoulder as she went past, reminding him to ring her about going out before she trooped out of the door. This was unbelievable, Liam thought. A couple more pints of Stella wouldn't do him any harm now.

The karaoke started as Bainesy was helped to his feet and taken to the toilets still staggering from the knock-out punch. Almost everyone was happy anyway. Simon sang an impromptu 'Three Lions on My Shirt' with everybody at some point joining in. As he looked round at all his mates laughing and joking and inspecting Paddy's arse, Liam just took it all in. What a night. Can life get any better than this?

9
The Pain Game

Sunday, 2 September 2001

'Liam, you're going to be late, love... Liam, you're going to be late, love.'

'What? What? Oh, mother, I just had the most horrible dream.' A photograph of his mum when she was young always reminded Liam of Dorothy out of *The Wizard of Oz*.

'Get off me, you wally.'

As she had stood over him shaking his arm, Liam had grabbed his mum for a laugh and pulled her towards him.

'Bloody hell, Mum, how many beers did you have last night?' He had gone to kiss her on the cheek, but the combined smell of alcohol and smoke on her breath had made him pull back.

'Only two or three cans, love.'

'Yeah, right, and the rest.'

His mum had started drinking a lot more lately. Liam didn't really want to have a go at her, though, because,

77

apart from going round to Mrs Mitchell's and the odd game of bingo, it seemed to be her only source of enjoyment these days. Her husband would leave her in on her own all the time and it was as if she had thought to herself, If you can't beat 'em, join 'em'.

Liam had tried to have a chat with her about it, but who was he to tell his mum what to do when his dad went to the pub seven nights a week?

'I'll go down and make you a cup of tea. Oh, by the way, love, your dad wasn't very happy when you tried to get in bed with us last night.' She said it in such a matter-of-fact way because it had happened a number of times over the years. 'He said you'd better find somewhere else to live, but I put him straight.'

'Cheers, Mum. I'm sure somebody must have spiked me drink. I felt great 'til the end of the game and then I can't remember anything else much after that.'

'You should watch how much you're drinking, love. It can't be doing you any good. Anyway, England won.'

He didn't tell his mum what had really happened. It was hazy anyway. He had remembered coming out of the Horse and walking on to the park with Paddy and Tony to find Mad Al swimming in the lake. A number of people were trying to get him to come back out but to no avail. Liam, not wanting to be outdone, had passed his keys and money to Paddy and ran straight towards the end of the pier before diving in. He had then seen his life flash before him as he smashed into the muddy bottom. It was only about 2 foot deep where he had dived in.

Everybody then cheered as Al and Liam swam to the middle of the lake, to the same platform they all had all swum to when they were kids. Liam had then realised that Mad Al wasn't that daft because, as he climbed on to the first ledge, he saw that his mate only had his boxer shorts on. Liam, the idiot, was fully clothed. Everybody had taken the piss out of him when they both re-emerged, but that was about all Liam could remember.

He looked at his bedside clock; it was only ten past eight. Perfect. He had told his mum to wake him early so he could prepare himself for the big game. He climbed out of bed and shook his head on seeing the mud on his pillow. He knew it was a stupid thing to do, but he'd had a brilliant night. England winning 5–1, the karaoke, especially Rob's rendition of 'Everybody', his Blues Brothers special, and Kate's telephone number.

Oh no... Kate's telephone number.

Liam picked up his sodden jeans and searched through the front pocket to find his personal jackpot numbers. He couldn't believe it; the piece of paper was now no more than a sodden lump of pulp with some indistinguishable blue dye streaked through it. Liam was absolutely gutted and the depression started to creep in as he made his way downstairs. He still felt drunk as he sat on the settee and was starting to think about being sick as his mum brought in his cup of tea.

'There you go, love. Do you want some breakfast?'

'No thanks, Mum.'

The state he was in he didn't think he would be able to keep anything down. He was just about to head for the toilet when the phone rang. Rob was already up bright and early.

'Could you nip round to me mum's house and check

on Giant's fitness? His hand was looking a bit dodgy last night, but we could do with him.'

'Yeah, no problem.'

'What a good night, eh? Can't believe you started walking home bollocky buff. I thought that copper was going to arrest you. Anyway, I'll round up our Paddy and some of the other lads.'

Liam got his footie bag from under the stairs, where he also found what must have been his mum's secret stash of cans of lager. He didn't want to start questioning her yet, but he knew she hadn't been telling him the truth about the extent of her drinking.

'See you later, Mum.'

He set off across to his old estate, hoping the brisk early September morning would bring him round.

When he arrived at the Johnsons', he knew the procedure. He didn't have to knock on the front door, but just went round the back, and picked up the key from under the dustbin to let himself in. 'Morning, Irene,' was met by a hug from his second mum as she came out of the living room. Her hair might have changed now, but it could have been any time from the last 20-odd years. She always greeted Liam with the same lovely smile and sincere hug.

'What the hell were you lot up to last night? Our Giant came in falling all over the place. I had to put him to bed.'

Liam laughed to himself at the thought of her having to put a 20-stone-plus dead weight to bed.

'I'll nip up and see if I can wake him up, Irene.'

She laughed knowingly, recalling the ridiculous nature of the many escapades the lads had been up to over the years.

Liam entered the bedroom where he had slept a number of times in the past. Good memories came flooding back; it was the others he didn't like.

'Giant, wake up, will you.'

He was just about to give up the shaking when Giant started his usual waking-up routine. He opened one eye before slowly opening the other and then shook his head vigorously before springing upright, finishing off with rubbing his face. He was doing this oblivious to Liam's presence.

He recoiled on seeing Liam. 'Have you been here all night?' He was still drunk.

Liam explained what had happened the night before as Giant clambered out of bed wearing just his T-shirt. On inspection, his hand was very swollen but he was still convinced he would be able to play. He attempted to put his jeans on, not even bothering with any underwear. Liam felt like he wanted to help as he saw his mate struggling to get his jeans past his knees. Giant stood up to finish wrestling with his jeans and asked Liam to pass him his trainers. As Liam bent down, Giant let out an almighty scream, the sort that Liam had not heard from him since he had fallen from his bike when he was seven years old.

Giant collapsed to the floor and was writhing about holding his hands in front of his crotch. Liam still didn't know what was going on as his mate was now incoherent but was at least managing to shout out, 'Mum, Mum...' in between gulps of air. Liam looked closer and the realisation set in. Giant had trapped his trouser snake in his zip. Not only had he trapped it but, as Liam peered even closer, he could see that part of his foreskin was zipped up, but still poking through the small metal teeth.

Irene was up the stairs like a shot to see what had happened. 'Oh my God, what have you done?' She looked down at her son writhing on the floor, although his initial pain had now seemingly eased somewhat. 'You'll have to try and unzip it, love.'

Giant looked at her then at Liam before looking down below. Liam knew that, at 28 years old, and built like a brick shithouse, he may have looked hard as nails and was in some respects, but John was the proverbial 'gentle giant'. His mum had a go, but Giant winced in pain. He had now also started to sweat profusely and had gone as white as a sheet. There was nothing else they could do; they would have to go to hospital. After only minimal resistance, Giant agreed to go.

His mum found him a big bath towel to wrap round his waist as he struggled to his feet. Liam could tell the pain must have been excruciating, so he held back from bursting out laughing, but he already knew it was going to be a great story for the lads.

He eased Giant into the front passenger seat of the big lad's car, and waved to Irene as he set off, doing his best to familiarise himself with the controls. Even Irene had struggled to contain her laughter, pursing her lips together tightly in between telling Giant he would be fine.

'I don't believe this... aaaahh...' was all that Liam got out of his mate in the short drive as he concentrated on the road. Liam began to worry. How would he explain this one if he got pulled over by the police? He could also do without the instant ban because he knew he was still miles over the limit. Naughty, but how many times does your grown-up mate trap his penis in his flies?

Arriving at the hospital, Liam followed Giant's instructions. John had realised that on a Sunday morning the waiting room for the Accident and Emergency would be packed with drunks and DIY injuries. He had begged his friend to go in first and explain to the receptionist and nurses what had happened.

Liam talked through the situation quietly with the receptionist who gave him the go-ahead to jump the queue. However, on seeing the packed waiting room, Liam decided he couldn't miss his chance. He went to the front of the rows of chairs and asked for quiet from the usual suspects of down-and-outs, domestic incidents and accidents that Saturday night/Sunday morning brought.

'Sorry to bother you all, but I thought I might be able to put a smile on your faces by telling you about me mate who will be coming through in a moment.' He explained what had happened and the chuckling started straight away. Before returning to John, he asked them not to let on they knew when he returned with the casualty.

Giant was just relieved he had been allowed to go straight through to see the nurses. As the two friends came through the double doors, Giant kept his head down and his hands round in front of him, holding on to the towel and what must now have been a throbbing piece of tender meat. Strangely, it must have been the happiest-looking Casualty waiting room in history. People weren't just smiling, they were giggling, and Liam spotted one bloke doubled over. Some of the women were grimacing but many of the blokes seemed to be taking pleasure in seeing somebody in so much pain. They were probably thinking back to their childhood, as most little lads must have felt the same pain; anyway, it seemed to be a man thing.

Giant was oblivious to the goings-on and Liam thought he'd got away with it until an old man stationed near the plastic doors they were heading towards shouted out, 'Don't worry, son, when it's as wrinkled as mine, you won't notice the scars.'

Giant looked at Liam and even managed a smile as he struggled to spit out just one word – 'Bastard.'

He was given his own cubicle to sit down in before one of the nurses took Liam to one side. By this time, there were about five or six nurses gathering round, giggling, all wanting a piece of the action.

'The doctor will be here in a minute, but somebody wants to ask you some questions.'

For a split-second, Liam thought he was going to be marched away to be interviewed by the police as he was taken to another cubicle. He started to read a magazine on the bed when he heard a cough behind him. This wasn't just any old cough, though... this was music to Liam's ears, as it transported him back to the warmth of his bed, and the face that he had dreamed of waking up next to for a second time.

'So, Liam, what have you been up to this time?'

Liam hadn't realised that Kate worked on the Accident and Emergency ward, but this must have been the luckiest break he had ever had. Giant probably didn't see it that way, but, if ever there was an up-side to catching your foreskin in your zip, then Liam was definitely reaping the benefits of his mate's misfortune.

Liam felt instantly at ease with Kate. She was absolutely gorgeous, but didn't seem to be like others who thought their looks meant everything.

'I am afraid my mate forgot to put his underpants on and ended up trapping his... er...'

Kate laughed. God, he loved that laugh, that smile.

'You and your friends seem to have a thing about not wearing any underwear.'

Liam didn't really want to tell Kate that he had lost her phone number, but he wasn't going to lose the chance of a date with his dream girl. 'Kate, I'm afraid I lost your phone number last night. I had a bit of an accident...'

He told her about the lake episode and, after she had spotted mud in his ear, she couldn't stop laughing. It was weird, he'd only met her a couple of times, but he was already noticing all her mannerisms and he liked everything he saw or heard. After he had arranged to meet her in the Gamebird pub on the following Friday night, he quickly had to say his goodbyes as the sounds from the nearby cubicle alerted him to Giant's increasing distress.

'No, you're havin' a laugh... I'm not havin' it... please tell me you're taking the mick.'

Liam walked back to the cubicle to see Giant surrounded by five nurses and an Asian doctor. The poor lad had just been informed that he needed a painkiller to help with the procedure. He had reluctantly accepted that before being told it would be in the form of an injection. He had always been scared of injections.

'Where?'

'In your doo-dah.'

'Jeeesus!'

He then had to be held down by the nurses while the doctor gave him the painkiller. That was bad enough, but the doctor then calmly looked at Giant and said, 'Please look at your friend.'

Giant hadn't realised what he was going to do as he obligingly turned his head towards Liam. In a flash, the doctor whipped down his zip, just like any mother would do. Giant screamed, and flung several nurses into the curtained walls as he instinctively reacted to the dramatic release of his mutilated manhood.

'Ahhhh, you bastard...' He stopped himself from continuing with the tirade and bent down, examining his foreskin. 'Sorry, doc. I didn't mean that.'

The zip marks were clearly visible, but incredibly everything still seemed pretty much intact. Giant just sat there for several minutes, breathing heavily, letting his red-raw willy get some fresh air before tucking it ever so slowly into his jeans. After shaking the doctor's hand and apologising to the nurses for any problems he had caused, Giant and Liam made their way back through the waiting area. Giant's pretend scowls made sure that nobody laughed again as they made their way slowly to the exit.

He wasn't embarrassed to have Liam help him fasten his belt or be asked whether he was comfortable and, when Liam began to laugh – no, cry – with the absurdity of the situation, he joined in.

The 'No wanking for me then' nearly made Liam crash and he was still laughing long after dropping Giant back home.

He couldn't wait to tell the boys as he headed for the changing rooms.

10
The Caribbean Disaster
Sunday, 2 September 2001

'Where's Giant?'

Rob didn't look happy and the story didn't go down as well with him as Liam thought it would. However, he could see that Spanish Phil, Rory and Wolfman, who were the only ones in the changing room, appreciated it.

'I don't believe this. Ten-past-ten and there's only four of you here. Have you seen those bastards outside? There must be 20 of them warming up, running around. It's like *Zulu Dawn*.'

Liam had noticed that the Caribbean Club were more than ready for the match and that Rob was right – he counted over 20 playing staff and other officials all warming up on their home pitch as he walked past.

'There's a full tribe of them out there.'

'Jesus, Knobhead, keep your voice down. We'll get strung up if they hear you.' Knobhead received a playful slap on the back of the head from Kenny as they both entered the changing room.

Rob was already pacing about with a notebook and pen in his hand. 'Right, get the strip out and get some socks and shorts on. Nobody put any shirts on.' He then marched out of the changing room shaking his head.

'Don't put your shirts on' had always been Rob's way of warning everybody in the old days that they shouldn't presume they were playing, but with the count now only up to nine players, it looked like everybody would be playing, even Knobhead and Wolfman.

The changing rooms in the massive pavilion were made up of 30 wire-meshed cages, each with individual doors. The communal showers at the bottom of the big old building were least close to their cage. As his bum started to go numb on the cold bench, Liam started to think about all the great laughs he'd had on the Park. He had always enjoyed the buzz and the banter coming from each 'changing room' as old friends and arch-rivals changed separately but together. The facilities hadn't altered in over 20 years; the lottery funding had definitely not made its way to Croft Park yet. Liam looked up, down and across, through the individual changing areas, and took in the atmosphere of the place as young and old players alike rummaged through kit bags looking for the best socks, shorts and tops as the banter ebbed and flowed.

It may be a shit standard, he thought, but football was definitely 'the beautiful game'. Then the ref entered their cage and Liam's idyll evaporated.

'Right, lads – no earrings, other jewellery, no swearing,

back-chatting or calling the referee. Remember, the referee is always right, even if he's wrong.'

The ref was oblivious to Browny pulling faces at him as he and young Gazza, other lions to the slaughter, made their entrance.

'Let me check your boots then.' The official had a face like a smacked arse as he studied each individual boot hoping to find a reason to show who was in charge.

Liam could tell his sort straight away. A bank manager or local council official. A man of importance, to himself anyway. His referee outfit looked like it had been ironed for an inspection and probably had been by his wife. He was definitely looking the part. Liam could see his notebook in the back pocket of his shorts ready to be used at the slightest misdemeanour. Another robot straight from the assembly line of crap officials; another ref who had most likely never played the game at any level but had passed some sort of exam to make him feel important. It wasn't that Liam was against referees. He knew they had a hard job to do and he also knew that the Chorley League was struggling for officials because of the abuse and various assaults some of them had suffered at the hands of some idiots, but Liam just knew instantly that this ref would be the most pedantic bastard you could meet. Fifteen years' experience was screaming this at him.

'Right, skipper, I want you to ensure you keep control of your team. I am being assessed today and will be acting accordingly. Any bad language of any sort and there will be an early bath for the player involved.'

Liam didn't know whether to laugh or cry. He knew the team were going to get hammered and the ref mentioning the early bath had reminded him of the luxurious freezing showers they could expect at the end of the game.

'I need your team sheet in the next two minutes and hurry up and get out on to the pitch. I don't want to have to call the game off for you being late.' He looked round, nodding his approval to himself before leaving, brand-new assistant referee flags – not linesman flags – in one hand and whistle in the other. He marched past Rob as the manager re-entered the changing room with his assistant Steve.

Rob looked gobsmacked. 'What did Councillor Wright want? Tell me he's not the referee. Tell me he was in fancy dress.'

Rob had his notepad with him and Liam could see he had a formation scribbled out. He hoped it was a defensive one because they were going to need it. He looked round the cage to try and assess the lads' fitness levels, and his heart sank – everybody looked absolutely knackered.

Riggers was the last man in to make it ten players at least, and then Black Wayne appeared at the entrance to the cage, as if to take the piss before playing for the Caribbean Club.

'All reet, Wayne, what position are you playing?' Tony had been in plenty of friendly battles with Wayne over the years.

'It depends where the manager is going to play me... eh, Rob?' Wayne then sat down.

Knobhead's face was a picture. Liam had managed to get Wayne to play for them after convincing him it would be a great laugh. He also told him Spanish Phil was going to be playing, which had closed the deal. Both of them loved dabbling with cannabis before, during and after the match. Both of them had only agreed to play if Liam could convince the other one back out of retirement.

After doing a very quick count-up, Rob began the pre-match team talk. 'Right, lads, seeing that there are only 11 here out of a squad of 38 I think it just shows you that people are not as committed as they say they are. I can assure you, though, that you 11 will not be forgotten for managing to make it this morning. Now I want you to think of how England played last night, mainly on the counter-attack, and I want you to get out there and make me – no, everybody – proud.'

Rob was still semi-drunk, but was deadly serious. He thought that they had a chance, but Liam knew for sure they were going to get hammered. After naming the formation and bollocking a few of the lads for smoking in the changing room, he headed out, dutifully followed by Steve, his secretary, assistant and 'bucket and sponge man'. It was lucky Rob didn't see Spanish Phil and Wayne rolling a spliff in the corner.

'Anyway, at least we won't have to call you Black Wayne this season.' Liam shook his mate's hand. The 'Black' had been added to his name when he and Liam had played in a junior team together along with another two lads both also called Wayne. 'I wonder if the other two still get called Fat Wayne and Little Wayne.'

'Call me anything this season and I'll be suing your white asses.'

For once, Liam couldn't even be bothered sticking in

his two penn'orth with the team. He could smell the alcohol on everybody and feel it sweating through his own pores already. At least they'd all made the effort to turn up. Out of the young lads, only young Gazza had appeared and a couple of the older lads who had said they were up for it were absent, which always drove Liam mad. He pulled his socks up, put on his tie-ups and headed out of the changing room, wondering where his brother Mick was.

The Caribbean Club looked keen to play. They were all now jogging round together, involved in a proper warm-up. Liam knew it was only Sunday League football but he hated losing and to know his team was going to get stuffed before he even stepped on the pitch really frustrated him.

The ref was waiting in the centre circle ready to go. A sharp shrill on his whistle and the shout of 'Captains here now, please' confirmed that he wanted to get the game under way. Liam looked around at his team-mates. Apart from Browny warming up the new keeper, Rory, by knocking a ball to him, the rest of the lads were just stood around with their hands down their shorts. Liam did a quick count-up; there were only eight including him out on the pitch. Kenny, Knobhead and Paddy had probably forgotten that it was an away fixture and were still in the changing rooms hiding, thinking they would miss out on putting the nets up.

'Captains, please.' The ref glared at Liam, but Liam knew all the stalling tactics.

'We've changed captains. He's still in the changing room, ref.'

'Well, we'll start the game without him, then. Either we start now or I abandon the match and give the points to the Caribbean Club... it's up to you.'

'Fuckin' hell, ref, you can't do that, you're out of order.' Rob was well on the way to disciplinary action before a ball was kicked.

The ref marched straight over to the touchline. 'What's your name?' As he reached for his book from his back pocket, it was clear he was going to stamp his authority early.

'What're you on about? I'm just walking me dog. I've got nothing to do with the team.'

The reply stumped the ref and, even with the lack of a dog, he didn't know what to do.

'Ref, are we going to get started or what?'

The remaining three players made their way on to the pitch, Knobhead finishing a cigarette as he trooped on behind Rory's goal.

'Come on, Horse. We can win this,' shouted the doggy walker as the Caribbean side kicked off.

It was a disaster from start to finish. The final score of 6–0 was flattering to The White Horse. Rory's heroics in the nets had kept the score down after Kenny had managed to get himself sent off two minutes into the game for a professional foul, hacking down the Caribbean's 18-year-old centre-forward. This lad was the fastest thing that Liam had ever seen and even he had applauded one of his goals when he had gone past five of the lads and stuck one in. The O'Shea brothers had argued from start to finish and were still arguing as the players made their way to the changing room.

'That second goal was your fault, Al... you should have got a tackle in on that lad.'

'Leave it out, Tony, you're doin' me head in. What about the other five goals then? I suppose they were my fault as well.'

And so it went on, the brotherly love drying up fairly quickly, whereupon they had to be separated by Rob.

Due to the match starting late, most of the other teams had left the changing rooms by the time The White Horse lads were back in their cage.

'Everybody sit down, lads. Nobody go for a shower. I want a chat with you all.' Rob had decided it was time for another motivational talk. 'Let's forget about today. You all did your best and we might have been all right if Kenny hadn't been unlucky to get sent off so early. Anyway, we'll get back to winning ways next week. We're only playing the Black Boy.'

Rob said the name of one of the Horse's local rivals at just the wrong time. One of the black lads whom Liam knew to be a bouncer in Preston was walking past towards the showers, and immediately glared in Rob's direction. 'What you sayin', man? You takin' the piss?'

He started walking towards the cage but luckily Wayne was walking in behind him.

'Eh, man, leave it out, leave it out.' Wayne pushed his former team-mate and friend out of the way. 'Leave the white boys alone. Do ya not think they've had enough?' He winked at the lads.

Liam smiled to himself. The Black Lad, as most people called it, had been a pub in Chorley for a good seventy years or so. In these times of political correctness, Liam couldn't believe that it was still getting away with the name, or – even more bizarrely – that it also still had a golliwog's head painted beneath the main sign that just looked like it had been taken from a Robertson's jam jar. He smiled to himself every time he went past the pub and saw the head peering down at the traffic. He laughed as he told Wayne who they were playing, reminding him of the sign. Liam wondered why the conscience police hadn't picked up on it yet.

With the ice-cold showers now in use, the prospect of hanging about to make a token attempt at cleaning some mud off didn't appeal to anyone.

'Back to the pub for the butties and soup then, lads,' Rob said. 'Jack's treating us.'

'I bet it's spam butties and watered-down soup.' Kenny was still not seeing eye to eye with Jack. Liam had heard him telling Rob he'd lost some more money in a late-night card school to him. 'Yeah, and I bet the football funds disappear down some handy little black hole, just like last time,' he continued. Some of the lads still remembered how the previous landlord had 'lost' the funds book before they disbanded.

Liam put his jeans over his muddy legs and started to put his socks on. He had personally not had a bad game but, in truth, had never really played well when he had a hangover. He was beginning to think that the treble dream was already over, but the thought was softened by the memory of possibly capturing an even greater prize – Kate. He couldn't wait for the date the following Friday.

11
Pub Politics
Sunday, 2 September 2001

The banter was already flying around when Liam got back to the pub.

'6–0, and I believe you were lucky to get nil.' Standing in his usual place at the bar, old Stan was already at it. He'd ridiculed the idea of the lads getting back together and was now having a field day as various members of the team ordered their drinks.

'What a great night last night, Liam.' Jack wasn't bothered about the score, just about making money. 'It'll be packed when we play Greece. I'll be doing butties again if you want to tell the lads.'

Jack must have made a killing on the bar takings and was keen to ensure another jackpot when England played Greece in the final group game – a win and England were through. Liam couldn't believe it.

'Is your Mick back from Spain yet?' Jack was after more cheap cigarettes and tobacco to sell on in the pub and

Liam's brother, it turned out, had been on another fag run. Steve had told Liam after the game that he had also taken two other lads with him. It was no wonder his business was going well.

'How much did we make on the raffle last night, Jack?'

'Arh... not checked it yet, Kenny, but we couldn't really get round much because of how packed it was in here.'

Kenny looked at Liam and shook his head.

'Hope you're in tonight for the draw before we start the karaoke at 9.30.' Jack then retired back upstairs before anybody could ask any more questions.

'No, it's not your blacks I'm that bothered about, it's more your Pakis and those illegal immigrants getting free housing all over the place.' Nicky, who had refused to come out of retirement and play again, but had agreed to be the official team supporter, was always in the pub for a pint or two of Stella on a Sunday and was already stoking up the fires for a debate.

'I think we should follow suit with those people in Oldham and Burnley and vote BNP at the next local or national elections.'

'That's a bit strong, Nicky.'

'No, it's not. What has Tony Blair done for us?' Remembering the Labour theme tune on the Election Day victory, he continued, 'Things can only get better? You must be joking. If things carry on the way they are with these asylum seekers and immigrants all coming into Britain, there's going to be riots like the '80s. Everybody's had enough but nobody will say anything.'

Liam always enjoyed a pint with Nicky who would have a discussion about anything, from his 'recreational' drug use being good for you right through to politics. Liam definitely wasn't a racist, but on the other hand he knew Nicky had a point. He knew that a number of people were disillusioned with the current situation and he didn't think it was really to do with racism, more that people wanted an equal playing field for everybody. Even members of the fitness club in Bury, clients whom Liam would say were mainly middle-class, were all dropping in 'this country's going down the pan' and 'between you and me, Liam' conversations with racist undertones. Of course, they ensured they were out of earshot of anybody who might be offended.

One of his lady members had come in to the club one day shaking her head and looking upset. She explained that she had recently been transferred to a different post office branch and, on one day the previous week, had recognised two Asian men who were regulars at the main Bury post office. She was disgusted because the men were claiming family benefit from her new branch under different names. She had told the manager who had first told her to keep her voice down and secondly that he would look into it. A week later, she still hadn't heard anything.

However, Liam also knew that half the drop-outs who went in The White Horse were claiming benefits and free housing and working on the side, so was there any difference? No, Liam wasn't a racist but he also feared that something serious would happen soon if the underlying racial tension continued.

'Fancy an all-dayer?' City Simon always managed to bring Liam back from the dark side.

'Yeah, come on, let's do it. Anybody fancy going to the

World Cup next year?'Tony and Rory had been to France '98 and had seen their dream of attending another World Cup rekindled the previous night.

'We've got to qualify yet.' Liam still wasn't convinced that England would get through.

'Talking about the prophet of doom, your Mick's just walked in looking like death warmed up.'

Mick gave the lads a wink before disappearing upstairs to talk business with Jack. Liam looked at his watch – 1.30pm. He was only working the afternoon shift the next day and he always liked a couple of pints the day after a good drinking session.

'I fancy a few pints, Simon. I'm going to go home for a quick bath and then I'll meet you in the Wine Lodge.'

'Don't be doing that, Liam, you'll be wasting valuable drinking time. It's not as if we will be out all day. Why don't you come down to the Wine Lodge now?' Rob, as always, had a valid point and, within minutes, the taxis were ordered and the lads were on the standard pub-crawl of Chorley. Nobody ever had to ask which pub was next because the lads always did the same route round the town and, as usual, it was the same old faces in the same old pubs.

Liam was starting to get bored with the same routine. He didn't know how Kenny remained enthusiastic about going out Thursday, Friday, Saturday and Sunday. Liam was now normally down to one night out during the weekend, and then went round to Kenny's to find out what he'd been up to the other three. After hearing about his friend's outrageous night-time antics, he felt as though he'd been out anyway.

As they made their way round the pubs, Liam couldn't

get Kate out of his mind and Paddy, who had got an all-day pass out from his wife, had spotted Liam's unusual seriousness.

'What's wrong with you, Liam... still not doing any shagging?' Paddy soon had Liam pissing himself as he made the most of the lack of bedroom activity among his team-mates. 'Just think about Nicky – two years without a jump. Talk about carrying your balls round in a wheelbarrow. Anyway, I've just got back from the World Championship Strawberry-Picking competition. Couldn't believe it... a woman with no legs won it – jammy cunt!'

Liam nearly spat his beer out as he burst out laughing. When he'd calmed down, he said, 'No, it's all right for you, Paddy, lovely wife and two beautiful kids.'

'Aye, if you say so, but you wouldn't be saying that if you had seen me at half-past-three this morning when Jake was puking and shitting all over me.'

'Point taken.'

The beer flowed as effortlessly as the banter, with the lads covering subjects ranging from piles to politics and wanking through to women. In what seemed like no time at all, they were back at The White Horse in time for the karaoke.

Liam checked out the pub for any good-looking women, but no sign of Kate, just the usual crowd. In the past year or so, all the better-looking local women seemed to give the pub a wide berth, and it had started to rival the Wine Lodge as the *Star Wars* bar of Chorley.

It was not long before some girls were up singing 'I Will Survive', and by the look of them they'd have to on their own, Liam thought. When another clambered up and started singing 'It's Raining Men', Liam whispered to Paddy, 'Not in your direction, love.'

Mad Al then jumped on the karaoke to sing 'Brown-Eyed Girl'. He soon had the pub rocking as he cavorted with one of the better-looking girls. As he finished the song, a big cheer went up, but it wasn't just for him. Giant had gingerly walked in. He wasn't going to let the fact that he had nearly lost his helmet stop him from doing his usual 'La Bamba' number near the end of the night. As he made his way over to the lads, he received some stick and cheers, as by now probably the whole of Chorley would have known what had happened. Rob and Kenny were on to him straight away.

'You soft bastard, we'd have won if you'd have played...' and 'I heard the doctor couldn't believe a 6-foot-odd giant could have such a small cock' were thrown at him but he lapped it up with his usual big grin. As he walked slowly towards his mates, Paddy was visibly bursting to take the mick out of his brother.

'Anyway, Giant, I believe they're going to make a film about your ordeal.'

'Yeah, go on then, give it to me.'

'They're going to call it *Free Giant's Willy*.'

Only Paddy, Liam thought, only Paddy could think up stuff like that.

'Come on, Liam, come and sing with me.'

'No chance, Kenny...' but, before he could do anything, Liam was stood in front of the screens.

Karaoke Dave introduced them. 'Next we have Liam and Kenny singing the lovely Rolf Harris number "Two Little Boys".'

Liam couldn't believe it. He'd sung it loads of times on numerous trips but never before with a microphone in his hand. What the hell, he thought. They both went for it and the whole pub started bouncing. Near the end of the song, Liam got the urge to drop his pants and Kenny didn't need any encouragement. They finished the song with their jeans round their ankles, revealing two pairs of very muddy legs, and everybody rounded things off with a massive cheer.

Liam loved the song. The lyrics probably didn't really mean much to anybody else but he sometimes became quietly emotional when he sang or heard the song. Without wanting to be known as a soft arse, he would do anything for his close mates and he knew deep down that most of them would do anything for him.

'Well done, Liam, you're no longer a karaoke virgin.' His brother Mick knew about Liam's fear of singing in public. 'You were superb, brother.'

Liam wasn't too sure, but he did feel chuffed with himself.

It wasn't long before Giant was up singing 'La Bamba'. 'You should be singing "Great Balls of Fire",' shouted Paddy.

'Fancy a curry and then a few beers at mine?' Kenny never wanted a night to end but Liam had seen enough.

'No, see you later, everybody.'

His mum was still up when he arrived home. She was really proud of him when he told her about his singing exploits. As she talked, Liam, even in his drunken state, could tell she had been drinking too much again.

'Mum, why don't you cut down on the beer drinking?'

'I'm OK, love, I only have a couple when your dad

goes to the pub and when you're out. I get bored just watchin' telly.'

Liam didn't really want to go on at his mum, but he knew that she was secretly drinking every night, seven days a week, but he still didn't say anything about her secret stash.

'I'm going to bed, love... I'll see you in the morning.'

'Love you, Mum.'

Liam went through the Teletext devouring the sports section, starting with the football. He couldn't believe it. Bolton had played two, won two. Rob must have been the happiest man alive. It was Rob who had converted Liam from a Liverpool to a Bolton fan at the age of 11 after taking him down to Burnden Park.

Liam's thoughts returned to his mum. He was genuinely worried about her. He had noticed since he'd moved back in that she spent most of her time in the kitchen, having taken to watching her portable television in there because his dad sat in the living room all day watching everything he'd taped from the night before.

'What a shit life for me mum.' Liam shook his head before burying it in his hands. All the family had tried their best to make their dad take her out more and do things during the day, without any success. His mum would also say that she didn't want to go to the pub and sit with all his dad's cronies and would rather stay in. She had told Liam that she was happy enough but he knew he had let her down by allowing his dad to treat her so badly in the past.

As he reached the top of the stairs, he heard her getting ready for bed.

'Good night, Mum, God bless.'

'God bless, love. You've not left your key in the back of the door, have you? Your dad will be home soon.'

'No, good night.' He wished his mum had locked his dad out of her life a long time ago.

Liam had a quick bath and was just leaving the bathroom when he heard his dad trying to get his key in the door. For a split-second, the noise scared him, bringing back memories of how all the family were frightened of hearing their father's key in the door. Nobody ever knew what mood he would be in when he arrived back from the pub, although it was not usually a good one.

Liam made his way quietly into his bedroom not wanting to speak to his dad. Once he was in bed, he couldn't stop thinking about how his father had treated the family, especially his mum. He tossed and turned as he listened to him banging about in the kitchen. Liam really wanted to confront his dad and ask him why. Why treat your wife like that? Why treat your own flesh and blood like he did?

12
An Eye for an Eye
June 1980 (Liam aged 10)

Liam woke up with the sound of his mum and dad arguing again. However, it was even noisier than usual this time. He slowly opened his bedroom door and realised with the different voices he could now hear that it wasn't just his parents involved in another alcohol-fuelled argument. He couldn't really comprehend what was happening, as only a few hours earlier his parents had gone out to the pub in a really good mood. His mum had given him a goodbye kiss and left him some chocolates and sweets after telling his sisters he was allowed to stay up to watch *Match of the Day*.

It was his sisters he could hear now, but it wasn't the laughter and silly screaming he had joined in earlier when they had played follow-the-leader all round the house. No, now it was also his mum's frightened screaming and the shouting he had heard before, when he was told to stay in his room. He made his way halfway down the stairs and sat in the darkness listening to the commotion. Cries of 'Get off her, Dad' and 'Please leave me mum alone' came out of the living room almost simultaneously. Liam didn't know what to do. He sat quietly for another minute or so before slowly sliding down each step of the stairs until he reached the bottom. He just wished his older brothers were around to help. Amid the screams, Liam could hear his dad shouting abuse.

'You fuckin' bitch, I'll kill you...' and then the distinct voice of his mum pierced the air with a desperate pleading.

'Please no, no.'

That was it; he would have to help his mum. He slowly opened the living-room door and peeped in to see her cowering on the settee, blood-stained hands covering her face. His dad was being held back from hitting her again. Jean and Fiona were grabbing and wrestling with their lurching, drunken father as best they could, as he tried to swing his arms towards his wife. Liam ran and rugby tackled his dad from the side and, along with his sisters, ended up with him in a heap on the floor. In an instant, the kids were scattered everywhere as Jim sprang from beneath them and made a grab for his wife's hair. When he pulled back his other arm to land another blow, all three children jumped on him with Liam and Fiona pulling at his hair and strangling him at the same time, while the stronger, older sister held back his arm with all her body weight.

Their mother managed to pull away from her husband's grip minus a clump of hair and ran upstairs screaming.

'Jean, phone the police, he's going to kill me this time.'

Jim was certainly not finished and he tried to stagger

after her, but was now being held back by two little bodies wrapped round his legs. However, he still managed to drag them to the table in the hallway where Jean had made it to the phone and was now trying to carry out her mother's wishes. Before she could dial the final nine, her dad ripped the phone out of the wall and threw it in the general direction of his wife's sobs from upstairs. Luckily, in his drunken state, he was now starting to tire, meaning that an eleven-year-old girl and a ten-year-old boy were now managing to hold on to him, preventing him from going upstairs. When the 14-year-old grabbed on to him once more, they all tumbled to the floor again.

Liam had had enough by now. He was not only terrified, but also angry that he couldn't protect his mum properly. He thought he knew who could, though, and, as his sisters started to beg his dad to stop, he seized his chance. He ran straight out of the front door directly in front of him into the darkness and pouring rain. He ran as fast as he could before he had to slow down to a walk, and then would run for a few more paces and slow again. It was only when he had stopped running that he realised how sore his bare feet were, and only then did he notice how much it hurt when he stood on stones and other objects on the path.

He thought he knew the way, but everything looked different in the dark and the street lamps only accentuated the pouring rain even more. His feet were grazed and his whole body began to shiver as he knocked on the door he hoped was his brother's girlfriend's house. An older man opened the door, which was the signal for Liam to burst into tears thinking he was at the wrong house. His brother must have heard the whimpers and came rushing out to see what was happening. Liam was then taken in, where, between blubbering tears and a change out of his soaking pyjamas, he managed to tell them what he had just witnessed. Within minutes, Michael and Dawn's dad had disappeared and Liam was being comforted with the assurance that he could stay the night and that his brother would be coming back.

The next morning, he was eventually, after a great deal of persuading, taken home by Michael after his mum had rung from a phone box to say she was fine and that she wanted her 'angel' to come home.

She met him at the front door and she gave him a reassuring hug and kiss on the cheek, but he felt like crying again on seeing close up her dark-blue-and-purple swollen and bloodshot eye.

Liam made his way apprehensively into the living room, expecting a bollocking off his dad, but the miserable old sod just sat there quietly in his chair.

It was only when Liam dared to look round a few minutes later as they watched television in silence that he noticed the black eye his dad now also had. Liam didn't say or do anything. He just slumped back even further into the settee, frightened. Deep down, though, he was happy and thought to himself, 'Is this what they mean when they say an eye for an eye?'

The black eye sustained by his mum couldn't have been as bad as his dad's because in the following days she got on with the business of going to work, looking after the house and children and generally doing everything for her husband as he sat in his chair watching telly. His dad didn't go to work the following week and didn't even go to the pub. Liam couldn't ever remember his dad not going to the pub before.

Within a week or two, the argument seemed to have been forgotten, but it wasn't long before the shouting matches started again.

His brother moved out of the house shortly afterwards to live with his girlfriend and her parents, which left only Liam of the three brothers at home. He cried when Michael shut the front door after telling his mum he would see her the next weekend. Liam also heard his mum crying in the kitchen, but made sure he was in his bedroom when his dad came home from work.

He listened at the top of the stairs as he heard his dad saying – no, shouting – that he didn't want to see Michael in the house again. Liam didn't dare tell him to his face, but he really hated his dad now and wished he was dead.

13
The Monday Blues
Monday, 3 September 2001

Why did alcohol make Liam so depressed? He could never understand how he could go from having a brilliant time on the beer with his mates to feeling like he wanted to top himself, all in the space of a day. Normally, he would remind himself that it was just the poison of alcohol bringing the demons into his head, but at other times he felt so melancholic that he doubted it was the alcohol. Sometimes, he thought he was on a collision course with depression. He should have learned from the experience he had gained from watching his poor mum in the past. Most of the time, he kept the sad thoughts well hidden from everybody, but there were some days when he would just lie on his bed all day and night and not want to speak to anybody.

At other times, like today, he told himself not to be silly and that once the alcohol was out of his system he could stop faking it with the Mr Happy smile every time he asked the customers if they had had a good weekend. This was in between making his excuses with them and the other staff and heading for the sanctuary of the toilets and his usual cubicle to read the *Daily Express* and get a quick 40 winks if possible. He didn't mind his dad's *Sun* during the week for the tits and the gossip, but he also enjoyed the football coverage in the *Express* and especially the day's headlines of England thrashing Germany 5–1.

Ever since he'd been a kid, he would read the sports pages from the back to the front and then start again and even now the headlines on the front page of the newspaper were left until after he had devoured the sports section.

Today, though, his head was mashed and the demons kept pestering him as he tried to read about how the 'Sven-Göran Eriksson-Inspired England Team' had demolished the Germans. The paranoia was digging into his brain, trying to spade out every reason to be unhappy. Who had he upset on Saturday night when he was drunk? Why had Spuggie, his friend from Newcastle, not returned his call? Did Kate really want to go out on Friday night or had she just been put on the spot? Why had his dad never taken an interest in him when he was a boy? Why had he not helped his mum more? And the last one which was nagging him more and more lately – Why me? Why me? Why me?

'Boss, just thought I'd better warn you that Ian's here and he looks like he's not slept for a few days…' came a voice from outside the cubicles.

Mark, one of the supervisors, knew the score when Liam had been on the beer at the weekend. Liam hated being called 'boss', but this meant that Mark called it him even more.

He got on really well with Mark who had been honest enough to tell him about his weekend drug habit. Ten years younger than him, Mark was from the new breed of lads, into Ecstasy and dabbling in cocaine. Liam had felt like he was his dad when he had first found out about Mark's weekend exploits and tried to lecture him about how some of his mates had seen it, done it and got the T-shirt in the late 80s and early 90s, only to be really feeling the effects now ten years later. But how do you convince a kid to lay off it when a tablet is as cheap as a bottle of Budweiser and gives you five times the buzz, as Mark had said?

Liam also liked the idea, if it was true, that these drugs didn't give you a hangover. It must have been an age thing but his hangovers were now lasting three days instead of the usual one.

Once he'd got used to the idea that most people were dabbling in recreational drugs now, he was happy to make sure that Mark wouldn't get into any trouble. If his supervisor was going on a 'Mad One' over the weekend, Liam would cover his shift, because he knew he could depend on Mark to cover for him when he was on one of his alcohol downers.

'Yeah, no problem. I'll be out in a minute.'

Liam walked into reception to find Ian rollicking Mark about the state of the staff kitchen. 'I'm not having it any more... I try my best for you lot and this is how you treat me, throwing it back in my face.'

'Ian, Ian, come on, let's pop into the office,' Liam suggested.

While Ian was banging a couple of the pots and pans

around in the kitchen sink, there were two or three customers at the reception desk waiting to be served. They had front-row seats as the owner blasted one of his best members of staff, employees whom in his advertisements he called the 'friendliest staff around'.

Liam shut the office door after Ian had trooped in, knowing he was going to get a lecture from his manager. Liam couldn't believe how rough Ian looked. His hair was sticking up without the aid of gel and his face hadn't seen a razor for three or four days. Liam tried to be sympathetic towards him. 'Ian, I know the staff get on your nerves, but you can't speak to them like that, especially in front of the customers.'

'I know, I'm sorry, Liam. I've had a bad weekend... I think I need to have my thyroxine levels checked again.'

'No problem, I've got everything in hand here. Why don't you go home and relax and I'll sort the monthly stats out for you?'

'It's me dad. He's been really getting to me again lately, and at church yesterday he spoke to me brother and sister and totally ignored me.'

Liam knew the feeling. He told Ian not to worry about it and gave him the old 'Don't think about the past but move forward' line.

When Ian had left, Mark came into the office. 'Thank God you got rid of him again, Liam. What did you say to him this time? On his way out, he thanked me for my good work and then said he would see us tomorrow. That religion shit really screws you up, doesn't it?'

Liam thought Mark was right to a large extent. He'd met a few really religious people over the years and they all seemed to have a screw loose. He'd also noticed that finding God had made Harty start to lose his friends. The last time he had been over to Bacup for a night out with him, a number of his friends had commented about how much he'd changed.

'Remember... religion is the opium of the people.' A quote he'd learned in Sociology A-level had somehow found its way back into Liam's memory. He laughed at Mark's reply.

'I think I'll stick to the Es, thank you.'

As they started to talk about the England game, the phone rang and Liam instinctively picked it up with the usual enthusiasm he had instilled in the staff – 'Thank you for calling Bodywise, Liam speaking.'

'Newcastle, Newcastle, Newcastle. How ya doin', man? Oh, Liam, I love you man.' The unmistakable tones of his Geordie friend sang down the phone. 'Did ya see the game, man? We wa' awesome. We're gonna win the World Cup, you knaw. Sorry I haven't called you. I was back in God's land for the Middlesbrough game, just got your message...'

'Spuggie, slow down, will you... you don't have to put your accent on for me.'

'Nah, man, ya cheeky bugger, what's happenin', anything new? I love the Toon, me. Are you goin' tonight, like?'

'Too right I am, if we beat Liverpool, we go back to the top of the League.'

'Aye, man, keeping it warm for the Toon.'

And so it continued.

Liam had met Spuggie – so called after a character out

of the children's TV series *Byker Grove* – while he was doing his degree at Warrington and they'd got on like a house on fire ever since. He was now a PE teacher in Manchester and had signed up for the glory season promised to him by Liam. That was as long as it didn't clash with any Newcastle games, because he followed them home and away. If they were playing on a Sunday, there was no chance of persuading him to play. Spuggie cracked his sides when he found out The White Horse's score and then went on to tell Liam how he couldn't even get out of bed on Sunday morning.

After a good 15-minute chat, Liam put the phone down and laughed to himself. If anyone could cheer him up, Spuggie could. He looked at his watch – 3.00pm, and the gloom was lifting.

The phone rang again and this time Mark answered it. Holding his hand over the receiver, he smirked knowingly at Liam before telling him 'somebody called Kate' was on the phone for him.

'Hello, can I help you?'

Mark had to stifle a snigger at his ultra-professional colleague before a 'V' sign sent him out of the office.

'Hiya, Liam, it's Kate. Sorry to bother you, but I just thought I'd check on how your friend was after his accident.'

'Oh, he's fine, Kate.' Liam wanted to say that Giant wouldn't be doing any shagging for a while, but he thought he'd try to be a bit more subtle. 'Giant said he was still sore down below when I saw him on Sunday night, but I think he'll live.'

'Oh good… are we still on for Friday night?'

'Yeah, course we are, I'll see you at the Gamebird at half-eight.'

'OK, see you then, bye.'

'Bye.' He'd forgotten he'd given Kate his work and home number after she had finally believed him when he told her that he didn't possess a mobile.

Are we still on? Are we still on? Liam wanted to do cartwheels round the office. The depression was rapidly lifting, as was the tingling feeling between his legs. The thought of a night out with Kate wasn't only making his spirits rise. He picked up the *Daily Express* and headed for the toilets again, although he wasn't planning on doing any reading this time.

14
The 'Hot' Date
Friday, 7 September 2001

L iam hadn't been this nervous since... well, he couldn't ever remember being this nervous. A night out with a girl who he thought was well out of his league had been the only thing on his mind all week. Anyway, he definitely knew he was on to a winner when Kenny, the ultimate 'blondes only' man, had agreed that Kate was a stunner.

Liam decided that he would make a really big effort with his appearance. A good hot bath was first on the agenda after the tiring 6.30am start at Bodywise. Finishing at 5.30pm and then getting stuck in the traffic on the way home had convinced him that it was time to start hunting for a job closer to home. It had also left him rushing around to ensure he would be on time to meet the goddess in the pub at 8.30pm.

After doing some nodding dog impressions in the bath, he set to his task of making himself look as presentable as possible. He looked in the mirror and was immediately conscious of his nasal hairs; he spotted some wiry little suckers in each nostril. Browny had obviously forgotten to check them on Sunday because he usually kept a grip on them for Liam. Countless times in the past, he had stood next to Liam in the pub looking for any protruding hairs before, without warning, ripping them out with expert precision. Liam had gone mad when he had first started doing it, but over the years he had now become accustomed to the sudden attacks. Even though his mate had recently presented him with a nasal trimmer for being his Best Man, Liam would still forget to trim them after a period of time before he received the short–sharp–shock treatment again.

Next, he attacked the blackheads that always seemed to reappear on his nose even after a few days of squeezing. Liam found it quite therapeutic watching how the white pus squirmed out of their holes. Luckily, there were no offending white heads to explode into the mirror. He continued with a quick shave of the bum fluff from his chin and around his lip and this made him think back to his first ever shave at basic training. He shook his head and smiled to himself in the mirror, remembering how naive he was when he joined the Army.

He had never even had a shave, but luckily his mum had bought him some Bic razors and shaving foam to take with him. The only problem was that Liam didn't have a clue what to do and had to watch the person at the next washbasin before he completely covered his face in foam and then gingerly pulled his razor across his skin. It was funny now, but it wasn't back then when you could be fined or even 'jailed' for not shaving correctly.

He finished the sprucing-up exercise by brushing his teeth. It really upset him that his teeth were yellowing after never smoking. Years of drinking tea and coffee, though, had taken its toll. He always brushed them as hard as he could until they bled. He knew he wasn't supposed to, but always felt he hadn't cleaned them properly if he didn't spit out some blood at the end.

He looked at his watch and, even though it was nearly 7.45pm, he still felt he had enough time to have a quick go on his secret weapon – his dad's recently acquired electric back heater, which doubled up as a face tanner. He had never used it before but it seemed easy enough to operate. His sister Fiona had warned him that ten minutes would easily be enough, so, after checking his watch again, he lay back as the tubes turned fluorescent. He put on some sunbed goggles he had borrowed from work and closed his eyes. Within a minute or two, he felt fantastic as the tubes gave off the warm glow. Liam then started thinking about the night ahead, hoping that everything would work out OK. Thinking of Kate gave him a hard-on, which he gently massaged through the wet towel draped over his legs. He then started to feel sleepy as he began to think back to all the good times he had had with different girlfriends. It was really difficult to decide which one was his favourite all-time shag... then...

Shit! Liam whipped off his goggles and opened his eyes, instantly realising he was in trouble. It was 8.15pm. He'd been grilling for over half-an-hour. Even as he looked in the mirror, he could feel his face tightening up and he couldn't quite believe the image staring back at him.

His face was bright red and burning, and all the more

striking for two little white circles round his eyes where the goggles had provided some protection. His face now began to swell, but not only that, as he looked closer, he realised his neck was still completely white as he'd fallen asleep and rested his chin on his chest. What the hell was he going to do?

He lay back down on his bed with a cold flannel on his face to try and stop the burning sensation. He felt like crying but his face was that tight he probably wouldn't be able to; the tears would have sizzled off his skin anyway. He was about to call Kate and tell her he had been struck down with something, anything, when he heard the front door open and the voice of his guardian angel speaking to his mum.

'Fiona, get your arse up here now,' Liam screamed.

After hearing her reach the top of the stairs, he lifted the flannel from his face. Fiona nearly wet herself laughing at her baby brother's predicament, but then set about assuring him he could still go out on the date.

'Give her a call and tell her you'll be late and we'll see what we can do.'

After leaving a message on Kate's mobile, he re-entered his bedroom where his sister was going through his drawers.

'Right, you'll have to wear a polo-neck jumper to hide your white neck. Sit there with the flannel over your face for ten minutes while I go and get some make-up and get Mum to iron your clothes.'

Liam lay back on his bed and reapplied the cold flannel to his face. In between feeling sorry for himself, he started to think how much his older sister had done for him in the past. There were only 18 months between them, although, in terms of maturity, they were years apart. Liam knew he was an immature 31, but Fiona had grown up quickly when their mum had become depressed, having filled the role of mother to Liam for a number of years. At the time, Liam was oblivious to how much his sister had actually done for them, but he knew as he grew older that he was indebted to her for everything she had done for him. She was happily married now, but was still very close to her family.

'Right, let's have a look at you then, Tomato Face. Oh, that's looking a bit better now.'

Liam still felt like a burns victim, but it had brought the swelling down. 'What are you gonna do about my eyes? I can't wear sunglasses.' The difference between his bright-red face and the white circles round his eyes made him look like a clown.

'Remember what I used to do with the make-up to cover up your zits? Yeah, well, let's see what we can do.'

She set to work with Liam, sitting on the same bedroom chair she'd used to put make-up on to stop him being teased about his spots when he had first started going out.

After what seemed like an eternity, but was actually about five minutes, he got the go ahead to open his eyes and examine the results.

'Perfect, sis. You're an absolute star.'

'Just don't get too close to her in the light or she'll think you are some kind of weirdo.'

'D'ya really think I can pull it off? Or should I give her a call and tell her I am not feeling so good?'

'Liam, you told me how much you were looking forward to tonight. I've never heard you talk about anybody the way you've talked about this girl. Now get out there and do your best. You finish getting dressed and I'll give your shoes a going over for you.'

When he eventually made his way downstairs, he went into the living room and, once the permanent fog of smoke cleared slightly, he received a wolf whistle from his sister and an admiring nod of the head from his mum.

'You look lovely, love... don't he, Jim?'

'Aye,' said his dad with his eyes fixed on the television. 'Make sure you take a key out with you.'

'D'ya fancy givin' us a lift, Fiona?'

'Yeah, no problem.'

As he closed the door to his sister's car outside the pub, he took a deep breath. He was determined to make a good impression and, luckily, he'd made the new time with five minutes to spare. He now felt like he looked the part; he just hoped he could play the part.

He walked in through the big oak doors and was relieved that it was relatively quiet and he didn't recognise anybody. He looked for the darkest part of the bar area and bought himself a pint of lager. He glanced round; there was no sign of Kate so he sat down on one of the big chairs. He took a large swig of his lager, hoping that he could get a pint or two down before his date for the evening arrived. However, just as he was about to take another gulp, he heard the entrance doors open and, as he looked round, Kate smiled at him. She looked absolutely stunning, wearing a slinky black dress. He noticed that a few other lads, even some who were with their girlfriends, were looking at her as she made her way over.

'Hiya!'

Liam jumped from his seat and pecked her on the cheek as she leaned forward. He just hoped he wouldn't be leaving her with any extra make-up on her face.

'Sorry I had to rearrange the time. What would you like to drink?'

'Oh, don't worry... it stopped me from having to rush around getting ready. Err, I'll have a lager and lime please. Anyway, are you all right? You look different today.'

Liam felt embarrassed but he couldn't go any redder. 'I'll tell you once I've got the drinks.'

When he returned, he decided that honesty was the best policy. He explained how tired he was when he had arrived home from work and how he had eventually fallen asleep under the sun lamp. He didn't tell her that, while his skin had been burning, he was dreaming that he had been making love to her on a deserted beach.

Kate couldn't stop laughing as he described how his sister had rescued the situation. 'Liam, I've only known you a week or so but I've already seen you naked twice and seen your friend with his tiddler trapped in his zip. Not forgetting seeing you with your ears full of mud... and now this. Is there anything else you want to tell me?' Luckily, she was giggling as she spoke.

'I know, I'm sorry. I'm quite quiet normally.'

'Don't be sorry. I haven't laughed so much for a long time.'

Over the next couple of hours, Liam and Kate talked and talked. Liam had never got on with anyone the way he did with this beautiful brown-eyed, black-haired, Catherine Zeta-Jones lookalike. He also made sure he was on his best behaviour all night. If he wanted to fart, he held it in until he excused himself and then let rip when he was having a pee. Failing that, if he couldn't hold it in, he made sure he got as far away from Kate as he could before emitting a silent one as he walked towards the toilets. He laughed on the journey back as he overheard a girl blaming one of his silent explosions on her innocent boyfriend.

By 11.00pm, he had nearly told Kate his life story. The good parts, anyway. She, in turn, told him how she had only recently split from her fiancée, whom she had been seeing since she was 14. She had been seeing the same bloke for 12 years. Between laughing and joking, she started to talk seriously about why she had decided to split up with him. Liam hadn't seen Kate before because she had lived in Saudi Arabia for five years working as a nurse – her gorgeous tan hadn't needed any artificial enhancement –and before that she had lived in Manchester. Her boyfriend was a doctor and they had moved to Saudi together.

'After I told him I wasn't happy, he accused me of having an affair. I couldn't get it through to him that we had just outgrown each other. I was so disillusioned and just wanted to be happy again, or at least to just start having a laugh again. He then started treating me really badly and became a complete control freak.'

Liam instinctively placed his hand over one of hers and gently stroked it as he spotted tears welling in the corners of her eyes.

'That's why I moved back to England.'

'Well, don't worry, you're back home in sunny Chorley now and, if the big bad doctor comes looking for you, I'll set the Giant on to him.'

He soon had Kate laughing again by telling her some more of the daft things that had happened to him in the past. One thing that Liam was quite confident about was making people laugh – even when he didn't mean to.

By the end of the evening, he was pleasantly pissed, but had made sure he had behaved and knew the night had been a success. In the taxi, Kate said that she had been embarrassed about how much she had opened up to him, but he told her not to be silly. He, for one, knew it was better to talk to someone than to bottle everything up, even though the guilt he had been feeling lately was still eating away at him. Liam had always been a good listener, but the opportunity to talk to someone about his own troubles had never really presented itself.

As the taxi stopped, Kate looked at Liam and thanked him for a great night. She then leaned forward and gave him an unbelievably sexy kiss. He responded for as long as she allowed, before she broke away. 'Give me a call over the weekend and we'll go out for coffee.'

He watched her as she made her way to the front gates before she turned round and gave him a wave and a gorgeous smile. Liam could feel himself stiffening down below as he gazed at her.

'She's a bit of a stunner, that one.' The taxi driver probably had a hard-on, too.

'I know, mate, I know.'

Liam couldn't believe it. It may have been five seconds

but she had put her tongue down his throat so seductively his face felt like it was on fire again. He'd behaved impeccably all night, but he was sorely tempted to head straight to the nearest phone box and call her to see if she fancied a coffee in the next half-hour.

15
Will Things Ever Be the Same, Harry?
Tuesday, 11 September 2001

'You'll have to take them, Liam... I've been booked in by Ian to do a fitness assessment.'

Mark usually took a group from the local secondary school in the aerobic studio for an hour on Tuesdays, but Ian, as usual, had messed the system up in his quest to get more money in. Normally, Liam would have been upset at having to take the 14-year-old lads – third years, or 'year tens' as they were now known. However, he was still on a high from his date the previous Friday, and then the subsequent coffee he'd shared with Kate.

'Only 45 minutes today, lads.'

'OK, sir.' Fifteen of the pupils walked into the aerobic studio along with Miss Eccles, their PE teacher, whom Liam always had a good flirt with.

Once he set each of them going with different exercises, he started the usual banter with her. 'So, miss, you've been out this weekend chatting up your students, have you?'

Before long, she was giving as good as she got. 'Mark tells me you've got yourself a lover then... is it true?'

Liam was about to reply, but spotted two of the young lads struggling with their press-ups. 'You two stop messing around and get on with it, proper press-ups. You're not trying to make love to the floor.'

The PE teacher threw him a 'You can't say that to the pupils' look, but Liam was having none of it.

'You... yes, you.'

One of the cocky lads who had been continually messing about eventually looked at him. 'Yeah? What's your problem?'

Liam couldn't believe what he had just heard. He walked over and crouched down, ending up with his face right up against the lad's head.

'Listen, you little shit, I'm not one of your PE teachers who you can take the piss out of. Either get on with the exercises or go and get dressed and see me later.'

Spuggie had told Liam how the kids at his school could get away with anything these days and the teachers couldn't lay a finger on them. They weren't even allowed to tell them off any more and that's why Spuggie, who had already been promoted quickly, was thinking of leaving the profession he loved.

Fortunately, the pupil backed down and started doing his exercises properly. Liam gave the PE teacher a wink.

'Come on then, Liam, is it true? Have you got yourself a girlfriend?'

'Well, you know, she'll do for now, until something better comes along.' Liam didn't want to tell Miss Eccles that he had really fallen head over heels for Kate and that he thought about her – and what they would end up doing together – for most of his waking moments.

Miss Eccles flashed Liam a look that unmistakably said, 'You male chauvinist pig,' but she knew he was only joking.

As the end of the session approached, Mark rushed in and gasped, 'You want to see what's going on the telly... there's a plane crashed into the Twin Towers in New York.'

Liam didn't have a clue what he was going on about and carried on with the lesson. He finished it with a few more bollockings before walking into the bar area. For the next two hours, he couldn't tear his eyes away from the television screen.

'What the hell is going on?'

Member after member came into the fitness club to exercise, but everybody became transfixed with the four television screens in the bar area. It was like watching a film in slow motion on each television station, be it Sky News, CNN or the BBC. They all showed continuous live coverage and re-runs of the planes smashing into the Twin Towers. Liam actually saw the second plane crashing into one of the towers as it happened. Various reporters started talking about the possibility of up to 100,000 deaths as various 'experts' were wheeled on to speculate about possible terrorist attacks all over America.

He watched in disbelief as the drama unfolded and felt totally sickened as the realisation kicked in that thousands of innocent people had been killed. Liam knew there and then that he was watching an event unfold that would sadly become a historic landmark.

When Barry, one of the members, came in and said, 'It's about time something like this happened to the Yanks.. it might wake them up,' Liam felt like turning round and smacking him. He was an annoying sod at the best of times, but no one was in any mood for one of his self-important 'look at me' comments

However, no matter how much Liam felt annoyed at Barry's insensitivity, later in the week, as he watched hours and hours of coverage, Liam thought more about what he had said.

Probably unknowingly, Barry had stumbled upon something potentially significant. Liam had missed out on an Ireland tour just as he was leaving the Army, but a day after his Regiment had arrived in Northern Ireland, a number of his friends had been helicoptered in to a horrific scene at which a coach bomb had exploded. Harty had recounted seeing all the charred bodies splattered all over the place and had told Liam that, even now, he still had nightmares about what he had seen. Liam had also been studying in Warrington when the IRA decided to detonate a bomb in the middle of the town, killing two innocent boys.

He remembered going into the town centre the following week and seeing the memorial of flowers that people had left and the boys' photographs. Tears had streamed down his face as he watched people, some the children's relatives, openly weeping outside shops. The valid point that Barry had probably not even realised he was making was that the Americans had never known terrorism like this, on a scale that was familiar to the British. Indeed, many Americans had unwittingly funded the terrorist cause in Northern Ireland by putting money in the charity boxes and giving money to the 'Free

Ireland' campaign when most of them had probably never been to Ireland. One American had once asked Liam, 'So whereabouts in England is Ireland?'

In the following days, Liam had started to feel sorry for himself, thinking about all the innocent people who had been killed. All the families left without their dads, mums, sons, brothers and sisters. He called Kate and she had said how upset she was watching and reading everything. But, for Liam, it became an obsession. It was sickening to watch but he was spellbound by the images of the victims jumping to their deaths. The tragedy of the firemen rushing in to try and save lives only to end up losing theirs made him wonder what the hell was going on in the world. The sadness of seeing people wandering round with photographs of their loved ones in a vain hope that they would still be found alive left him feeling empty.

He watched the television every day and bought a couple of broadsheet newspapers to read anything and everything to do with the 9/11 events. The whole thing started to depress him, and make him wonder what the point of everything was. For some reason, he began to take the disaster and its aftermath really personally. And all this at a time when things were going so right for him in all other respects – finding a beautiful girl and playing football again. It just didn't seem worth it, when all you had to look forward to was the death and destruction of innocent, law-abiding people.

It was Harry the Lollipop Man, on duty on the crossing outside the fitness club, who brought him out of his depression and back to the reality of routine life. On the Friday, as he walked into the club, Harry – the 78-year-old World War II veteran – shouted his normal 'Morning, Liam, sir...' greeting, clipped his heels together in perfect military style and waited for Liam's usual 'Carry on, chappy...' reply. But this time he got more than he bargained for.

'What's it all about, Harry? All those innocent people... Words fail me. It's not worth it, is it? The world will never be the same, will it, Harry?'

'Now, Liam, lad, I've never seen you without a smile on your face. I know you're upset. We all are with what's happened in New York. But you know what, lad? They said things would never be the same after the Second World War when there were millions of innocent people killed, and nowadays most people want to forget about it, and some kids don't even know it happened.'

Liam could see Harry's eyes welling up. 'All I can say to you, lad, is enjoy your life because it goes quick. You can only worry about the environment around you – you can't put right what's happening in New York, can you?'

In an instant, Liam knew what Harry meant, and he was so right.

'Harry, you are the man.' He held out his hand and Harry took it, Liam feeling the strength in the ex-coalman's grip.

'OK, enough of that, make sure them boots are bulled better tomorrow or you're on a charge.'

'You cheeky young...'

Before he could finish his sentence, Liam was through the fitness-club door. As he opened up, he thought again about what Harry had said. He still couldn't get his head round why war veterans and their families – and, for that matter, older people, were not treated with greater respect. Harry was nearly 80 years old, but was still having to stand out in all weathers 'for a little bit of extra cash'.

By the time he had finished the opening-up routine, Liam felt ready to take on the world again. He made Harry and himself a cup of coffee just as Julie, one of the reception staff, was arriving.

'Me Julie... me Julie... I love you, Julie.'

'Shut up, you silly bugger.'

Liam then made his way back outside into the cold. 'There you go, Harry, you little star. He who saves one man saves the world entire, sir.'

The phrase – believed to have been said by Oscar Schindler, the man who saved hundreds of Jews from the concentration camps and immortalised in the novel *Schindler's Ark* – held a great deal of significance for Liam, who was utterly sincere when he continued, 'You may have just saved my life, Harry.'

'Well, get yourself inside while I go and save some more.'

Harry then went into the centre of the road to cross a couple of kids over.

What a man, Liam thought. What a man. He went back into the fitness club and tried Kate's mobile phone number.

'Hello?'

'Hello, Kate, it's Liam. How you doin'?'

'I am just about to go to work. Are you all right?'

'All right? I am feeling one hundred and ten per cent. Will you give me the pleasure of your company this weekend, or do I have to stay in on my own with me mum watching *Parkinson*?'

'You sound more cheerful than the other day. What about Saturday? Fancy a quiet drink in the Swan with Two Necks?'

Liam fancied a great deal more than that as he held his new mobile phone, which Kate had embarrassed him into buying, in one hand and, without realising it, gently tugged at his crotch with the other.

'Yep, definitely, see you about seven–thirty?'

'Yeah... and don't go under the sun lamp again.'

'Very funny... bye.'

'Bye.'

Julie was looking at him as he struggled to find the 'off' button on the mobile.

'Liam, do you mind?' She laughed, as he followed her eyes down to his tracksuit bottoms before realising his hand was down the front of them.

'Sorry, Julie... just making sure it's still there.'

16
It's Not a Matter of Life and Death
Sunday, 16 September 2001

'Keep still, Kenny, it's definitely broke.'

Steve, whose role for the day was the bucket and sponge man, was rather stating the obvious as Kenny's lower left leg was facing the opposite way to its usual position.

'I know it's fuckin' broke, but try telling the rest of me body... I can't stop shaking.'

Liam looked round the lads to gauge their reaction as to how bad his mate's injury was.

'Bloody hell, Kenny, you won't be doing any shagging for a few weeks,' Mick joked, trying to make light of the situation.

'It could be worse.' Nicky, who'd run on to the pitch, can of Stella in one hand, roll-up in the other, was only trying to raise Kenny's flagging spirits.

'What do you mean worse?' spat Kenny, wincing as the pain grew in intensity.

'Well, there's a turd about six inches from your head... you could have landed in that.'

'Oh, there is as well.'

'I thought you'd just shit yourself, Kenny.' Giant joined in, attempting to keep the banter going, trying to keep Kenny talking.

One of the League officials, who'd been observing that morning, arrived with some news. 'The ambulance will be here in ten minutes, once the park gates have been opened.'

'The tossers have forgotten to open the park gates again. Who's in charge of that shit, Mick?' Rob turned round but Mick was already running towards the gates.

The manager was getting more and more wound up not only because one of his friends had probably got a compound fracture, but also because the game was in danger of being abandoned with The White Horse leading 3–0 against, of all teams, the Black Boy.

The referee was also looking at his watch as it had started to pour down. It looked like he didn't want to get his uniform wet or dirty. 'I think I'll have to call the game off. We can't move him and if the ambulance is going...'

'You fuckin' well won't. We were called off last week because we didn't have a ref and the fixtures will get well behind later on in the year because of the weather, so we're not going to stop this one.' Rob looked round and spotted that pitch number 6 didn't have anybody playing on it.

'Right then, if we can't move Kenny, we'll move the game.'

Rob took his brother Giant to have a chat with Jim, the

Black Boy's manager, and, after some gentle persuading, he agreed to change pitches.

Within minutes, Kenny had only Steve for company, and the game was up and running again with 20 minutes to go. By this time, the rain was hammering down and the pitch was deteriorating into a mud bath.

The opposition weren't up to much and Liam heard one of them asking the ref to blow his whistle early. Of course, the Jobsworth wasn't having any of it.

Jogging about to keep warm, Liam looked over to Kenny. He was now covered in everybody's coats, spare tracksuit bottoms, tops and subs kits that Steve had laid over him to make him as comfortable as possible. He also looked like he was on fire as Wayne had given him a spliff and a cloud of smoke was hovering over him.

The game finished with Spuggie and Wayne completing the rout with a couple more goals piece. Liam made his way over to see how Kenny was just as the ambulance men started to make their way across with a stretcher.

'What the fuck you doing? You can't drink that.'

Liam couldn't believe his eyes – in between puffs, he was drinking from a can of Stella given to him by Nicky.

'Too right I can – painkillers.'

Within minutes, the ambulance men had manoeuvred Kenny on to the stretcher and were marching with him across the sodden field. By now, the patient was as high as a kite, as the cocktail of drugs now included permanent lungfuls of gas and air.

'Bloody great this...' he giggled uncontrollably as he went past the pavilion.

'I'll see you lads later in the pub... tell that tosser Jack to save me some of that piss soup.'

Mad Al seized his chance. 'What size boots are you, Kenny? You won't be needing them again.'

Even after seeing Kenny carted away in the ambulance, Rob was surprisingly still in an upbeat mood. 'First win on the board... we're back on track.'

He grabbed hold of Liam round the neck and Liam could see the excitement in his face; it was as if they were all teenagers again.

'Not only that, the best thing possible has just happened to us.'

All the lads, who were by now starting to freeze as they awaited the opening of the changing-room doors, looked at Rob for the punchline. He didn't disappoint.

'Kenny breaking his leg means I don't have to tell him I was dropping him next week.'

As Liam walked into the pub a while later, he could tell Jack already knew about Kenny's leg.

'Shame about Kenny... he's knackered now, being self-employed and all that.'

At first, Liam thought Jack was revelling in Kenny's misery. However, after the landlord had served Stan, who was again arguing with his mate Harold, he made his way back over to Liam. 'Listen, I know I've had the odd argument with Kenny and we don't always see eye to eye, but for the next few weeks I think we should organise a few whip-rounds for him, and any money we make on the raffles should be given to him. I know what it's like working for yourself, Liam... the lad'll need some help now.'

Liam couldn't believe what he was hearing. He turned to Rob to see if he'd put him up to it and they were just taking the piss, but Rob was nodding in agreement.

'Yeah, I'm going to sit down and start trying to sort out something for his business. Me and Knobhead are going to work out what jobs he's got on at the moment and Knobhead's going to sort them for him. He's going to be knackered for a couple of months. Oh, I'll see about his insurance as well. Knowing Kenny, he'll end up making some money out of this.'

Liam was really moved at the togetherness of everybody and even though he knew Jack was a good bloke underneath he never thought he would want to help Kenny out. He was just about to shake the landlord's hand when Stan and Harold started pushing and shoving each other at the bar.

'Eh, eh, eh... you two, sort it out. What's going on?'

Liam couldn't believe it as Stan and Harold, with a combined age of about a hundred-and-fifty, were now wrestling at the bar.

Jack split them up. 'Right, you two, sort your differences out or you're barred.'

There were a few sniggers as Jack continued. 'What's the problem, Stan? Has he been shaggin' your missus again?'

'No, I've just bet him a tenner that I'll die before him and he's not having it.'

Harold burst in. 'Come on then, let's make it 20 quid.'

'How are you going to collect your winnings?'

Jack liked a bet, but even he was amazed at the wager. Both pensioners looked at Jack with bemusement.

Harold suddenly had a bright idea. 'Well, whoever wins

the bet, the other buys the dead geezer's wife a bunch of flowers and some chocolates then.'

Stan seemed satisfied with this compromise.

'Reet, get your money where your mouths are then.'

The two old war horses then shook hands on the bet and carried on drinking at the bar.

By now, all the lads were grouped round a few tables and the usual post-match chat was in full flow. 'See, boys, you needed Spuggie Shearer to sort your team out. Some Geordie pride. Shearer... Shearer... we are Champions League, said we are Champions League.' There was no stopping Spuggie once he got going. 'Aw, man, my mate Alan would have been proud of me today, like. Just call me God Number Two if you want.'

Spuggie was not only obsessed with Newcastle, but even more so with their famous number 9.

'Well done today, lads,' said Rob, raising his glass. 'Unfortunate Kenny breaking his leg, but it'll hopefully make us more determined next week. We're going to be doing a few things to help him out, so if any of you have got any ideas, let me know. Man of the match and two free pints to young Gazza.'

'Fix... fix.'

Spuggie pretended that he wasn't happy with the manager's verdict, but Gazza had played superbly. Liam was really pleased that he had taken the trouble to coax the young lad into playing.

As all the lads started chatting to each other about their teams' performance the day before, City Simon started singing 'Blue Moon', a tune he put on the jukebox every week. Liam smiled to himself. Two weeks into the season and everybody – bar Kenny, of course – was having a great laugh.

'Bit of news from the hospital...' There was a lull in the chatter as Jack continued, 'Kenny's going to be in for a few days because of how bad it is, but Steve says the dirty dick has already come close to shagging one of the nurses.'

'Hope it's not Kate, Liam.' Rory then ruffled Liam's hair. 'Ah, no, stupid of me... she's not blonde enough, is she?'

17
Beckham the Saviour
Saturday, 6 October 2001

Liam was having one of his really dark days. No, the darkest day. Even a phone call from Kenny telling him about his fling with a nurse despite his broken leg had been unable to lift his spirits. Kenny usually couldn't fail to cheer Liam up with updates on his antics and questions like 'How you going on with Iron Knickers?' but Liam's usual laughter was half-hearted today. Kenny couldn't believe that Liam wasn't going to the pub, and preferred instead to stay in bed, claiming that he was knackered. He finished the phone call reminding Liam that he was out of order for saying England would get beaten anyway.

As the phone started ringing again downstairs, Liam slumped back into bed. He decided he wasn't going to answer it any more. He had arranged to meet a number of the lads in the pub at 2.00pm to watch the build-up to the Greece game, but it was now 2.50pm and his bedroom was still in near darkness, a suitable match for the thoughts that were spinning around his head.

Liam closed his eyes. What was wrong with him? How could he contemplate committing suicide when he apparently had so much going for him, perhaps the most he had ever managed to achieve? He now had the gorgeous girlfriend he had always dreamed of meeting. He may not have slept with her yet, a fact that Kenny never let him forget, but he didn't mind. Four weeks into the relationship and Liam was besotted and knew that Kate also genuinely felt something for him. The way she spoke, looked at him and even kissed and touched him was different from anything he had ever experienced previously.

Today, though, even this didn't seem to matter now. In the last couple of days, he had started thinking more and more about the painful memories from his childhood and this had started to weigh heavily on his mind. Everything that had happened to him had become more vivid and Liam didn't like what he saw. The fact that 99 per cent of the time he was more than happy didn't matter today. The one per cent of depression had hit big time, and it wasn't just a niggling one per cent today... no, today it was up there in neon lights.

This was not the first time Liam had contemplated suicide, but this time it was for real. Past occasions had surfaced more like passing thoughts, but rarely imposed themselves. He thought back to the 'Dear John' letter he'd received during basic training that had nearly sent him over the edge, which, coupled with the bullying he experienced, had made suicidal thoughts all the more persistent. He laughed to himself now, thinking how heartbroken he was at the time to lose his first girlfriend and believe that, at 17, he had nothing to live for. The second time was more serious, but was still a major source of piss-taking with the lads, who even now didn't appreciate the full extent of Liam's one and only dabbling with drugs.

He had come out of the Army in late 1990 when quite a number of the lads had gone into the rave scene while the rest stayed on the beer. Liam had stayed a 'beer-head' because he liked alcohol, but also because he was always paranoid that he'd inevitably be the one to take the bad E and end up dying from it. The fact that some of the lads were taking five a night and not dying didn't come into it.

However, one night the lads had gone out on a stag do as a group of 'beer-heads' and 'E-heads' together. Liam had played football earlier in the day and was feeling absolutely shattered by about 9.00pm.

'Take a bit of speed to get you going,' Paddy suggested, aware of Liam's non-drug-taking policy, but he wasn't dissuaded by the dirty look Liam flashed him. 'No, honest, it'll just get you going again, perk you up.'

Liam had then been passed a moneybag of speed from Billy, one of his other mate's older brothers, a giant of a bloke who had just done a five-year stretch for drug-dealing. As soon as he had the speed in his hand, Liam had panicked. He tried to act cool and collected as he headed for the toilets, but inside his heart was pounding.

First, he was scared to death of getting caught with the illegal substance and, second, he was worried about the effect that the speed would have on him. He had then locked the toilet-cubicle door and opened the moneybag, before taking out the entire lump and chewing the chalk-like substance. He struggled to swallow it, but managed eventually and even licked the money bag clean before flushing it down the loo.

As he made his way out of the toilets, the gorilla was waiting for him. His smiling face turned to disbelief as he realised what Liam had just done. 'Where's me shit?'

'I've eaten it.'

How was Liam supposed to know how much to take? He'd never seen speed before, never mind taken it. Billy did a quick exit as Liam made his way back to the lads. He could just about remember answering Paddy's 'Are you all right, mate?' with a 'Think so...' but the rest of the night and the next couple of days had been pieced together for him numerous times.

In the days and weeks to come, different friends recounted what had happened. Paddy told him how he did the *Exorcist* vomit scene all over the dance floor in the rave club as he sprayed the contents of his stomach – lager and speed – over everyone in the immediate vicinity, an act that had probably saved his life. Giant told him how he wanted to fight everybody in the club, mostly people who were all loved up on Ecstasy. Tony explained to him how he had tried to grab hold of every girl whom he thought was giving him the eye, something they all did when raving, lost in their 'I love the world' state.

All the stories seemed hilarious now, but not at the time when his sister Fiona had found him in the back garden with his eyes popping out of his head. She then had to look after him for two days in his bedroom as he went on the biggest downer of his life. This wasn't at all funny. The paranoia had been real and only she and Liam knew how close he had come to topping himself on the second day. She had promised not to tell anybody what had happened and had always kept her word. He, in return, had never taken drugs again, telling everybody that 'beer was enough for him' – and it was.

The depressive thoughts he was having today, though, were different. He was sober, he'd had another great night with Kate and he should have been happy. On top of that, work was going OK, he had the best set of mates he could hope for and The White Horse had won the last four games on the trot with, as Spuggie kept reminding him on the phone, 'Spuggie Shearer scoring ten goals'.

Today, though, no matter how he tried to make light of everything, he felt down; no, not down, today he felt like he didn't want to be a part of the world any more. Of course, he felt guilty about what he was going to do. When he went to the cemetery to visit his nana and saw the gravestones of the three lads, all at different ages – 19, 22 and 27 – who were past pupils of his school, he had thought what a waste it was. He always read the inscriptions and thought how sad it was that they had become so desperate that they didn't want to live any more... but now it was Liam's turn.

From 3.00pm onwards, he heard the phone downstairs but he just kept ignoring it. He knew the lads would be ringing to see where he was and, for a split-second, he wondered what the score was before returning to his desperate state, and the task in hand. Eventually, he brought the shoebox out from under his bed and took the boxes and tubs of tablets out. He knew it was the easy way out and the least painful, but his thoughts were to take the pills and then go to sleep thinking about all of his happiest moments from his childhood and later years.

He knew on the face of it he'd had a great life. Everybody had always seen the good in Liam ever since his school days. He may have been a bully sometimes, which he regretted, but at one of the school reunions recently even the former nerds said they had still liked him. He may also have got himself into trouble in the Army, but he left there a blue-eyed boy with an exemplary record. Even at college, where Liam got into a fight with a lecturer, he had also really enjoyed studying.

No, he'd had a great life, but deep down he was sick of the dark secret. Yes, if he really thought about it, it was the 'things' that his uncle had made him do and did to him that were driving him to suicide. He knew there were people who were worse off than him, but the mental pain of what his uncle had said and what he had encouraged Liam to do was just as bad, wasn't it?

It was weird that everything was becoming more vivid as he got older. He sometimes woke up in the night after dreaming about what had happened and what his uncle had actually said to him. Was it his own fault? Should he have known it was wrong? He'd thought about telling Fiona many times, and he knew she would probably understand, but he had never wanted anybody to know.

As he sat in near-darkness, the house was totally quiet. His mum had gone round to Mrs Mitchell's and his dad had gone to the pub for the afternoon. Liam thought about his mum. She wouldn't understand why, but she would understand. She wouldn't want any of her children to be in pain, be it physical or mental, Liam reasoned. He felt guilty and he had thought about leaving a simple note saying, 'Sorry, Mum,' but he didn't want her to think it was her fault, far from it.

He started to pop the tablets out of a packet into the pint of water his mum had left for him, his last request. One after the other, the white disks fizzed and dissolved. He lost count, but could see the water changing colour and becoming cloudier and cloudier. Liam then grabbed a pen and slowly stirred the milky liquid, getting ready to down the pint glass in one.

Just as he started to raise the glass to his mouth, he nearly had a heart-attack as the shrill ring of the mobile under his pillow shattered the silence, causing him to spill the mixture all over the place. 'Bastard!' he shouted out loud, but it could only be Kate calling as he hadn't told anybody else he had bought a mobile. He searched round for it, thinking she could be in trouble. In the mobile's glowing face, the name 'Goddess' shone out at him. He pressed the green button. He couldn't hear anything for a second or two, except for something that sounded like background interference.

'Kate... Kate... are you all right?'

'Liam, it's Kate...' Her excited voice punctuated the random noise. 'I can't hear you, but I'm in The White Horse. You should be here. David Beckham's just scored for England and we're through to the World Cup Finals. I'll be round in two minutes.'

Liam's bed was wet through. He opened the curtains to

allow some daylight in and spotted his mum coming up the garden path. She smiled and waved to him.

'Liam, David Beckham's got England through to the World Cup, love.' His mum sounded like she'd been on the pitch celebrating with the team, she was huffing and puffing that much. 'Are you all right, love? Are you still feeling rough? Can I get you anything?'

As he made his way to the bottom of the stairs to get a cloth, the phone rang and Tony was on to him. 'Why are you not here celebrating?' He didn't wait for a reply. 'Beckham's done it for us again.'

Liam could hear Giant in the background eager to get his expert analysis in. 'Fuckin' hundredth free kick he'd took, the tosser.'

'We're going to Japan.'

Liam didn't get a chance to offer his thoughts, as there was a knock at the door and, within seconds, Kate was in his arms.

'I love you... I love you...' She was hugging him close and thrusting against him, saying, 'Yes, yes, yes!'

'He's a good 'un, that Beckham, in't he, Kate?'

Kate looked at Liam in total shock. She hadn't realised his mum was in the kitchen.

Liam could see the newspaper headlines in his mind: 'DAVID BECKHAM SAVED MY LIFE'. He looked at Kate and grabbed her, nuzzling into her neck. Everything would be all right, he thought. What the hell had he been thinking?

18
She's the One
Sunday, 7 October 2001

'Come in and stop looking so jumpy... my mum and dad aren't back yet.'

Kate's voice was calm and reassuring, but Liam felt anything but calm. He was really nervous. He'd had a fantastic night with Kate and she had loved listening to his mum's stories of what she had got up to when she was a young girl. Liam had heard them a thousand times, but he still enjoyed hearing about a time when his mum was at her happiest.

When Kate had left, he had sat on the end of his bed and cried his eyes out. He couldn't believe how close he had come to being another sad statistic.

As soon as he had woken up the next morning, he had wanted to see Kate and was really chuffed that she had replied to his text message with a 'CMON ROUND'. He was really apprehensive about meeting her mum and dad for the first time, though. Half of him was looking forward to seeing

Kate's parents because of her good reports about them, but the other half was, for some reason, very uneasy. It was all about creating a good first impression because he already knew Kate was the one for him. Anyway, it looked like he'd got away with it again because there was no sign of her parents, even though it was barely after 8.00am. He wasn't sure what Kate had meant when she had said they weren't back yet. Where had they gone so early in the morning?

'Would you like a cup of coffee?'

Liam knew what he would really like, but he'd waited five weeks so far and was enjoying practising on his own, so it didn't really matter. He was just waiting until whenever Kate gave him the nod.

'Yes, please... black, no sugar... I'm back on a diet.'

Liam was aware that his voice sounded different in this huge house. And it wasn't just the acoustics – his accent had changed. Just like he did in the fitness club when he was talking to one of the posher members, he was adjusting to his audience or, in this case, the environment.

Kate laughed. 'What's with the posh accent all of a sudden? I've already warned Mum and Dad you're from that rough council estate, so I don't want you talking all la-di-dah when you meet them.'

She walked towards him and grabbed both his hands and moved her head close to his. 'Relax, will you?'

Before he could reply, she kissed him. Liam responded and, without realising at first, he placed both his hands on her gorgeous bottom. She pushed her hips into his. She carried on giving him a really sensual kiss before breaking free and tickling him under his chin. She disappeared into the kitchen.

'Err... d'ya mind if I put the Teletext on?'

Liam could feel his hard-on straining against his jeans. It was absolutely rock hard. He sat down and quickly fiddled with the remote control to see what position Bolton were in the Premiership. He knew exactly where they were really, but it would take his mind away from what had just happened and hopefully his bulge would become less obvious. He flicked through all the football results and tables, even though he knew every one anyway. By every Monday morning, he could tell anyone which teams had played, won, lost, scored and who had been sent off. He knew he was slacking, though, because, when he was younger, he and Rob would have competitions to see if they could remember the crowd figures from each match.

'Thanks for a lovely night last night... your mum's absolutely brilliant. I couldn't believe how pleased she was about England winning. Your dad's not as bad as you make out, either,' Kate continued.

Here we go again, thought Liam. His dad was managing to pull the wool over somebody else's eyes. Liam hadn't told Kate about the really bad things that had happened in the past, but had just told her that his dad had not been the best in the world. Liam looked at Kate as she passed him his coffee. He still couldn't believe how beautiful she was and still felt out of his depth. She sat down on the settee and patted the seat next to her. 'Come on over here.'

Liam didn't have to be asked twice. He sat down and Kate placed her legs over the top of his legs. Liam was trying to keep calm as she talked to him, but he wasn't really listening to what she was saying. First, he was trying to control himself, as with no boxer shorts on an unmistakable pyramid had started to form again in his jeans. Second, he was thinking, Is this it? Should I make a move or am I going to blow it here? He couldn't remember the last time he'd been in this position – fully sober and with the very realistic chance of making love to a beautiful woman.

'Are you listening to me, Liam?'

'Yeah, yeah... sorry. I had a great night, too.'

'I was upset that you didn't want to come back here last night. I told you last week my mum and dad were away at their cottage for the weekend.'

Shit! Bollocks! Liam had forgotten and hadn't wanted to go back because he had felt drunk after the large amount of wine they had consumed. He wanted to be on his best behaviour when he first met her parents.

'Anyway, lucky for you they're not coming back until tonight, so you've got a chance to redeem yourself.' Kate then took the coffee cup out of Liam's hands and started kissing him again. He responded in kind, but she must have been able to tell he was nervous.

'We could go upstairs if you like.'

He looked into her stunning eyes. She was taking the lead. Liam couldn't believe it. 'I would really like that.'

Too right he would. He would love to ride her on the beautiful leather suite but he needed to stall for a while. It would give him a chance to comprehend what was happening and help him gather his thoughts.

'D'ya mind if I get a drink of water first?'

'Yeah, but just relax will you, I'm not going to bite you... well, not straight away.'

Jesus Christ, she wasn't a nympho, was she? He was starting to panic. As he looked for a glass, he checked the tent pole in his jeans – nothing, it had disappeared. The panic really set in now as his usually trustworthy mate had gone soft on him. At the bottom of the stairs, he could hear himself talking to his penis. 'Please don't let me down, please don't let me down.'

He repeated this mantra over and over as he made his way up the stairs. He just wanted everything to be perfect. Then his thoughts suddenly swung the other way. He knew he could last a good while when he wanted to, but he still knew that he was sometimes prone to a quick release if he was really excited, and a re-examination of his package confirmed he was now very excited. He would have to initiate Plan A, which meant as much foreplay as possible.

'I'm in here.'

As he pushed Kate's bedroom door open, he took a big gulp of water. She was sat on the edge of the bed waiting for him and she must have been able to see the fear in his face. She patted the space next to her again. 'Relax, will you?'

Liam placed the water on the bedside cabinet and sat down next to her. 'I really, really care about you, Kate.'

'I know.'

As they lay together with their legs entwined, Kate with her head on Liam's chest, he felt like passing out. He looked at her bedside clock. He couldn't believe it was nearly half-past-twelve. He'd never made love for so long before – yes, making love, because that was what it had been. Nor had he caressed somebody so gently and had never felt as sensual as he felt now, ever. He stroked Kate's long hair. He felt like the proverbial cat that had got the cream and scoring for Bolton couldn't possibly have made him feel any better than he did now, surely.

'Are you all right?'

'Yeah... that was unbelievable.' She held Liam even more tightly.

They didn't have to say anything else – actions speak louder than words, Liam thought. But, while he revelled in the glow of that moment, the paranoia gently tugged at his consciousness.

'I hope I did everything right... I mean... I hope I didn't come too loud.' He was speaking to himself again. Natalie had always told him to be quiet when he was coming, especially when they were at her parents' house. Quiet! She was having a laugh! Coming was the greatest pleasure ever given to man. How could anybody be quiet? He continued to articulate his thoughts as he gently massaged Kate's neck, while she gently stroked his chest. 'Kate, I've never made love to someone like that before.'

He meant it, but, even as he said it, Liam almost wished he hadn't. What if it was just another day at the office for Kate? She'd been seeing her boyfriend since school, so they were bound to have perfected the act.

'Liam, I never realised I could feel like that. I never knew my body could react in that way. I've never had sex – no, made love like that before.'

They looked into each other's eyes before they started kissing and hugging again. This is it, thought Liam. This is it.

'Listen, my mum and dad will be back from the Lakes tonight and I would love you to meet them. I've told them all about you and my mother has been nagging me to bring you round. Why don't you go out for a drink to The White Horse and I'll make you some lunch?'

Liam couldn't believe it. Not only had he just had the most incredible sex with the goddess, but she was now telling him to go for a beer. He shook his head as he walked along the path to the pub. He felt 10 feet tall and couldn't believe the difference a day could make. If he ever met Golden Bollocks himself, Liam would definitely buy him a pint.

19
A Real Family
Sunday, 7 October 2001

'Pleased to meet you, Liam.'

Within a few minutes of meeting Kate's mum and dad, Liam felt totally at ease. Kate gave him a smile and a few 'Told you you'd be all right' looks as Liam told them about his background. He threw in the 'going back to college after being in the Army' story and how he went on to do a degree after passing his A-levels. He could tell he was quietly impressing them. That is all he had hoped for, not in an arrogant way, but he did want them to consider him a suitable candidate in the son-in-law stakes.

'Kate tells me you've had a look round this morning. What do you think?'

Roslyn wasn't bragging about the fantastic house, but Liam could tell she was proud of her home, and why not?

'It's absolutely beautiful and you could have a football pitch in your back garden, couldn't you?' Liam didn't really want to tell Mrs Davidson that he'd had a great view of the garden from Kate's bed as he took her daughter from behind.

Ken carried on the football theme. 'Oh, Kate tells me you're a Bolton fan. They started off well but they're struggling now, aren't they?'

'Yeah... but we're hanging on in there. Newcastle at home next week. Hopefully, we'll beat them.' He didn't want to tell Mr Davidson that Spuggie had said that, if Bolton beat Newcastle at the Reebok, he would run from one end of the Tyne Bridge to the other and back bollock naked. Liam was going to hold him to it.

'I used to follow Preston when I was a young lad,' Ken went on, 'but I don't really bother much now. It's all changed... none of your local lads playing and the money they're on... aren't fit to lace Tom Finney's boots.'

Jesus, thought Liam, trying not to get too irritated by the 'grumpy old man' attitude, but Ken did have a point. 'I know. It's gone silly now with all the money involved.'

What Liam meant to say was that he was thoroughly demoralised with Premiership football. Some of the jammy bastards were on 20–60 grand a week and couldn't even be bothered chasing the ball if it wasn't straight to their feet.

'Would you like to see some photographs of Kate when she was younger, Liam?'

'Mother!'

'Yes, I'd love to.'

Roslyn soon had the family albums open, exposing Kate's formative years to all and sundry. Liam had already noticed loads of photographs of Kate and her only brother Andrew around the house, recording their progress from babies up to the present day. He was amazed at the collection and brushed aside Kate's embarrassed 'Mother, Liam doesn't want to see any more...' with a 'No, I do, honestly...' and he did. He wanted to hear about Kate growing up in a loving family and he wanted to hear how proud her mum and dad were of her and her brother. As he was looking at the school photographs of the children together at primary school, he was reminded of the happy times he'd had with his brothers and sisters. Unfortunately, when his mum had been going through one of her 'bad patches', she had ripped up every single family photograph and thrown them in the bin without anybody realising. Hardly any of them had been of the whole family anyway, but seeing Kate's mum's collection did offer a poignant reminder to Liam of his mum's condition.

By the end of the night, he knew the full Davidson family history and, far from being an ordeal, it had been a revelation. He meant it when he had hugged Kate on her doorstep and told her he'd had a 'fantastic night', even though she wasn't convinced. As he drove away with Kate still visible in the rear-view mirror waving, he felt a little strange. He had just been in a 'real' family environment where he could feel the genuine expression of love and care that Kate's parents had for her and her brother.

He thought of his friends' families and it was a few minutes before he remembered that Wolfman's mum and dad were still together. Most of his other mates' parents were separated. Yes, Liam's mum and dad may still have been together, but they shouldn't have been.

'You still up, Mum?'

His mum was sat in her chair, rolling up a cigarette with a can of Spar lager and a half-full glass on the table beside her.

'Hello, love... have you had a good night?'

'Yeah, Kate's mum and dad are lovely.'

He sat on the settee and picked up the newspaper, going straight to the back page. His mum was looking into space again.

'Are you all right, Mum?'

'Yeah, love.'

'How much have you had to drink tonight?'

'Only two cans, love, I don't drink four any more.'

Liam didn't have to check the bin in the kitchen to confirm that his mum was lying. He could tell by her slurred speech and her struggle to roll her cigarette that she'd had much more.

'Mum, I had a really good childhood, you know. I loved growing up on the Elsmere Estate.'

'Did ya, love? I always tried me best, love.'

Liam smiled. 'I know you did, Mum. I've had a great night tonight. Anything on the telly?' He reached for the remote control to go through the Teletext.

'Not really been watching it, love.'

Liam knew his mum was a lot better than she had been a few years ago, but he could still tell when she wasn't fully there sometimes. He also knew that she didn't always take her anti-depressant tablet and this sometimes affected her behaviour. 'Have you been taking your tablet every day, Mum?'

''Course I have, love. D'ya want a cup of tea?'

'Go on then. Cheers.'

She struggled out of her chair and staggered towards the door.

'Bloody hell, Mum... how may have you had really?'

She laughed. 'No, me legs have gone numb from sitting down.'

It was frustrating because his brothers and sisters did still try to get her to go out more, but she didn't want to. She enjoyed having her grandchildren round and, when they were brought down or visited for a short time, it was as if she was young again, but then she would go back to sitting in the kitchen watching telly with that vacant look on her face, or sitting in the living room when Liam was in or when Jim went to the pub.

'Mum, I'm sorry you've had a crap life.'

'I haven't, love... your dad's all right, just stuck in his ways, but you've all done well, haven't you, and that's all that matters to me.'

Same old mum, he thought, she never had a bad word to say about anybody.

'Anyway, I'm going to bed, love. Goodnight.' She leaned over after passing Liam his cup of tea and kissed him on his forehead. She smelled of cigarettes and booze, but Liam didn't mind as she gave him a hug. As she walked out of the living room, she offered her usual parting words of wisdom. 'Keep hold of Kate... she's a lovely girl.'

'Don't worry, Mum, I will.'

He lay in bed comparing his upbringing to Kate's. He'd loved growing up on the old estate and Kate had commented about how she couldn't believe how close he was to his friends. She had continued by saying that, in some ways, she wished she had grown up in such a close-knit environment. Liam had nodded, saying that he would never have changed that part of his childhood.

He was beginning to think he had found his soul mate. Maybe one day he could tell Kate the other aspects of his childhood he *would* have changed.

20
Respect
Sunday, 11 November 2001

By early November, Rob's prediction of disruption due to bad weather was already coming to fruition as, for two Sundays on the trot, all the games on the park were postponed.

Liam normally hated the autumns and winters in Chorley due to the total bleakness that these seasons of the year brought to the town. Autumn was bad enough, for, when the clocks went back, it was usually a sign for everybody to begin their hibernation period as the darkness took over and the gloom set in. Some years, Liam would not see a number of his friends, especially the married ones, from the end of October until Christmas Eve afternoon in the Wine Lodge. It would then be a week or so of partying before 2 January arrived, and everybody would return to their nests until April. This period was probably the most depressing for everyone as they all tried to cope with the after-effects of their Christmas spending.

TELL SOMEONE

It wasn't just the dark, dreary nights that did Liam's head in. Everybody in Chorley seemed to suffer from the SAD syndrome – Seasonal Affective Disorder – over the autumn and winter period. This was due in part to a huge grey cloud that hung over the town because it was overshadowed by the Rivington hills.

It was the same in Bury, and Liam would often get out of his car outside work, stand momentarily in the rain, take a deep intake of breath and then sigh as he knew the major topic of conversation in the club would be the crap weather. The previous year, the raindrops on his face could easily have been tears of frustration, as, one after the other, members started with the weather, and then moved on to their particular concerns – it was astonishing to Liam just how troubled some of his members were. Liam was not only a fitness club manager, but had to take on the role of doctor, social worker and psychologist as well, as he was consulted on a variety of subjects, from in-growing toenails to several members justifying their ongoing affairs.

Although he had been told hundreds of different tales, none of them could match his all-time favourite from a guy called Damien who had confided in Liam that he really wanted to be called Doreen. The harshness of the previous winter and the subsequent predictable and boring conversations had been saved by the body-builder whom Liam had thought had just taken the wrong steroids. Week after week, Damien would arrive at the club and inform Liam of the latest developments in his quest for a sex change. He even confessed that he had started going out in his wife's clothes and a rather fetching wig. Liam, the consummate listener, would stand there sympathetically nodding and shaking his head at the appropriate moments to make his client feel better. "Course it's confidential... top secret, Damien,' he would say.

The lads in The White Horse would then crease themselves laughing as Liam told them the next instalment and they were gutted when the saga eventually finished. Damien became Doreen and split up with his wife but, thankfully, he had left Bury, which Liam was rather pleased about. Telling people they had a body odour problem that was offending other fitness club members was bad enough, but even someone as diplomatic as Liam was starting to get worried when Damien had asked whether he'd be able to use the ladies' changing rooms when the sex change had been completed. Nothing that the fitness-club members did or told Liam surprised him any more.

This winter was going to be different. He wasn't going to mind if the single lads said they were staying in the pub all night because they didn't want to get wet going into town. He wasn't going to bother if the couples didn't want to go out because they were saving up or were skint after Christmas. No, Liam was going to concentrate completely on making sure that he wasn't going to mess up his relationship with Kate. He had already cut down on his drinking and he had taken another massive step towards full maturity – he'd been to see an estate agent.

With the games being called off, he hadn't seen the lads for a few weeks and had started staying at Kate's at the weekends. It was great that her mum and dad went up to their cottage in the Lakes every weekend because it meant that, if Kate wasn't working, they spent most of the weekend in bed. Liam believed in keeping in touch with his mates, though, and his mobile now made it much easier for him to remain in contact, particularly by texting. He was still by no means an expert, but he was far less cynical now of the little device. The mechanical tone that signalled an incoming text message even made him feel a little more wanted, and he especially looked forward to receiving some 'special', X-rated messages from Kate.

One person whom he regretted having texted was Spuggie. '4–0', the scoreline by which Newcastle had beaten Bolton at the Reebok, flashed up regularly and he didn't have to look to see that the sender was 'Shearer'. Mind you, in turn, had Liam not had his phone, he wouldn't have been able to text Tony with the 2–1 scoreline that Bolton had beaten Man United by. He had laughed to himself as he sent it, knowing how much the United season-ticket holder would sulk.

'Come on, Kate, we're going to be late.'

'Ohhh...'

Kate loved her bed and her sleep, having earned every moment of it after the hours she put in at the hospital. Ten minutes earlier, Liam had disentangled himself from her beautiful body and headed for the shower. As usual, she had wrapped the double quilt back round her with a plea for 'five more minutes'.

Liam loved the power shower in her en-suite bathroom. He blasted the showerhead into his face as he thought of the great sex they had had in there the night before. Then he began to feel a little tingle of emotion as he anticipated the special event he was taking Kate to — the Remembrance Sunday commemoration at the Cenotaph in Croft Park.

He'd been there every year for the last eight years, but usually went on his own. He would see the same people there, year in, year out, apart from those who had sadly passed away. Liam would stand in awe of the spectacle and, closing his eyes, would try to put himself in the shoes of those still alive, and those who had died so heroically. He would take time to think about his granddad, whom his poor mum never got the chance to meet. He always shed a tear at the end of the ceremony. Remembrance Sunday didn't seem to mean a lot to some people, but to Liam it meant a great deal. His nana had made sure of that.

A slight drizzle, suiting the mood of the occasion, fell lightly on Liam and Kate as they stood holding hands, watching the parade march through the town centre towards the park and the final destination of the Cenotaph. Liam loved watching all the different groups of people who made up the parade. The young army and navy cadets made him feel proud, but also always made him laugh as the young ones looked left and right for their parents. Then there were the veterans. Liam hadn't been able to explain to anybody before how the hairs on his neck stood up when he saw these proud old soldiers. The amount of people taking part had been increased by the more recent conflicts Britain had been involved in, and quite rightly so. Nevertheless, it was the proud old men and women whom Liam felt the most compassion for. These people should be afforded the greatest respect, almost like royalty, Liam and Nicky had decided together. Instead, this proud, courageous group of people, now marching past him as if they were young again, were often the forgotten victims of modern society, many of whom had been subject to muggings, burglaries, surviving on meagre pensions, growing cold in winter and having to suffer the indignity of enduring hardship and neglect.

Liam may not have been an angel when he was younger, but he always respected the elderly. The night before, Kate had teased him when he had explained his feelings, and how he cried every year at the playing of the 'Last Post' at the end of the parade. Now, though, she squeezed his hand hard before kissing him on the cheek and whispering in his ear. 'I know what you mean, now, Liam.'

They made their way through the park gates and joined the rest of the people who had come to pay their respects. Liam spotted Paddy and Anna and their children who were now waving and shouting to him. Anna's mum and dad were also there, as usual. After the parade, Liam always went for a bacon butty and coffee at their house next to the park.

As they made their way round to his friends, Liam winced as a sneaky kidney punch hit home from another old friend. 'Ohhhh, eh up, Liam... you're slowing down.'

Davey would always give Liam a friendly dig when they met. As he quietly introduced him to Kate, Liam couldn't resist telling her about Davey, and how he was one of his living heroes. The former soldier was always embarrassed when people spoke about him in such terms, but to Liam it was the truth. This guy, who was not yet 40, had fought in the Falklands War with the Parachute Regiment. He had then gone on to be the British Lightweight Boxing Champion. This made him a hero in Liam's eyes, especially as they were from the same estate. Kate kept hold of her boyfriend's hand as Davey left them with a friendly parting shot: 'Anyway, you're too good for him, love.'

At the end of the parade, Kate placed her arm protectively round Liam. She had said the night before how different he was to her ex-boyfriend; how she could talk to Liam so much more easily. She'd also been surprised at just how sensitive he could be. As Liam wiped his eyes, he gave her a smile and she responded by giving him another soft kiss on his lips.

'Kate, one thing...'

She looked at him, concerned. 'Yes, what?'

He looked at her sadly before continuing, 'Don't tell the lads I cried, will you!'

As they both started to laugh, Liam received a push in the back.

'It's not a bloody youth club you know.' It could only be Paddy.

'Uncle Liam, are you coming to my nana's?' Before he replied, little Emma continued, 'Hello, Kate, are you going to marry Liam? My mum said he needs somebody really badly.'

Anna's face was a picture as they all burst out laughing. 'Bacon butties at me mum's it is, then!'

21
The Winter of Love
November 2001 – 31 January 2002

The rest of November and December passed unbelievably quickly with Liam seeing a great deal of Kate. He had now been introduced to her brother, who had flown home from New Zealand for a three-week break. He'd also met Kate's nana and granddad. Meeting them had been another revelation. When Liam had left their beautiful bungalow, he had said to Kate, truthfully, that they were the loveliest couple he had ever met. They had recently celebrated their sixtieth wedding anniversary, and Liam could tell as they recounted some favourite memories that they were still very much in love. It had been as if they were still teenagers as they shared their reminiscences, still teasing each other at every opportunity.

Unfortunately, Liam had seen less and less of his mum over the last two months. When their paths had crossed, though, he had been constantly reassured that she was

OK, and was told, 'I've had my life... you go out and enjoy yours,' which only confirmed to Liam just how wonderful she was. He'd also seen less of the lads but, as he'd told Nicky, 'D'ya think I'd want to sit in The White Horse with you and Rory while you complain about the latest changes to the offside rule, or be round at Kate's giving her a good seeing-to? And that's off the record, of course.'

'Point taken.'

Luckily, Nicky could be trusted not to tell Kenny or Mad Al about his exploits. Liam knew that, if they found out the details of his and Kate's sexual chemistry, there was a good chance their comings and goings would appear in the next edition of the *Chorley Guardian*. No, the lads were no different to the rest of the inhabitants of Chorley in the winter; everybody did their own thing.

On Christmas Eve, Liam found himself out with some of the single lads because Kate was working the night shift at the hospital. He'd had a great night with Rory and Nicky, but nevertheless, as the night wore on, he found himself feeling really strange. At first, he couldn't put his finger on it but, towards the end of the night when they had a choice between another hour in the Tut 'n' Shive or a trip to the Academy nightclub, he realised what was bothering him – he was completely lovesick. He'd had a great laugh with the lads in the Wine Lodge about it still being the number-one *Star Wars* bar. He'd danced with a few girls in the Prince of Wales, but he hadn't really looked at another girl all night. Well, not in a 'Fancy a shag?' type of way.

Rory, Giant and Nicky had been trying their best with anything that moved, but all that Liam could think about was seeing Kate again the next morning. He'd never felt like this before. On the contrary, he was usually the last one who wanted to go home. Now, all he could do was keep looking at his watch and try and hurry the time along.

'What's the score then? The Academy or are we staying here? I've got to get a shag tonight.'

It had been obvious all evening that Nicky was gagging for a jump.

'Academy it is then,' chirped in Rory.

Nicky hadn't had his leg over for ages, mainly because he was choosy and his drug habit also kept him in the back room of the Horse chilling out. However, he knew that, if he wanted to break his lean spell, the Academy on Christmas Eve was the perfect place to guarantee that, like Santa's sack, his would be empty by the morning if he played his cards right.

'Come on, Liam, you soft bastard... are you coming or what?'

Wolfman had walked forwards three paces before realising that Liam wasn't following the group.

''Course I am... just finishing me pint.' Liam put his glass to his mouth and pretended to sup the last drops as he watched his mates make their way out of the heaving pub. He looked at his watch again: 12.35am. Kate's shift didn't finish until 4.00am and he could have gone straight from the Academy to her house. Instead, he checked his pocket for the front-door key she had given him earlier and made his way to the taxi rank. He would take all the abuse from Giant on Boxing Day when they met for their official annual all-dayer. For now, though, he was ready for bed, but not to sleep. He would wait up for Kate and be ready to give her his best. He always felt at his peak when he'd had one or two beers because he always lasted longer. Over the years, he had sort of worked out when he was at his optimum sexual level and it was definitely when he had had around six pints. Not enough alcohol and he really had to work on the foreplay and think of every football team starting with A right through to Z so he wouldn't explode too early. Too much, and he knew he was a goner. He'd fallen asleep a number of times when he was supposed to be having a wild time with Natalie, and that's what had happened on that fateful night. He had not only fallen asleep when she had climbed on top of him for the first time ever, but, an hour later, he had unfortunately decided in his sleep that it was time to go to the loo... and that had been that.

However, it wasn't just thinking about sex that gave Liam this constant warm inner glow he was now experiencing; no, this was different. The first two or three times he and Kate had had sex, he had been so nervous and tried to put every move he'd learned over the years into practice. Now, everything just seemed so natural and both of them would tell the other what turned them on, and they now had a real understanding of the best way to excite the other.

With Natalie, it had been so different. The usual missionary position was all right at first but two years of it had dampened Liam's desires. It wasn't as if he had wanted S&M or anything too outrageous. If he suggested anything different, like sex outside or over her parent's kitchen table when they were out, she would always give him a look of disbelief, and tell him that he was seeing too much of Kenny and Mad Al. As his relationship with her had deteriorated, his one-handed pursuit had become more frequent. He would find himself driving to work or even walking down the street in a state of heightened alertness, and simply seeing an attractive woman or hearing a sexy voice on the radio brought him to attention down below. Even now he still indulged. However, he had reduced all solo activity from a peak of a couple of times a day before he met Kate to now only two or three times a week. Mad Al didn't believe him at first and thought he must have been ill, but even he had to admit that he was slowing down since he had moved in with his girlfriend Maria. Liam had even started to feel guilty as he prepared for another five-fingered shuffle, but he always reconciled himself with the fact that it was enhancing his and Kate's sex life because it was just another tool he used to make himself, and their lovemaking, last longer.

His relationship with Kate was in direct contrast to his and Natalie's. He had put more into the current relationship in two months than he had in two years with his ex. The break-up had been his fault because of the emotional stress he was experiencing, but he had never been in love with Natalie. He was head over heels already with Kate, and everybody seemed to like her.

Anna had commented after he and Kate had been round for a meal that she was the best thing to happen to Liam for years. He always took Anna's advice on board, because he really respected her and Paddy, who had started seeing each other at school, and they'd been through a great deal together. They had also been one of the first of his friends to have children and Liam was honoured when they had asked him to be godfather to Emma. He loved going round to their house playing with her and her younger brother Jake.

Paddy and Anna had had their arguments as a couple, but Liam looked up to them because of what they had built together. Deep down, he knew that he wanted to get married and have kids. He had recently mischievously told all his married friends that he didn't want to end up manacled and miserable like them, but this was far from the truth. He was waiting to meet the right woman... and Kate was definitely the one.

Liam knew the one person he would be able to pour his heart out to – and start to talk about his past – would be Kate, but not yet. For now, all he could think about was how much he really cared about her and how scared he was of losing her. How long do you wait to ask someone to marry you? He'd barely been seeing Kate for three months, but it already seemed like three years. And he knew he wanted it to be even more special than it was already, if that was possible.

He sat in her dad's chair and put on the huge, wide-screen television. Her mum and dad had gone to Marbella for a week to celebrate Christmas with friends, so once again they had the house to themselves. He couldn't believe how good her parents had been to him. They hadn't even minded when he'd started sleeping in Kate's room during the week.

He looked at his watch; it was already nearly 1.50am. He picked up the phone, wondering if his mum would still be up. He was just about to put the receiver down after at least a minute of ringing when she answered.

''Ello?' She spoke slowly with a definite slur.

Liam started singing, '*I just called to say I love you… I just called to say how much I care…*' Over the years, he had often sung the Stevie Wonder classic to his mum. Every time he'd rung from her from Germany, he had started with the song before bursting into laughter.

'Is that our Liam?'

He could tell his mum was drunk again, but she was allowed to be on Christmas Eve. 'Have you not been out, Mum?'

'No, love.' She was croaking as if she was struggling for breath. 'I'm not going to that dive and sitting with your dad and his mates. I'd rather sit on me own and watch telly. It's been great tonight… Oh, I've just been listening to that Frank Sinatra tape you got me as well, it's brilliant.'

'I knew you'd like it. Mum, I'm staying at Kate's again tonight. All right?'

'All right, love, don't worry about me, I'm all right.'

'Love you, Mum.'

'Love you, Liam. See you tomorrow… Merry Christmas.'

He sat back in the comfy armchair with his can of lager. He thought of his mum sat in on her own, not just on Christmas Eve, but all the time. Liam couldn't help himself making comparisons again between his and Kate's respective parents. Not the material differences, although it was true that his dad could have bought a lovely house with the money he had earned from long-distance lorry driving. Liam briefly allowed himself a smile as he thought of Rob pointing out that his dad had trodden a path all the way through the park pitches to the pub, and it was true, he had done. The standing joke was that he could have bought the pub with the money he had spent in there.

If – no, *when* – Liam married Kate, he would do his best to make her happy. He knew that he was no angel but, as he scrolled through the Teletext, he thought about how his dad's behaviour had affected all the family. Liam himself had inherited his father's Irish bad temper, especially on the football pitch when he was younger, but there was no doubt that, out of the five kids, his older brother Mick had been treated the worst. What Liam still couldn't understand was why, after seeing what his dad had done to his mum, Mick should, to a lesser extent, do the same to his wife. He also had his kids, whom he adored, but again, by treating his wife badly, Liam could not understand how he could fail to see the effect it would have on them as they grew up, just as it did to him. His brother had even been out with the lads earlier in the evening saying that Dawn wanted him out of the house so she could wrap the kids' presents. Liam wasn't too sure, though, if she would be happy if Santa Claus beat her husband home before the morning, which could happen.

He was struggling to keep his eyes open as his thoughts drifted to his oldest brother. James was 41, unmarried and a teetotaller who'd sensibly paid off his mortgage. He couldn't be more unlike his dad and Mick. In fact, he was totally different to the rest of the family. Liam's mates always gave him some stick whenever they saw James out on his own or with the two mates he went to quiz nights with. He wasn't just tight with his money, he was downright stingy. Liam laughed to himself because his brother knew the price of a glass of Coke in every pub he went into and would hand over the exact change, much to the amusement of his mates. Liam also knew that, when he opened his present from James, it would be some Lynx deodorant he had bought in the January sales when he always did his Christmas shopping for the following year. The previous Christmas, Liam had nearly wet himself laughing when he realised that the gift he had received from his brother was wrapped in the wrapping paper he had sent him the year before with 'To James' crossed out and 'To Liam' added in.

Liam had just started analysing the effect their upbringing had had on his sisters when he heard a key in the door. He couldn't believe how quickly the time had gone. Kate literally jumped on him as he tried to get out of the chair. After a passionate kiss, she whispered seductively in his ear, 'Merry Christmas... let me take you to bed for your early Christmas present.'

It was just what he wanted to hear.

Once Liam had undressed and pulled the duvet over himself, he took a deep breath. Why wait any longer, he thought to himself. It all seemed so simple. 'Kate?'

'Yes, honey?' she shouted back from the bathroom where she had gone to get his surprise.

Sitting up in her bed, it would have been the easiest thing in the world to say, 'Will you marry me?'... but he didn't have the bottle. Instead, he called out, 'Hurry up, will you... I've missed you.'

As he said it, Kate emerged from the bathroom wearing a silk dressing gown. 'Merry Christmas,' she purred, and with that she let it slip down from her shoulders to the floor to reveal a pair of skimpy red knickers and red Santa-style bra. She dived under the bottom of the quilt. 'Merry Christmas!' she giggled.

Liam felt like all his Christmases had come at once.

The Christmas and New Year celebrations sealed it for Liam. Kylie Minogue's single 'Can't Get You Out of My Head' had become Liam's all-time favourite record, as it neatly summed up his feelings about Kate. He was completely in love with her, and in many ways she had hinted that she had the same feelings. They would spend hours together, just chatting, and they had both become very tactile with each other. It was the smaller details that Liam noticed, such as how they both grabbed for each other's hands whenever they were together and played footsie all the time. Lately, every day seemed a good day. Just seeing her or even hearing Kate's voice on the phone made his heart beat that much faster and he was enjoying doing things with Kate that he would never have considered before. Sales shopping in Manchester had never been Liam's idea of a great day out, but for now it was up there with Rob's stag do to Blackpool. He never thought he'd be comparing a day out with the boys to a shopping trip with a woman, but it was true. They had now become inseparable and Liam's friends had become her friends, and vice versa.

Rob's annual Christmas house party had, as usual, been brilliant. It was also a real test of their relationship as Kate got the chance to meet everyone – friends, partners, hangers-on – in one fell swoop. She was also told every embarrassing story about Liam that his friends could recall. Wolfman, Paddy and their wives were unrelenting in telling her what Liam had been up to for the past 25 years, and she and her friends Alison and Susan had giggled their way through all the anecdotes.

Spuggie had also made his way down from Newcastle with Heidi and, in between coming up for air, took Kate through a blow-by-blow account of Liam's entire three years at college. Liam was just hoping that Kate couldn't understand his machine-gun Geordie accent as he condensed three years of studying and partying into 20 minutes. Even then, he still managed to tell her how much he loved Newcastle Football Club and Alan Shearer and how he and his missus were considering getting married at St James' Park.

The party had been a wonderful success as Kate had fitted in perfectly with everyone. She didn't even seem the least bit fazed as the atmosphere became more and more outrageous and explicit as the night developed into the early morning. She laughed and shook her head as Rob, who always had sole control over his music, went through his Premier League of party hits, ranging from Madness, The Blues Brothers and Tom Jones to his Seventies' Greatest Hits albums. She also looked on incredulously before joining in the cheers as Browny was announced, as he pranced downstairs in nothing more than Karen's knickers and bra and a Scouser curly black wig. Even Karen and the culprit's wife Jill thought it was hilarious, until Karen realised that it was one of her Christmas presents from Rob. Browny then had to make a swift exit to the garden to join the cannabis smokers before he suffered the full force of his victim's anger.

Wolfman was next with his usual party piece – Michael Jackson's 'Thriller', which always finished with him completely starkers. This was always a sight to behold as he had the hairiest body anybody had ever seen. Newcomers to the spectacle were always amazed, and Kate and her girlfriends were no exception when they saw the full extent of his body hair. Kate also continually reassured Liam that she was having a brilliant night, and whispered that she had never met so many friendly people. Even more confirmation – although none was really needed – that she was definitely 'the one'.

She took everything in good spirit and, by 4.30am, she was even being introduced to a Cat Stevens album. The whispered 'I love you' as they subsequently smooched to an Elvis track had made Liam feel fantastic. Nicky and Rory had, by this time, moved in on Kate's friends, and they gave it their all, bumping and grinding.

At the end of the night, everybody had given Kate a kiss or a hug. Liam then left hand in hand with Kate at about 5.00am.

After only a few hours' sleep, Kate had listened intently as Liam gradually mentioned more and more about his childhood and some of his concerns, and explained what had happened to his mum and how he felt really guilty that he had not helped her more. Kate had held him close as his tears had welled up and he had clenched his teeth to stop breaking down. And as he eventually gave in to the tears, she cried with him, consoling him, soothing him.

She also disclosed more about herself, explaining how badly her ex-boyfriend had really treated her. It was only a matter of time, Liam decided. He didn't mind if he would have to wait a year or two, but Kate was the one with whom he wanted to share the good times, the bad times and hopefully have his babies, as he had told Anna the night before. Besides, Kate had now seen everything, been told nearly everything about him by the people who mattered, and Liam had told her almost everything about himself. Almost.

He had thought about asking her to marry him right there and then while they were lying in bed together, but the timing wasn't right. Particularly after the previous night's eating and drinking finally caught up with him, and he failed to hold in a rather toxic fart for the first time in their relationship.

'Oh my God, Liam, that's disgusting,' she shouted before scrambling out of bed. 'I'm going to be sick.'

Liam opened the bedroom window while she was in the bathroom and wafted the quilt around. He felt apprehensive about Kate's reaction because it was the first time he'd let one slip in her company, and had not been able to blame it on anyone else. However, he was also giggling to himself as he buried his head in the pillow, wondering if everyone really liked their own farts as much as he did, but weren't prepared to admit it. Kate returned from the bathroom and bravely jumped back into bed, pinching her nose but laughing at the same time.

Liam had a flashback to Rob's house the night before and a Madness track started playing in his head. '*It must be love, love, love…*' and it *had* to be, didn't it? If she could put up with that smell, he thought, she could put up with anything.

22
The Charge of the White Horse
Sunday, 3 February 2002

'Goin' down, goin' down... Shearer, Shearer.' Liam had been dreading Spuggie's call, but persevered as the mad Geordie talked him through Bolton's 3–2 defeat the previous day at St James' Park.

'Aw, man, you were unlucky, but we are Champions League... I said we are Champions League...'

'Spuggie, it's eight o'clock in the morning... have you been takin' drugs again?'

'Aw, man, I'm on't best drug in the world, Newcastle United FC. We're all goin' on a European tour... a European tour... a European tour. I'll be at the Horse by nine-thirty, man... watch me pop some goals in... Shearer, Shearer.'

Spuggie was on his way back down from Newcastle after watching the game. He would also have his girlfriend Heidi with him. Liam had a cunning plan to convert Kate into a football fan to rival Spuggie's and City Simon's girlfriends. Both had managed not only to convert their girlfriends to their football teams, but also to be season-ticket holders. Liam had already tried with Kate, taking her to watch Bolton, but they had got stuffed 3–0 at home to Leeds on Boxing Day.

The previous Tuesday had been even worse. He had been stupid enough to take Kate to watch Bolton play Manchester United, thinking the atmosphere would be fantastic. However, when they'd put the fourth goal in, even he felt like joining in the 'Hate Man United... we only hate Man United' chants. He'd then sulked all the way home and told Kate that she was an unlucky omen and wasn't allowed to go again.

Liam picked up the *News of the World* from behind the front door just as his dad came out of his bedroom in his chewing-gum-coloured Y-fronts and matching vest. Between wracking coughs which made his cheeks puff out as if his head was going to explode, he gasped, 'Make us a cup of tea,' before coughing and disappearing with a farewell, rasping fart into the bathroom.

Liam couldn't believe what his dad was up to. Only a week after being told that if he didn't give up smoking he could lose a leg, after a scan had shown that he had blockages in his arteries, he was back smoking. He'd lasted six days before the smell of his wife's cigarettes had got him back on the tobacco again. Liam had tried to tell his mum that she should give up, too, but she had said simply, 'Well, I don't smoke as much as your dad and it's the only pleasure I get.'

What could Liam say or do? They were both in their

sixties and he knew neither of them had any intention of giving up.

He put the kettle on and then started reading through the match reports. He knew that Bolton hadn't won since November and that the Newcastle result meant that they had gone 12 games without a win. He felt gutted, not really for himself, but mainly for Rob and Paddy who had travelled up to St James' Park. His mates were season-ticket holders and took defeats as if their lives were going to end. Liam didn't know if they would be able to cope with Spuggie's banter for the next couple of hours. United had also hammered Sunderland 4–1 at Old Trafford, so he was not looking forward to meeting up with everyone at The White Horse.

After looking at the Premiership table more closely, he was now even more upset. Bolton were third from the bottom with Man United, Newcastle, Liverpool and Arsenal occupying the top four spots. He also couldn't believe that Bolton had played 25 games already. He laughed at the difference between the Premier League and the Chorley Sunday League. The White Horse were just about to play their fifth League game of the season in February. Thank God it was only a small League or they'd still be playing through the summer.

Liam had phoned Rob the night before from Kate's to get confirmation that the match was on, to be told that they had been given the green light and they were playing The Eagle. Liam knew the landlord of The Eagle. Actually, everybody knew Trelly. He had been a great footballer when he was younger, but had been 'retiring' for the last ten years. He had started off plying his trade as a speedy winger when he was a young lad, but was now manager/substitute. He always played if the team was short, and he'd even been in the nets a number of times. As he stood at barely 5 feet tall, this had given the other teams a distinct advantage.

Wayne was already outside The White Horse having a toot with Spanish Phil, and Liam was surprised to see his brother Mick sitting next to them on the wall.

'Thought you were in Spain for the weekend?'

'Got back this morning, bro', so, if you know anybody who wants any goods, wink, wink, say no more.'

Before long, all the lads started arriving with the updates on their previous night's exploits. Kenny always had the strangest stories and Knobhead was never far behind, but he was known for exaggerating.

'City... City.' Simon blasted his horn as he arrived with the O'Shea brothers in the back of his works van. 'We'll see you on the park.'

The combination of a City and two United season-ticket holders meant that they would probably be having a heated difference of opinion as usual. Simon would be happy because Liam had also noticed that his team had won nine out of the last ten games and drawn the other, although it didn't really matter if they were winning or losing to Simon. He did bite back, though, when the others pointed out that City's results didn't matter because they were in a rubbish League.

By the time Spuggie arrived, yelling unintelligible about Newcastle and shaking his fist in triumph, Liam realised there were 17 players to choose from, nearly the full squad. Then again, Knobhead turning up in his Arsenal top eating a bacon barmcake didn't suggest to Liam that he was available for selection.

As he made his way through the changing rooms, he was pleased to see Trelly getting stripped. Over a 15-year span, he had played with and against him plenty of times and they always had a good laugh.

The changing-room cages had the usual buzz around them. The smell of winter green and the fact that you could see your breath added to the ambience of Sunday League football for Liam. The Eagle had lost all their five games but this hadn't dampened Trelly's enthusiasm, especially now his two sons were playing in the same team with their proud dad. As he came past The White Horse's cage on his way to the pitches, he shook hands with Rob and gave Liam a hug.

'You still going, Trelly?' shouted Kenny from the back of the cage.

'Said I'd see you into retirement, didn't I, Kenny?'

Rob's team talk was even longer than usual. He had pages of notes, which he was now working his way through as the lads fought over the best socks and shorts. He finished with, 'This is the start of something big; I can feel it in my bones. Right, everybody, stick your valuables in the bag and get out there and give them a good hiding. Come on... any wallets, keys, false teeth or other valuables, give them to Steve. Riggers, make sure you give Trelly a kick.'

Steve had burst in late, as usual, as Rob had finished the motivational speech that would have made Sam Allardyce proud.

As they walked out of the changing rooms, Liam

realised that, except for young Gazza, who had not turned up, they could field their strongest possible team and he knew that they were going to hammer the Eagle. Giant was now officially fit and Riggers, Simon and the O'Shea brothers made up a strong defence. Liam also had Paddy with him in the centre of the park, which was superb because they had played together all the way through school.

At the end of the game, the 8–0 win was not even flattering to The White Horse. Liam still couldn't believe how well they'd played. The Eagle may not have been much opposition, but the lads had played brilliantly. Trelly had even come over at the end and congratulated Rob on his team's performance.

Apart from Giant, who hadn't had anything to do, the rest of them had surprised Liam with their fitness and willingness to chase everything. The seven-a-side games and training through the weather-imposed 'winter break' had done its job. Spuggie and Spanish Phil had been brilliant up front scoring two each, but everybody, including the three subs, had played their part. For once, young Gazza, who hadn't been down to the indoor training, wasn't really missed. Liam didn't say anything to the other lads, but he was really upset with Gazza. He had been shocked recently when his young neighbour had been round desperate to borrow £150 to go on holiday. Liam didn't even know him that well, but had felt sorry for him. He hadn't seen him since.

In the changing rooms afterwards, Rob was singing everybody's praises and talking about a squad-rotation system to give everybody a chance. It was a far cry from when Kenny had broken his leg and they'd had to finish the match with ten men.

'We've got eight games to go and we're going to win every one of them. Everybody here has got a part to play, even you, Knobhead. Now make sure your socks, shorts and tops are all the right way round because I know which numbers you played in and I won't be...'

Rob tried to battle on, but he was bombarded with muddy kit before Spuggie broke into 'Toon army... Toon army...'

Tony picked some mud off his boots and splattered it straight into Spuggie's face, which led to a full-scale mud fight. When they had finished, five or six of the lads had their faces completely covered in mud before Mad Al turned to Wayne and started dancing.

'Wayne, man, it's your brother Al here.' His attempt at a Caribbean accent was quite convincing. 'Let's dance together like we used to.'

They then started a little body-popping routine that they had last done together on a piece of lino in Chorley town centre in 1984. Before long, half the lads were joining in.

Rob tried to restore order. 'Hey... you lot... quiet. Remember, it's Wayne's real brothers from the Caribbean Club who we'll have to beat to win the league. Now come on... who's coming for a pint?'

Rob would no doubt keep his serious head on for at least three pints before he would be dancing and singing himself.

As they sat around the tables in The White Horse, Rory shouted to anyone who'd listen, 'Who fancies staying and watching Liverpool destroy Leeds?' He then looked at Liam, once a usual suspect for staying out. Liam pursed his lips together, sighed and shook his head.

'Liam you need to sort your act out. You're becoming as boring as these married tossers.'

'Get stuffed.'

Paddy wasn't having any of it. 'Just 'cause you can't get a bird, Rory.'

Liam let the banter die down before telling Wolfman that he was covering the early-morning shift in the fitness club the next day.

When Kate arrived looking as stunning as ever, she received a few friendly whistles from some of the lads. Liam tried to act cool as he bought her a drink, but underneath he was bursting with pride. Kate was only wearing casual clothes, but she oozed sex appeal. She had that natural dark look and figure that turned heads.

'Eh up, Kate, you look a million lira today.'

She smiled, but Liam had heard Paddy's next line a thousand times.

'All green and wrinkly.'

By the time Rob had drunk his third pint, he was in a buoyant mood. 'It was absolutely brilliant today, Kate, you'd have been proud of Liam. He's a midfield dynamo, never stops working.'

Nicky jumped in. 'It's all the exercise he's getting.'

Liam flashed him the daggers, but luckily the comment went over Kate's head.

'Anyway, Kate, you better look after my mate because this win is just the start of The White Horse charge to glory.'

Liam couldn't help but laugh. It may have only been Sunday League football, but to Rob it meant everything. As he got up to leave, Rory was at it again.

'Don't you fancy staying out, Liam?'

Liam just smiled and shook his head.

'OK... See you next week, captain; we're playing the Morris Dancers at home.'

As he walked out of the door, the chief supporters, Nicky and Knobhead, were dancing about with napkins in either hand trying to do some traditional Morris dancing.

'I swear this place gets crazier by the second,' Liam muttered.

He looked at Kate to see her reaction but she didn't have to say anything. The look on her face said it all.

23
Smackheads Rule
Sunday, 10 February 2002

Liam had another hectic week at work and couldn't believe how quickly Sunday had come round again. The January and February months were always hectic with everybody trying to stick to their New Year's fitness resolutions. The busy club at least kept his conversations with Ian down to a minimum. Liam still felt sorry for his boss, but he didn't really want someone else's misery in his life at the moment. Everything was going fantastically well with Kate, but he was now becoming more concerned about his mum and dad.

For some strange reason, he was starting to worry about his dad's health. Liam hadn't been that interested initially when his mum said that his dad had begun complaining about being tired all the time. He had even missed going to the pub a couple of times during the week, so something must have been wrong. Liam then started to wonder how his mum would cope if he suddenly died. How upset would she really be?

TELL SOMEONE

The thought of his father dying gave Liam mixed emotions. He had tried to talk him into going back to the doctor's but to no avail. Luckily, he'd been given the all clear after the dye tests for his legs, but this unfortunately meant that he had started smoking heavily again. For some reason, though, he had been treating Liam's mum better since he had been ill. He was speaking to her more, without shouting. He was actually listening to her when she was talking and he'd even started to help her around the house. It was strange behaviour from his dad, but Liam could see that his mum seemed happier because of it, which was all that mattered.

Liam had also begun to worry about his mum because she still insisted on walking to the local shop every night to buy her shopping. 'Gets me out of the house,' she'd say. But a few days earlier, two well-known alcoholics who usually hung around the park had asked her for some money and became aggressive when she refused. It was only on the intervention of another customer leaving the shop that they had done a runner. Liam had always thought that he was very lucky having been brought up in Chorley compared to the inner cities, but he knew that his hometown was becoming less safe with an ever-increasing number of smackheads and alcoholics now roaming the streets.

This was on his mind as he and some of the lads entered the park gates. The normal pre-match banter had already started. Kenny was telling all and sundry about his latest shagging exploits, as usual, Big Rory and Giant had been trying their best and Knobhead was trying to tell Tony how he had just left two beautiful girls in his bed.

Tony was taking him on until his brother Al had intervened.

'Thought you'd gone home on your own, Knob? I saw you leaving the Horse and there were no birds on your arms then.'

'Yeah... er, they came back to me mum and dad's all loved up after they had been clubbing. Mad for it they were, bit of Charlie and away we went, all night. You're lucky I'm here this morning, I'm knackered.'

Liam was about to whistle the theme tune from *Jackanory*, but he was suddenly so shocked by what was going on in front of him, it stopped him in his tracks. At first, he couldn't take it in. Three blokes, clearly drunk, were urinating on the Cenotaph. Liam dropped his football bag and ran up behind the unsuspecting vandals and lunged two-footed, Cantona style, kicking two of them in the back at the same time.

They smashed into the monument as Liam landed flat on his back. He wasn't finished yet, though. The other startled drunk turned round, penis still in hand, wondering what was going on, only to be caught full in the face by a punch from Liam. He collapsed to the ground. Liam's head had completely gone, and the adrenalin was really kicking in now.

Browny and Rory, having seen what was happening and racing to help their mate, jumped on him and held him down, trying to calm the situation. Pinioned under 30 stone of prime beef, Liam peered up at his captors, knowing that he was going nowhere. He'd made a right mess of the two bastards he'd laid out with his first attack, and the third one was still motionless on the ground. Liam realised one of them was Stringy, who had lived on his estate when he was younger. Was this the lad who used to bully him when he was a boy and call his mum names? Liam was surprised to see him, as he knew he had been in prison for drugs and was a heroin addict, but he hadn't realised he was back in Chorley.

After having to reassure his mates that he wouldn't start kicking off again, Liam was allowed to his feet. Paddy had managed to bring the other scumbag round. It looked like Liam had broken the guy's nose as blood was pouring over his hand, with which he was trying to stem the flow.

Liam grabbed Stringy by the scruff of the neck. 'Read that, you dickhead... Thomas Robert Lee, died 1942. That's my granddad you're pissing on.' Liam let go of him before the heavy mob jumped back on him and Stringy walked away.

'Jesus Christ, Liam, you could have killed one of them... what's going on?'
Browny was shaking his head, concerned for his friend.

Liam knew it could have gone badly awry, but he had become disgusted with everything that was happening lately. The smackheads had started leaving their syringes in the park and even in the streets. The park was now becoming more and more deserted and had become a no-go area at night. Where were all the kids? When Liam was younger, there had been football teams from each street in the neighbourhood playing each other every Saturday and Sunday, games that would go on for hours. Lads of all ages would play all different kinds of sports on the park, but now he hardly ever saw anybody except for the drunks and smackheads who hung around the park gates.

The only real enjoyment Liam had down the park

now was on Sunday mornings when all the teams were turning up to play. He still loved the atmosphere, but he was becoming disillusioned with the state of Chorley and, in particular, the amount of drugs flooding the town. Was he looking back through rose-tinted spectacles about how good it was when he was growing up, or were things really getting worse? Was he just becoming older and more cynical? Maybe, but he also knew that the rave scene from the late 80s onwards had a lot to do with it all. Most of the lads in the pub who had become entangled in the scene had managed to come out of it relatively unscathed, except for the odd bout of paranoia, but for a number of people in Chorley it was different. Liam knew lads and girls who had started with Ecstasy and had carried on into heroin. Ten to twelve years later and these idiots were still dabbling in anything they could get their hands on. Not only that, but it was these people whose kids were now starting to get in on the act. A case of 'My mum and dad do drugs so it can't be that bad for you'.

Then again, Liam might have had a lucky escape with his one and only dabble with drugs, but some of his team-mates were not that reluctant when the speed, cocaine and Ecstasy were being handed out, so were they any better? There was a fine line, but it was the lowlife smackheads that Liam, possibly naively, thought were the real problem. There was also the fact that, if he'd had a policy of not speaking to anybody who took drugs, then his social circle would be severely diminished.

While the ref was inspecting the pitch, Liam explained to Mad Al and Spuggie why he had had a go at the three blokes. 'Me nana used to bring me down to the Cenotaph when I was a young lad and tell me loads of stories about me granddad. He was killed in the Middle East when me nana was pregnant with me mum. Never even got his body back.' He looked at Al and Spuggie as they shook their heads. 'The Cenotaph was her place to remember him.'

Spuggie and Al carried on listening with the odd nod of the head and an understanding 'aye' as Liam explained how the red mist had come over him and he'd just lost it. 'Where's all the respect gone? Ex-servicemen dead and alive should be treated like royalty, not have their memory pissed on, be mugged and get treated like a piece of shit by the Government.' Liam was into his stride now. He had no particular political sympathies, believing that all politicians were only in it for themselves. 'The politicians don't give a shit about the little people as long as they are in power, picking up a good wage, travelling between their various houses in their different cars and shagging each other... or even shagging strangers down parks like this.'

Spuggie started to laugh before realising Liam was on a mission. Liam and some of the lads, including Paddy and Giant, had even been talking about doing something about it more recently, because somebody knew which smackhead had been carrying out some of the recent break-ins.

'What the fuck do we do? Become proper vigilantes and kick the shit out of all the thieving bastards and the dealers?'

'Videos and tellies being sold for 30 quid for their next

hit,' piped up Giant, who'd had enough of retrieving the ball from behind the nets and had started to listen in.

'You want to have a word with your mate Gazza, Liam,' interrupted Steve. 'I've heard he's got back on the heroin.'

Liam looked round to see the reactions of the other lads and the nods confirmed that someone whom Liam had taken under his wing and had a good laugh with had gone a step too far. No wonder he hadn't been to the football lately or been round to give him his money back.

'Get the nets up, you tossers.' Rob was getting upset with the inactivity. 'Come on, we're going to stuff this bunch of pansies. They probably play like Morris dancers, anyway, so just get stuck in, and we'll do 'em easy.'

Liam's head was throbbing. He couldn't remember much of the game – a 2–0 win with Spuggie scoring both. He would usually enjoy listening to Spuggie compare his goals to ones that Alan Shearer had scored for Newcastle, but he hadn't really been concentrating on the match. His back and head had started to ache from the abrupt landing of the Cantona kick. The lads were also now calling him Hong Kong Phooey.

After getting changed, he walked back past the Cenotaph. Liam poured some of his water over the bloodstains on the monument and used his towel to clean it away before reading the inscription yet again.

They shall not grow old, as we that are left, grow old.
Age shall not weary them, nor the years condemn.
At the going down of the sun and in the morning,
We will remember them.

Liam felt the usual tingles down his spine. 'Proper heroes, the lot of them... forget your football superstars. These are the real heroes.'

'Come on, you soft get, let's get to the pub... I've got a mad thirst on.' Nothing got in the way of Wolfman when he was gagging for a pint.

As they reached the pub, the banter was flowing again, but Liam's thoughts were all about Gazza. Within an hour or so of pub chat, he had built up enough anger to realise he had to have it out with him and find out for himself if he had gone on the smack.

Liam turned suddenly to Giant, who was sitting next to him, and muttered, 'I'm going round to Gazza's.'

Before the big man could say anything in reply, Liam was out through the door.

24
A Waste of a Life?
Sunday, 10 February 2002

Liam thumped on the front door – no answer. He looked up to the first-floor windows, but, just like the downstairs, all the curtains were closed. He knew Gazza lived alone, so he wouldn't be disturbing anyone else in the house.

'Gazza.., are you in?' Liam bellowed through the letterbox. He then stepped back and shouted up in the direction of the bedroom windows before banging more forcefully on the front door, hard enough for his knuckles to hurt. His mind was starting to go into overdrive. 'Bastard must be out getting money for his next hit.'

He went through the back gate and into the garden – although 'garden' was stretching it a bit. The back yard was just one concrete slab with dog turds everywhere, helping to match the smell of the front garden. The curtains round the back were also drawn.

Liam made his way back to the front door. He tried

the door handle as a last resort, but he knew any sensible person wouldn't leave their doors unlocked any more. However, to his amazement, it was open and the force he had used on the handle meant that it flew backwards, smashing something behind the door as it hit the inside wall.

A different smell hit him straight away as he made his way in. The stench was unbelievable. What he thought was the smell of all the dog dirt in the front garden was masking an appalling aroma, which was now starting to make him heave. He covered his mouth and nose in an attempt to lessen the stink and prevent him vomiting, but it was too late.

After spitting out the last remnants of puke, he looked round the hallway and into the kitchen – what a shithole. He still felt anger, but also some pity at the state of Gazza's living conditions.

The layout of the house was exactly the same as his mum's, so he knew where he was going. He opened the living-room door and immediately wished he hadn't. It was either a dog or a cat, but Liam didn't wait to find out. The flies and the maggots were one reason for closing the door, and the now unbearable stench was the other. 'It' must have been what was left of Gazza's pet dog, but Liam didn't think it was the best time to check for its dog collar. There was still no sign of the owner. Liam started to make his way upstairs.

'Gazza... are you up there?'

No carpet on the stairs made his voice echo and his footsteps sound as if he was wearing clogs. He went instinctively to the equivalent of his own bedroom. Liam

– a rough, tough ex-soldier – was now starting to feel quite scared, although, if he'd actually crapped himself, it would probably have passed unnoticed in this particular environment.

He tentatively put pressure on the handle, opened the door slightly and peered in. There was nothing at all in the room except net curtains. They had probably been white at one stage, but the dirty grey now kept the daylight to a minimum.

At this point, he felt like leaving, but part of him was determined to sort things out. As he reached the other bedroom door, he felt a genuine sense of fear. He slowly opened the door but stayed outside, pushing at the bottom of it with his right foot, fists raised boxing-style. This was getting stupid; he could hear his own heart beating, for Christ's sake. Nothing jumped out from behind the door, so he felt brave enough to peer slowly inside, fists still raised. A double bed with a crumpled quilt were the only objects visible in the near-darkness as a ray of sunlight pierced the partly opened curtains. He switched on the light, more out of curiosity than anything, as it was clear that Gazza had vacated the premises.

The room was in a hell of a state. All over the floor there were cigarette stumps, tin foil and even a couple of syringes. How naive had Liam been? He had befriended a scumbag of a smackhead. He turned back to the door, already running through what he'd like to do to the little shit when he got hold of him.

'Liam, wait a minute.'

Liam nearly jumped out of his skin as he spun round, fists raised, more in shock than anything else. Gazza's face was peering out from under the quilt – or what was left of it, anyway. He was greyish-white, and all his features stood out sharply beneath the tightly drawn, sallow skin.

'What the hell are you doing, Gazza?' Liam wanted to rip into the kid and give him a verbal roasting, but his instincts told him that this went way beyond that sort of treatment. This lad was 19 years old and was on his way out if he didn't get some help.

'Sam's dead...' Gazza said softly, and then he proceeded to sob gently as he buried his head into the grubby pillow.

Confirmation that the carcass was Gazza's pet dog who'd gone everywhere with him meant that even Liam felt a twinge of sympathy for the animal. He picked his way carefully over to Gazza, and sat on the edge of the bed.

'Come on... you'll be OK, yeah?'

He tried to sound sympathetic, but underneath Liam was thinking, 'It's only a bloody dog.'

'Liam... I've lost me mum, dad and now me best friend. I've got nothing to live for.'

Liam couldn't believe what he was hearing. 'Don't be so stupid. You're 19 years old... you've got *everything* to live for. You've just got to get off the drugs and out of here.'

Liam hadn't raised his voice, but the strong, confident tone he used made him seem very assertive. He knew he somehow needed to shake the young lad out of his depression. Steve had given Liam the low-down on Gazza, having told him that Gazza's mum had died of cancer when he was a baby and his dad had died when he was about ten – the poor bastard had had it rough. For some reason, he had been in care homes since then, but he could still make a go of it... couldn't he?

'No, you don't understand – I've had enough.'

Liam was trying to think on his feet. 'Gazza, I don't know much about your past, but surely you've got to give it a go. What do you think your mum and dad would want you to do?'

'Me dad, that bastard... he's the one that's ruined me life.'

Liam now began to wish that he hadn't started with the emotional manipulation as the stench from downstairs was slowly drifting into the bedroom.

Gazza continued, 'I've never told anybody what happened between me and him – the dirty bastard.'

'Hang on... what are you talkin' about? I thought your dad died when you were a young lad?'

'Yeah, not before he...'

Gentle sobbing then started again. Gazza now sounded more like a child than a young adult. The realisation of what might have happened to Gazza began to hit Liam and he wasn't sure if he wanted to hear any more in case it brought to the surface some of those suppressed memories from Liam's own past. It was too late, though.

'I loved me dad before he started touching me.' Gazza then proceeded quite matter-of-factly to list the disgusting, perverted things that his dad had done to him. He sobbed more, every so often, as tears streamed down his face. 'I never told anybody what he did to me, but I knew it wasn't right. I was scared, Liam.'

Liam became oblivious to the smell as he sat listening to the poor lad's story. Gazza told Liam that the abuse had carried on in the care homes when his dad had died, but by then he knew what to expect, so it wasn't as shocking and things weren't as bad.

TELL SOMEONE

Liam knew he had been through some rough times, but he knew it was nothing compared to what Gazza had been subjected to.

Gazza then revealed that he didn't care at all when his dad had died. 'I'd had enough, Liam. I was ten years old and been getting abused regularly since I was about seven. "Don't tell anyone," my dad would say, "they'll take you away from me and we won't be able to see each other again..." were some of the things the bastard would say so I would keep me mouth shut, but, after three years or so, Liam, I knew it was wrong, I'd had enough. That last night when he came in drunk and he sent the babysitter home all happy and smiles, I knew what was comin'. I could hear his footsteps comin' up the stairs and knew what was going to happen – the usual stuff. I can remember what happened next like it was yesterday. I can still see him doin' the things to me. His breath stinking of alcohol, and then the kiss goodnight. But that night I followed him as he staggered out of me room and seized me chance as he took the first step back downstairs.' Gazza's face twisted into a half-smile as he carried on. 'I pushed him as hard as I could and hoped it would be enough. He groaned as he lay at the bottom of the stairs, but I left him there and ran back into me bed.' He sobbed again. 'I looked down the stairs the next morning and he was still there. I remember standing over him and seeing how different he looked, his eyes wide open, staring out. I rang for an ambulance and that's when the social services came.'

Liam rubbed his eyes, kidding himself that it was more from tiredness than from what he had just heard. He searched hard for the right words. 'Listen, we can sort this out... your dad deserved it for doing that to you... We just need to get you sorted out,' he muttered.

'Thanks for listening, Liam... I've been wantin' to tell somebody for years, I feel better already. I promise I will sort meself out now. I'll get cleaned up and come round to your house tomorrow for a proper chat. I really want to get back into everythin'... football, work, the lot. I'll get that money back to you as well.'

'Don't worry about that.'

Liam made his way down the stairs somewhat shocked, a little dazed, but glad that Gazza had confided in him. He was sure he could help the lad.

As he opened the front door and he squinted into the dazzling sunlight, Liam rubbed his eyes hard, taking in a deep breath of fresh air. He would be good as his word. He wouldn't tell anybody what Gazza had told him, not even Kate.

25
Like Father, Like Son?
Sunday, 10 February 2002

'What's the matter with you?' Tony and Mad Al could always tell when something was wrong with Liam and they had both uttered the same words as he sat down on his return to the pub.

'Nothin'. Who fancies staying out for a few beers?' Liam was in the mood to forget what he had just seen and heard.

'Ooooow... got a pass out then, have you?' Paddy was, as usual, only joking, but Liam's mind was still buzzing about his visit to Gazza's.

'Yeah, yeah, whatever, Paddy.' Liam glared at his friend. On his return from the bar, he took a massive swig of his pint of Stella, downing nearly all of it in one go.

'Didya see that goal, man? I am awesome, me. My mate Shearer would have been proud of that one.' Spuggie jumped on Liam's lap and tried to get Liam in the party mood, but Liam wasn't having any of it. He was now uncharacteristically brooding and preoccupied, so when Spuggie started saying, 'I love you, man,' and bounced up and down on his mate's lap, accidentally knocking the table over, spilling the drinks, Liam snapped.

'Will you piss off, you tosser.' He shoved Spuggie away.

'Whoah, man, take a fuckin' chill pill, will ya? It wasn't me pissin' on the Cenotaph, man... I'll get the beers in.'

Giant, on seeing what had happened, walked over from the bar. 'Are you all right, mate?' He understood Liam's connection with the war, and his family background.

'Yeah, I'm all right... just pissed off with what happened.'

'What did that piece of shit have to say for himself?'

'Wasn't in,' Liam said, taking a mouthful of Stella, 'but don't worry, I'm going to sort him out one way or the other.'

It sounded like a threat, but Liam actually meant that he was going to help Gazza. For the moment, everything he said was sounding aggressive and hostile.

Spuggie placed a pint of Stella on the table. 'I've got to get goin' now, Liam mate. See you next week. See you later, boys.'

'Spuggie... Spuggie.'

Liam could tell he'd upset him and had wanted to say sorry, but, before he could get out from behind the table, Spuggie had walked out. He knew he should have followed him, but Liam's dark mood prevailed.

Nicky was the next person to end up on the receiving end of Liam's troubled state. Liam had finished his pint and made his way to the bar, just as his friend entered the pub. Nicky's face was showing the telltale signs of another hard night, and an early morning foray into a cocktail of drugs.

'Good night, Nicky?' Usually, Liam would say this and mean it.

Even though he was still coming down, Nicky had already spotted that Liam wasn't in a good mood. 'Yeah, yeah... you all right, mate?'

''Course I'm all right, why shouldn't I be? I'm not taking drugs, am I?' As soon as he said it, Liam wished he hadn't, but it was too late.

'Fair enough, but sounds like you need some. Did you lot get beat or something?' Nicky didn't hang around for a reply.

'Pint of lager, Jack, please.'

As Liam waited for the landlord to serve him, Mick was the next to have his ear bent as he approached the bar and cheerfully acknowledged his brother. 'All right, bruv, good win this morning... you lot played really well.'

'They weren't exactly Man U, though, were they? Anyway, I didn't think you were watching... you seemed more interested in getting round the other pitches selling your tobacco.'

Mick was now chasing every avenue to build up his flourishing business and a few hundred blokes all together at the same time was an opportunity he could not miss. Unfortunately, he hadn't recognised Liam's fragile state.

'Yeah, it's going really well. I'm going to Spain again next week and taking Knobhead with me.'

'You want to take Dawn and the kids away for a change. You remember... your wife and two children you sometimes live with.'

Liam had a point, but it was the wrong time and place to start talking about his brother's marriage problems.

Mick looked at his brother with surprise and resentment. 'Yeah, right. Who do you think you are, you self-righteous prick? OK, so everything's going well with your life, eh? Give me a break, will you?' He then walked straight out of the pub.

Liam stood at the bar and finished another pint as Tony made his way towards him. Tony never took any grief from Liam and had always been able to calm him down, either on or off the football pitch. He stopped five yards away from his mate at the bar, next to old Stan, and gave him the eyes. The look and the shake of the head that said calm down, don't take anything out on your mates. He then did his usual trick of making Liam laugh to get him back into his usual good mood.

'Eh, Stan... Liam's been reading them books again.'

'What's he been reading this time, *Playboy* again? I could do wi' that to get me goin' again. Old pecker's stopped working now. I think I need some more of that Viagra.'

'No, he's been reading *How to Win Friends and Influence People*, but I think he's going to write his own if he's not careful – *How to Lose Friends and Piss Them Off*.'

As Stan looked at him, confused, Liam smiled. 'Point taken.' He slowly made his way over to the lads who were busy tucking into the butties and soup. 'Paddy... Nicky... I apologise for my childish behaviour.'

'No problem.' Paddy never took Liam on anyway and, along with Browny, he still ribbed him about his first year of the army phase, where they, as civilians, were inferior to their military friend. Or, as he quite rightly pointed out, 'That time when you were an obnoxious little shit.'

'Sorry, Nicky.'

'No probs, Liam. Wayne's just told me what happened. They should have let you carry on kicking the shite out of them dirty smackheads.'

Liam decided he would give Spuggie a call later as he'd left his mobile at home.

'Brotherly love with your Mick?' Rob had had enough silly arguments with Paddy and Giant to know that everything would be forgotten in a day or two, but he still took Liam to one side. 'Your Mick's told me that him and Dawn haven't been getting on for ages. Been like that for years. Between me and you, they are only together for the sake of the kids, anyway. He was telling me the other night and he was really upset, so go easy on him... shit happens, you know.'

Liam instantly felt mad at himself. He would try to have a chat as soon as possible with his brother to see if he was all right.

'Anybody for another pint of wife-beater?'

Liam always laughed at Paddy's usual description of Stella.

'Anna's the only one who does the beating in your house. You best be getting home before you get shouted at again.' Nicky never missed an opportunity to rib his former classmate. Paddy had never lived down the 1996 European Championships when Anna had marched into the pub and ordered him to get outside to talk otherwise their relationship was over. He'd managed to smooth things over but, in the short time outside the pub, Paul

Gascoigne had scored *that* goal – that wonder-goal – against Scotland and Paddy had missed the biggest bounce the lads had ever had.

Although Liam's façade improved as the day went on, his mind was still working overtime.

'You white lads just don't have that speed that we do.' Wayne was being mischievous again.

Nobody dared argue, until Wolfman, who loved stirring it with Wayne, jumped in. 'I'd take Spuggie to whip you any time over 50 yards, Wayne.'

Wayne fell straight for the bait; he couldn't get his words out quick enough. 'Get your money where your mouth is. You're on... I'll give him ten yards' start and I'll still whip his little white ass.'

In his absence, Spuggie was christened 'The Great White Hope' and 'The White Flash' by some of the lads as Wayne was reeled in and bets were laid down for the future race.

As the day wore on, the number of lads around the tables slowly diminished. Mad Al noticed that Liam was steadily getting drunk. 'You all right, Liam? Aren't you supposed to be seeing Kate tonight?'

'Yeah, later on.'

Liam hadn't realised that it was now 7.00pm and he'd arranged to be at Kate's at 6.00pm, but he carried on regardless. By 9.00pm, the all day-drinking had taken its toll. Liam had made his way into town with Mad Al and Kenny, but the mixture of his first proper beer session since Christmas and not having had anything to eat had taken him past the point of no return.

The rest of the evening passed in a blur, until Liam

found himself rubbing his eyes and trying to work out where he was. It was pitch-black but he instinctively knew he was in his own bedroom. After a vague feel around to orientate himself, he switched on his bedside light and saw the back of Kate's head, her hair just about visible from beneath the duvet.

He tried to think back, but he couldn't remember anything at all from the night. He'd blanked out again. He didn't have a clue how he had got home or how Kate had come to be in his bed. *Déjà vu*. He smiled and thought about their first meeting in his bed nearly six months previously. Gently, he lifted a corner of the duvet, and slid as silently as could into the bed. Kate mumbled something sleepily and turned towards him.

'Jesus... Fiona! Wha... what the hell are you doing here?'

His sister had turned round to face him as he looked round again to make sure he was in his own bedroom and to confirm that he wasn't dreaming. He then clambered out and sat on the side of the bed and, before long, was shaking his head in disbelief as his sister filled him in on what he had been up to in the last 12 hours or so. It was now 7.00am on a Monday morning.

Fiona told him she had been in the living room with his mum when he had crashed through the front door paralytic at around 10.00pm the previous evening. 'By the time me and me mum had come out of the living room to see what you were up to, you had gone into the kitchen and had started banging about trying to make a drink.' Fiona said it was quite comical at first as he had fallen against the cooker and dropped a pan on the floor, but, instead of laughing along with her and his mum, he had turned nasty, telling them both in no uncertain terms where to go. He had even become aggressive to his mum as she tried to help him.

'We both decided that it would be best to just let you get on with it and mum said she would clean up after you. As we were going back into the living room, there was a knock on the door.'

It had been the unfortunate Kate, who explained to Fiona that she had been worried because she had called Liam a number of times on his mobile, to no avail. She had also seen Al and Kenny in town who'd told her they'd lost Liam in one of the pubs and they were worried about him because he'd been acting strangely, and was the worse for wear.

'I warned Kate that you were really drunk and told her that she might be better leaving you to it, but she then heard you smash a glass and rushed into the kitchen to see if you were all right.'

Fiona had followed closely behind to see Liam standing among shards of glass, totally out of it, with another glass in one hand and a carton of orange juice in the other.

'Kate asked you if you were all right. You looked straight through her and pulled a stupid face before telling her to piss off.'

Liam started to shake his head, but he told Fiona to tell him exactly what had happened.

'It got worse because Kate tried to help you and started to pick up the glass, but you told her again to piss off. I told her to leave you, but she tried to take the glass from you before you dropped it and that's when you pushed her away.'

'Ohhh no.'

'You pushed her quite hard, but she still tried to talk to you. You just told her again to go and then mumbled to her a number of times that you didn't want to see her again.'

'What? You can't be... What the fuck have I done?'

'You finished by pushing past us both and then you staggered upstairs before collapsing on your bedroom floor. Poor girl was in tears but she still wanted to make sure you were all right. I said I'd stay the night in case you were sick in your sleep, you were that bad.'

Liam couldn't believe what he was hearing. He had done stupid things before, had had blackouts and been told the day after how he had fallen out with mates, but nothing like this. He had never laid a finger on any previous girlfriends, so to do it to the girl he adored made him feel utterly disgusted with himself.

'When she left, she said she'd give you a call today to see if you were all right. What happened to you, Liam? I've never seen you like that before... you reminded me of Dad when we were kids.'

'I am so sorry, sis; I can't believe what I've done. I've probably just lost the best thing that has ever happened to me.'

'No you haven't... just give her a call and sort it out. You better not lose her, she's an absolute star.'

After Fiona had gone, Liam slumped into his bed. He still couldn't believe what he had done. He knew seeing Gazza the previous day and his pitiful story had upset him, but there was no excuse for what had taken place. Then he started to mull over what Fiona had told him, and what might happen as a consequence. Was he really good enough for Kate? Could he guarantee that he would never do anything like that again? Had he inherited that trait of assaulting your nearest and dearest? Could he really tell Kate about his uncle and would she stay with him after what he had just done?

Various scenarios ran through his head and it wasn't until his mum was halfway into his room that he realised she was trying to speak to him. 'I said are you all right, love?'

'Mum, I'm so sorry about last night... I can't remember a thing. I'm really sorry.'

'Don't worry, love. I told Kate I'd never seen you like that before and that you must have something on your mind. When she left here, I told her that you'd regret what you'd said and it was just the alcohol talking.'

'I know, Mum, but it's no excuse; I think it might be better if we split up.'

'Listen, love, don't get so upset. You've made a mistake, but everybody makes mistakes. You're a good person, Liam, and Kate can see that. She was still worried about you when she left, love. She wasn't mad at you... she just kept saying that she hoped you'd be all right. Just learn from your mistake, love. Learn from your mistake.'

'I am sorry I shouted at you, Mum, I didn't know what I was doing.'

She flashed him one of her maternal, loving smiles. 'At least yer didn't try to go to sleep with your head in the fridge.'

It was true. Liam's mum had found him asleep in various different places, from the front lawn to the back garden, but finding him with the fridge door open and his head perched next to a block of cheese with a bite out of it was probably the strangest.

'Come on, I'll make you a cup of tea. You think of what you are going to say to Kate. Eh, and don't listen to what our Fiona said, it was nothing like your father was with me.'

Why do mums have that knack of being able to say the right things when you need them to? Liam thought. No matter how old you are, they are still there for you, always sticking up for you. His mum had made him feel better, but he was still dreading speaking to Kate.

26
Sorry

Monday, 11 February – Thursday, 14 February 2002

By lunchtime, Liam felt like his insides had been torn out. It might have been the alcohol, but to him it felt more like a premonition that he was going to lose Kate. His stomach was churning and his heartbeat was racing as he lay on his bed staring at a dirty mark on his bedroom ceiling. Should he call Kate or should he wait for her to call him? What had his sister said? Then he remembered he had left his mobile phone on charge next to his stereo. He sighed as he realised there were two missed calls and a text message.

At about 7.00pm, Kate had rung to ask, 'What time are you coming round, lover boy? I am waiting,' and then at 10.00pm, she left a second message, sounding more worried than annoyed: 'Liam, hope you're all right... give me a call.' The text message was from 5.30am that morning: 'NOT SLEPT. HOPE U R OK.'

After picking up the messages, Liam buried his face in

the pillow. His head now started to feel like it was going to explode. How could he have been so pathetic? He still couldn't remember a single thing from the night before and this was making him feel even worse.

The noise of the telephone ringing downstairs made him feel physically sick, but he knew he had to answer it. His mum had gone to get him a newspaper. He jumped out of bed and staggered downstairs before taking a few deep breaths. After another couple of rings, he picked up the receiver.

'Need a new left-back now, Liam.'

Rob's voice surprised Liam for a second, as he tried to take in what Rob meant. On this occasion, though, Liam wasn't in the mood to talk football. Then Rob got his full attention.

'Young Gazza's gone and topped himself.'

'What?'

'Well, Steve rang me last night and told me some drug-dealer found him in his front room next to the remains of his dog. Apparently, the dealer told the girl next door, who raised the alarm. Just had a sheet of paper in his hand with the words 'Sorry' wrote on it. Weird, innit?'

'Yeah, errr, I'll speak to you later, Rob. I'm feeling a bit rough.'

'No problem, mate.' The line went dead.

'Eh, Liam, you're not going to believe what I've just been told by Graham at the shop.' His mum breezed in and passed him the *Daily Express*, not giving Liam a chance to reply. 'They've found that young lad dead in his house. Graham said he'd heard he'd killed his dog and then himself or somebody's murdered him – all to do with drugs or something. Anyway, I'll make you some breakfast.'

The rumour mill had started already.

Liam decided to take the day off. He didn't want to speak to Ian and was glad when Mark said that their boss had already rung in to say he wouldn't be in for a few days.

'No problem, Liam. Eh, good win for your lads on Saturday and we did you a favour stuffing Ipswich 6–0.'

Bolton beating West Ham and Liverpool trouncing Ipswich would usually have made Liam's Monday, but football seemed insignificant at the moment. Liam trudged back upstairs. His day was going from bad to worse. 'Sorry'? What had Gazza to be sorry about?

He didn't know how long he'd been asleep when the sound of his mum's voice woke him. 'Liam, love, Kate's on the phone.'

He took a deep breath before picking the phone up. 'Kate?'

'Hello... er... are you OK, Liam?' She didn't sound angry, but she didn't sound too happy either.

'Kate... I'm so sorry about last night, I can't remember a thing. I'm really, really sorry. I'm ashamed of myself... I didn't hurt you, did I?'

'No... um... anyway I've got to go. I'm working 'til six. I just wanted to make sure you were all right. I've been worried about you all day.'

'Kate, will you meet me at the park gates tonight and give me a chance to explain myself. I wouldn't blame you if you didn't want to see me again, but... I just want to talk.'

'I'm sorry, Liam, but I'd rather leave it for now. I need a few days to... think things over.'

Liam was totally stunned and didn't know what to say. 'OK, I'll... speak to you soon.'

'Bye.'

He had really wanted to hear the usual 'love you' at the end of the call and became increasingly paranoid within minutes of their conversation. He didn't know why he'd said to meet at the park gates, other than being too embarrassed to go to her house in the unlikely event that Kate had said something to her mum and dad. He didn't want her to come back to his mum's house because it was where his 'crime' had taken place. Liam now felt physically sick as he made his way back up to his bedroom. He was still finding it hard to comprehend what he had done. His mum tried to help in the only way she knew how, by pampering him all afternoon, bringing him cups of tea and butties.

For the next few days, he walked round in a complete daze. Was he going to lose his soul mate? Was he going to lose the best thing that had ever happened to him? He didn't tell anybody about the situation except his mum.

'She'll come round, love,' she had said supportively.

But would she?

In between working, Liam stayed in his room within constant reach of his mobile. When Al had called to see if he'd got home all right from the night out, Liam was very brief.

'Yeah, good night. Anyway, speak to you at the weekend, I've got to go, mate.' He didn't want to tell Al that he was scared he might miss Kate's call.

By Thursday night, Liam was at his lowest point. He hadn't eaten anything for two days and he was physically and mentally drained.

'Liam... Liam?'

'Yeah. Mum, come in.'

His mum had stayed outside his bedroom door and Liam had ignored her at first, but she had persisted. He tried to raise a smile as she opened the door and peered in.

'Listen, love... this is no good, you moping around like this. You've got to give her a call. Tell her how you feel about her.'

His mum didn't wait for an answer but turned round and left the room. Liam lay on his bed for another ten minutes before he plucked up enough courage to call Kate. What would he do if she said she never wanted to see him again? His chest tightened and he cleared his throat in anticipation of speaking to her.

'Hello.'

'Hiya, Kate... I... er... just wanted to tell you again how sorry I am for Sunday night.' He paused desperately hoping for a positive response.

'Liam, I need to talk to you... You've upset me... really upset me... but I've really missed you over the past few days.'

'Kate, you wouldn't believe how much I've missed you. Can we meet up tonight?'

'Yes, OK.'

'I'll meet you in the park car park at 7.30pm. Is that all right?'

'Yes... see you then.'

Liam would never be able to express just how much he

had missed Kate over the last four days. Burying his face in his pillow had brought some comfort, as traces of her Eternity perfume were still recognisable. He had looked over the photographs she'd taken of them together and he had gone over and over the happy, laughter-filled experiences they'd shared. They had not had one argument since they had met.

Before he went to meet her, he sat at the end of his bed and gathered his thoughts. At that moment, he felt as if he was about to find out the results of some dreaded test —cancer or similar — but he tried hard to put things in perspective. He knew of a beautiful girl from school who had recently died from a brain tumour at 28 years old. Unlike him, she was no longer in a position to make any more mistakes, and then pick herself up and get on with life. Liam had probably made the biggest error of his life and he was dreading the consequences, but, whatever happened, he would dust himself down and, like his mum said, 'learn from his mistake'.

As Kate's car pulled into the car park, Liam's chest began to tighten again in nervous anticipation. He took a deep breath and blew out his cheeks in the cold, damp night air. His stomach was tying itself in knots again.

'Love you...' she said softly. Kate didn't realise how much her saying those words meant to him.

'I'm sorry, Kate... I am so sorry.' They had started hugging each other as soon as she had stepped from the car. 'I've missed you so much. I can't tell you how much I love you.'

Kate didn't say anything else at first, but just held on to Liam as they kissed and cuddled. In that one embrace, in those few seconds that felt like hours, he knew that everything would be all right.

As they walked through the park holding hands, Kate disclosed to Liam a little more about her feelings. 'Liam, I have never been as happy as I felt up until Sunday, but you scared me with your behaviour.'

'I am...'

'No, let me tell you why.' She squeezed Liam's hand as they walked. 'Liam, when I was in Saudi Arabia, Gareth didn't just become possessive...' She stopped talking and Liam knew instinctively what she was going to say.

He placed his arms round her. 'He hit you, didn't he, Kate?'

'I was so scared, Liam. In the end, I didn't dare say anything to him, I was that frightened. I never even told him I was leaving. I just left him a letter when he went to work and flew back to England.'

'Kate, if you give me another chance, I promise you I will never ever do anything like that ever again. I'll never get that smashed again.'

It was really quiet in the park as they walked round the football pitches.

'Liam, I don't think for one minute you are like him. I have never laughed as much, ever, as I have in the last six months when I have been with you. You're so different. Sunday night, I was so worried for you but you upset me. I wasn't sure if I wanted to see you again but the last four days have been a nightmare. I've not been able to concentrate on anything, eat anything...'

'Kate, I am so sorry. I haven't been feeling too good about myself lately and, on Sunday, everything just got on top of me.' He explained what had happened to Gazza and how he had gone back into the pub and upset everybody before drinking too fast and losing all self-control.

'Liam, it's all right, don't worry about it... we all do daft things, and we all make mistakes.'

'No, it's not right, Kate. I wouldn't have blamed you if you didn't want to see me again.'

'Don't be stupid, I just want to help you...' She squeezed his hand. 'I love you.'

The way she said 'I just want to help you...' made Liam feel as if she knew he needed help. Liam didn't know what to say and walked on in silence as they crossed the park towards the gardens.

'Your mum told me you must have been upset about something or had something on your mind. Was it speaking to Gazza or are other things getting you down?'

Liam had always managed to mask his deep-seated unhappiness with everyone else. Always the joker, always smiling, up for the craic... but, with Kate, it was different. He normally felt comfortable telling Kate that he was just feeling a bit down, but that was as far as he'd comfortably go. It was different this time.

'Come on... a penny for your thoughts?'

It was all Liam needed. 'Can we sit down?'

They headed for one of the benches. Liam was always comfortable in the park, so many wonderful childhood memories. But now he couldn't even look at Kate.

'Kate... I don't know what to say.'

'Come on, Liam, get it over with. If you want to split up, just tell me.'

Liam looked round and saw that she had tears rolling down her cheeks.

'Kate... oh, Kate.' He hugged her again and started to kiss her. He could taste her salty tears on his lips as they kissed. He looked into her eyes. She didn't have a clue what he was going to tell her, but somehow Liam knew she would understand. There was no going back. Hearing about his visit to Gazza's, and then his suicide, was the turning point and it was as if the enormity of that gave Liam the licence to dig deeper, much deeper, than he'd ever been willing to go before, and release some of those buried memories and feelings that dragged him down. Perhaps confronting those childhood memories was what Liam needed.

He had only recently started to read more about child abuse cases. It was weird how he had never really thought about what had happened to him until recently. It was just like he had seen it on television or read about it in the newspapers, an occurrence in which the child abuse victim only starts to recall later in life what had happened to them as a child. He had always had recollections, but it was as if, when his uncle had died, the 'problem' went away. Liam had been too young to understand fully what had happened at the time, but it was as if nobody needed to know and he could get on with his life. It was only in recent years he had started questioning it, and knew that the memories of those times were starting to affect him and the people around him.

Why had he never wanted to talk to anyone before? He had even considered ringing the Childline number once after watching a programme about abuse. At one stage, he'd thought of telling one of his friends, but would they have seen him in a totally different light if they found out? The thought of what had happened not only Liam disgusted him now but it also embarrassed him... and what about his mum if she found out? How would she feel? He never wanted his mum to find out because he knew it would break her heart. She still blamed herself for her depression and had constantly asked Liam if she had been a good mum. Of course, he told her that she had been the best mum in the world and she had been but, deep down, Liam felt guilty that he might have helped to tip her over the edge – an edge she had fallen dramatically from in her late thirties and had never really been able to climb back up from.

Kate knew all about his mum's problems but now it was time to tell her his secret. Liam knew he could talk to Kate about anything, and she would never tell anyone. Even if they were to split up, he was sure she would never disclose what he was going to tell her.

He didn't know how long they then talked for, but they had both cried at different points. It was strange how they seemed to have the park to themselves; there didn't seem to be another living soul in the park that night as Liam told her everything. When he'd finished, they just hugged and Kate told him gently how everything was going to be all right. Liam explained how he had been scared to tell her in case she wouldn't want to see him any more, and they both laughed at how each one of them, for a moment or so, had thought it was the end of their relationship.

'How do you really feel about us together, Liam?'

Liam had long ago stopped being Jack-the-Lad with

Kate and explained how he had never had feelings like he had now, and it wasn't bullshit. He really did mean it.

'So... what would you think if I said I would love to marry you?' Kate said, wiping away a tear.

'What?' He looked at Kate and realised she wasn't joking. 'Are you sure you mean what you're saying?'

''Course I'm sure, trust me, I'm a nurse. It's Valentine's night as well, and you don't seem to have bought me a present, so you'd better redeem yourself.'

Liam didn't waste any time. He jumped down on one knee. 'Kate, will you marry me?'

She gave him the biggest, most beautiful smile he'd ever seen. 'I thought you'd never ask! 'Course I will.'

The tears welled again, and were rolling down both their cheeks as they hugged.

'Come on, let's go and tell your mum,' Kate laughed.

She knew how much it would mean to Liam telling his mum first. Liam knew he had made the right decision. Telling Kate was as if he had been set free from what was fast becoming a living hell. He knew that it would still take time and that he would never forget what had happened to him, but he'd taken a step forward, and he already felt free.

27
Wedding Bells
Thursday, 14 February 2002

As they walked out of the park hand in hand, Liam had a flashback to when he was a boy walking along that very same path. It was very dark now, but he still looked round and thought to himself of how beautiful it was without the lowlife and scumbags who seemed to have gone into hibernation with the rest of Chorley. This was the place where he had dreamed about his future, a place where he had imagined himself being Kevin Keegan running round opponents as if they were statues, a place where he had been a soldier hiding in the trees, waiting to pounce on his enemy, usually made up of the O'Sheas or the Johnsons, depending on which sides they had picked. Here was the place were he had kissed his first girlfriend and even had his first tentative sexual experience at 14. Yes, the park had been a magical location and now the girl of his dreams had asked him to marry her there.

TELL SOMEONE

As they walked past the Cenotaph and out of the big iron gates, Liam squeezed Kate's hand tighter and she gave him that big to-die-for smile. He looked at his watch; it was already 9.00pm. Perfect, he thought. He couldn't wait to announce the news to his mum but he wanted her to be alone. He wanted to see the look on her face without his dad piping up in the background, 'You what? It's a bit soon, isn't it?' – assuming his dad even noticed them in the room as he watched the television, with the volume up loud enough for the next-door-but-one to hear *EastEnders* whether they liked it or not.

After buying a couple of surprise presents from the local shop, they walked round the corner and bumped straight into his dad.

'Now then... what are you two love-birds up to?'

'All right, Dad, where you goin'? The White Horse for a change?' Liam knew very well his dad never went anywhere else but The Wheatsheaf.

'Hello, Kate, love... anyway, I'll see you later.'

His mum already had a glass of beer on the table next to her chair. Liam left Kate hidden behind the living-room door. His mum's face dropped as she saw her son's look of mock anguish.

'How did you go on, love... what did she say?' She didn't give Liam a chance to say anything or change his expression. 'Oh, love, I am so sorry... but, if she wouldn't listen to you, it's her loss.'

'Mum... Mum.' Liam burst out laughing and stopped her before she could put her foot in it even more. 'I've got a surprise for you,' and with that he opened the living-room door. Kate was stood there with a tentative, shy smile.

'Hello, Mrs, O'Sullivan.'

'Oh, hello, love. He's always having me on... come on in. It's a pity yer dad's not here.'

She leaned forward and gripped the arms of the chair, ready to launch herself out of her seat.

'Hang on, Mum, sit there a minute, will you... we have something to tell you.'

'Oh, lovey, you're not pregnant, are you?'

'Mum!'

Liam picked the flowers up from the bottom of the stairs and took the bottle of champagne out of the plastic bag Kate was now holding. 'No, Mum, not pregnant yet, still only practising.' He looked at Kate and laughed at her embarrassed look. 'No, Mum, it's the best news I've ever had to tell you. These flowers are for you as the future mother of the groom.'

'What, love?' His mum's face was a picture and Liam couldn't remember the last time she had looked so happy as she burst into a gigantic smile. 'Oh, love... I – I can't believe it.' She jumped out of her chair and into her son's arms as if she was 20 years old again. They hugged each other and, when they eventually stopped, Liam pulled away and looked at his mum. Her eyes were shining and she was grinning from ear to ear as joyous tears coursed down her face. She then turned to Kate. 'Oh, love, you don't know how happy you've just made me.' She hugged Kate and, as Kate's head came over her shoulder, Liam could see that his fiancée was feeling the emotion as well.

'Come on, ladies, calm down, will you? Let's get the champagne out and celebrate. Mum, you can tell Kate how lucky she is to marry me.'

'Oh, Kate, I hope you know what you're letting yourself in for. He never stops acting the fool you know.'

The bride-to-be just stood there smiling, taking it all in as mum and son grabbed each other again.

By the end of the night, Liam had run up a phone bill that would give his dad a heart-attack. He had gone through the phone book and even informed a wrong number that he was getting married. No one he spoke to could believe it, but sounded unbelievably thrilled. His sisters and Anna had even started with the waterworks as they spoke to Kate. The most excited of Liam's close mates was Rob, whom he could hear going ballistic on the other end of the phone.

'Ooohhh... fantastic... we needed another stag do. Oh my God, I'll get organising it now.'

It didn't matter that Paddy would be the Best Man; Rob would still be chief organiser. When Liam explained that they were looking to get married as early as June, he was straight to the point. 'I think you might struggle with a venue, but, whatever you do, don't book it when England are playing their World Cup group games – that's Tuesday the 4th against Sweden; Saturday the 8th against the Argies; and Tuesday the 11th against Nigeria. Apart from any of those dates, I would be thrilled to be invited.' He finished with a 'Get in there, my son... I can feel a jolly boys' outing coming on.'

Before Liam could get another word in, Rob had put the phone down and was probably already writing a list of possible stag venues.

By the end of the next day, Kate's mum, dad, nana and granddad had been excitedly informed. Liam had never been as scared in his life when he had asked Kate's dad if he could he marry his daughter. However, his reaction had been fantastic and he had even produced his 25-year-old whisky to celebrate. Kate's mum had burst into tears and rung Kate's brother within minutes. Both parents had already taken to Liam and were now telling him how happy they were and how they had never seen their daughter so settled.

Everything seemed unreal to Liam. He knew he was going to get some stick from the lads on Sunday, but he also knew that every one of them would be pleased for him. Anyway, they all loved a good stag do and then meeting up on the wedding day to pick over the events.

Within two days, everything was set. Before the excitement had died down, Liam had sat Kate down and asked her if she was really sure what she was doing and even told her they could have a longer engagement if she wished, but she was adamant she wanted to get married as soon as possible.

'Liam, don't you know it's every girl's dream to meet her man in shining armour and choose her wedding dress? Do you think I'm going to let you go?'

He had been gobsmacked at the speed of everything and even Mad Al had phoned Liam telling him the same thing. 'She could have any bloke she wants, Kate, including me, so what is she doing marrying you?' he had joked.

Liam had thought the same. He couldn't believe he was marrying the goddess he had found in his bed. He hoped one day he would be able to find and thank the young lad who had put his hand up her skirt that Sunday night. He would buy him a pint. This wasn't a dream though – it was a fantastic, amazing reality.

The engagement ring was bought and the wedding venue was booked for Friday, 7 June at 1.00pm, with a £1,000 deposit to secure the Old Manor in the park for the reception. It was fortunate that the wedding was on a Friday, because the Manor was booked up for the next two years' worth of Saturdays and this was the only available Friday for the next four months. It must have been fate they had said as they booked it over the phone.

Neither family were disappointed that Kate preferred to have a civil wedding. She had explained to Liam that, at her degree ceremony, she had come out in a nervous rash so she thought the less formal the wedding, the less chance of it reappearing.

Liam was secretly ecstatic with the date and with his input on the honeymoon destination because he had made sure that he would be able to watch England v Argentina with the lads on the Saturday. They would then be jetting off on their honeymoon to the Caribbean on the Sunday.

Since he had met Kate, Liam's life had changed completely. Six months had seemed like six years and he felt really good about things for the first time. His brothers and sisters were made up for him and even his dad had said it was great news before mumbling on about not being able to afford a new suit. Liam knew underneath that he was really pleased, as his dad ran up the phone bill even more, ringing all his family in Ireland with the good news.

Liam didn't really know if he believed in God.

Sometimes he did, sometimes he didn't, but at that moment in time, as he lay in bed thinking about the past two or three days and how his life had turned out, he felt as though there had to be someone looking out for him. He felt an unbelievable sense of peace with himself and everybody. He had so much love to give to Kate. He would repay her faith in him by making her the happiest bride ever.

He also thought of the new lease of life his mum now seemed to have. She had already organised a day out shopping for her wedding outfit with his sisters and had been in touch with her brother Brian to give him the good news. He'd also overheard her talking to Mrs Mitchell telling her how proud she was. Liam would definitely make his mum proud. He had already determined that he would treat Kate with the utmost kindness and respect – in direct contrast to the way his father had treated his mother.

One minor concern still lingered in the background, though – he hoped Kate wouldn't stop him playing or watching football once they were married. He had already had a word with Rob and some of the lads, and they had thought it was a brilliant idea to get Kate and him two season tickets for Bolton as a wedding present. Roll on 7 June, he thought.

Just as he was nodding off, the phone rang. He jumped out of bed and bounded downstairs.

'Liam, it's Rob.' His tone was worrying; something had to be seriously wrong.

'Are you all right, mate?'

'Yeah, but I've made a massive mistake.'

Liam thought he could detect a slight slurring in Rob's voice, and suspected that he'd had a drink. 'What have you done now?'

'I've fucked up on the date of your wedding. We play the Argies on Friday, 7 June at 12.30pm, not Saturday the 8th. I don't know why I thought it was the 8th.'

The potential football quiz champion of Britain had, for once, got it wrong.

'Oh shit... we'll have to try and change the wedding day.'

'I'm so sorry, captain.'

'Don't worry... we'll sort something out.'

'Cheers... sorry.'

Liam put the phone down and immediately rang Kate.

'Don't worry, we'll work it out one way or the other,' she said.

Liam just hoped she would understand. Getting married was important, but England v Argentina in the World Cup Finals... well, it doesn't get any more important than that...

28
The Beautiful Game
Sunday, 14 April 2002

The next six weeks, culminating with The White Horse reaching the semi-final of the District Sunday League Cup, was by far the best time of Liam's life. He'd had good and bad times in the Army and had enjoyed going back to school and being a student, but nothing matched the happiness he now felt with Kate.

Even work seemed more enjoyable as Ian had been reconciled with his father. Liam hadn't told Ian that he'd spoken with his dad and had diplomatically told the old guy about how his son had felt left out as he grew up. For some reason, Liam's pep talk had done the trick. Recently, instead of being upset, Ian couldn't wait to tell Liam how he'd spent the weekend fishing or on a church expedition with his father. Liam enjoyed helping out other people but, in a way, in this instance he felt a pang of jealousy that Ian had become close to his father. He had long given up on his own dad, one who had never seen his son play any of the sports he'd excelled in at school, and who had never taken him fishing or on trips apart from the annual holidays to Rhyl, which usually ended in disaster. What with him nearly drowning one year and his sister Jean cutting her leg open on another holiday, much to the annoyance of their father, they weren't exactly good times.

Now, though, the past didn't matter. Liam was moving forward and part of this more optimistic attitude was his renewed policy of taking every day as it came and enjoying it. He'd written down his favourite quote by Gandhi and pinned it on his bedroom wall:

Live as if you were to die tomorrow.
Learn as if you were to live forever.

Now he was with Kate, he was looking at everything differently. Problems now seemed more trivial, and a chat with his fiancée was usually enough to put things right. Liam wondered at his good fortune, at last having someone he could talk to about anything and everything, and knew now how essential it was for people to experience that. It made him reflect on how many desperately lonely people there must be out there in the world who had troubles to impart to someone, anyone, but who hadn't found the right person to share them with.

He and Kate would now spend hours in bed, legs locked together, warm bodies leaning into one another, as they talked of their past, and their hopes for the future.

Liam's mum said she'd miss him when he announced that he and Kate had eventually seen the house they wanted, with the added bonus that they could be in it within the next month or so. His mum couldn't stop talking about how much she was looking forward to the wedding. Liam promised her he would try to get round to see her as often as possible to make sure 'the grumpy old fart' was looking after her. She'd even said she was going to cut down on her drinking so she would lose weight for the big day.

Even his dad had started smiling more and was really pleased when he received the news that two of his sisters were coming over from Ireland for the wedding. Not surprisingly, he never said he was going to miss Liam when he found out about the move.

On the football front, things could not have gone any better. The win against The Eagle and The Morris Dancers had set the lads on their way. Spuggie and Wayne had been unstoppable up front and Liam had never seen Spanish Phil playing so well. It may only have been the First Division of a pub league, but some of the things he could do with a ball were amazing. In fact, the entire team had really gelled, because they were playing week in, week out, even though the pitches were a disgrace. Liam laughed at the thought of a Premiership player turning out on a Sunday morning and playing with his ankles up to 6 inches in mud. At the end of most games, the pitches would resemble a mud bath and you sometimes couldn't tell your team-mates from the opposition.

Wayne loved it. 'You boys just want to be like me. Don't deny it. I know there's a bit of a black man in all you white boys waiting to get out.'

By the weekend of the semi-final, when they were due to play The Golden Lion from the Premiership Division, The White Horse had chalked up five consecutive victories in the league, including wins against local pub rivals The White Hart, Tut 'n' Shive and The Red Lion. Every game may have been a local derby, really, but these were teams with whom most of the lads had friends and even family playing against them. The White Horse had done the double over The White Hart who were managed by one of Rob's friends, Mully. They had a big bet on the outcome and, Rob being Rob, he had shared the winnings out with the lads.

It wasn't only the winning that Liam was enjoying. The laughing, joking and camaraderie had been everything he had hoped for and more. Mad Al and Tony had even started bringing a blow-up rubber doll with them, which they sat in the changing room with the team before every game. They put a strip on her one morning and tried to get the ref to let her have a game. Mick, who had decided very early in the season that he didn't fancy the muddy pitches, and Knobhead were also vying with each other to be supporter of the year.

Liam joined in all the antics but he was still deadly serious during the games themselves. On the morning of the semi-final, he couldn't believe how pumped up he was. If the team managed a shock result, the weekend could turn out to be perfect.

The previous day, Bolton had beaten Ipswich 4–1 to more or less secure Premiership survival, and to be there with Paddy, Rob and Nicky had been fantastic. They had been like kids jumping all over each other. Liam loved watching Bolton, but Paddy and Rob especially worshipped them and took everything to heart when the other lads goaded them if Bolton got beaten. Hammering Ipswich and the incredible noise from the Reebok crowd had even put a lump in Liam's throat. Sam Allardyce had performed a miracle once again by keeping the Whites in the Premiership.

To make Liam even more pleased, he and Kate had picked up the keys for their new house, a three-bedroom semi. Kate's dad had been unbelievably generous not only helping with the deposit, but also persuading an estate agent friend to speed up all the usual red tape. After the semi-final, Liam was going to spend the first night there, and had been quite unfazed when Kate had said she was going to stay at her parents until after the wedding day.

By 9.00am, he had already been through Ceefax and read the *News of the World* twice. Man City had beaten Barnsley 5–1, so Simon would be bouncing as his team homed in on the Premiership.

Liam decided to focus on their opponents, to whom they had given home advantage because they had a lovely, mud-free pitch. Rob thought the small pitch would suit The White Horse style of play and was in much better condition than any of the park pitches.

The odds were stacked against The White Horse beating The Golden Lion because of the calibre of their opponents. Liam knew the locally famous Barrow brothers, who had all played professional football at some stage and now enjoyed playing for their local pub. They may have been in their late thirties, but Liam knew they were still class. Even so, he still thought the Horse had a chance. He'd been through the formation with Rob a hundred times on the phone the night before, eventually going to his house at half-past midnight and staying 'til 2.00am before they had finally agreed on the team. With everybody except Kenny available, they were able to field their strongest line-up.

When he arrived at the pub at 9.20am, Liam was amazed to see everybody was already there, either reading papers or kicking a ball around. Even Kenny was bright eyed and bushy tailed and Liam counted 18 players plus himself. It was amazing what a big game meant to everybody. Knobhead was the only one not there, but had asked to be picked up on the way. Anyway, they couldn't go without another one of their chief supporters. Liam just hoped he wasn't expecting a game.

The lads had just started arguing about who was driving when Steve came round the corner in the minibus. A massive cheer went up on the realisation that they would be travelling in style. Rob had hired it for the day and Steve had volunteered to drive after promising he wouldn't have a drink until after the game. He didn't tell them he would be smoking cannabis all day, though, to make up for it.

As they began the 20-minute journey, Liam could sense the tension on board. Even Spuggie, who was never usually still for more than two seconds, was quiet. Giant soon changed the mood with a massive fart and then a roar of 'Come On You White Men...'

As everybody tried to waft the smell away, he soon had all the lads humming the *Great Escape* tune. The more serious Rob went round having individual chats, explaining what he expected from key players. When the minibus pulled up outside Knobhead's house, both Liam and Rob jumped out to knock on his door and talk tactics.

'Shit! What's Knobhead's proper name?' Rob asked quickly, realising that he may not answer the door. As

Liam knocked louder, he also realised that he didn't have a clue what Knobhead's real name was. He was a mate but hadn't grown up with the two of them. He had only started coming in the pub the previous year and, when Liam had asked why everyone called him by that name, Knobhead had simply replied, 'Because I am.'

Before they could go back and ask one of the lads on the bus, it was too late – the front door opened.

'Er, er... is your lad in, love?' Rob asked the middle-aged woman in front of him, whom he recognised as Knobhead's mum.

'Oh, hello, lads. I've been trying to get him up for the last half-hour, the lazy bastard.'

The two of them were a little startled at this, but what happened next would go down in White Horse folklore. The woman, dressed in what looked like a dinner lady's outfit, marched upstairs before screaming, 'Knobhead... KNOBHEAD, are you getting up, love? The lads are here for you.'

She repeated this a number of times as she closed in on his bedroom, and then burst into it, by the sound of things.

Liam and Rob returned to the bus and told the others what they'd heard before Knobhead stepped on to the bus having obviously just stumbled straight out of bed.

'Knobhead... Knobhead... Knobhead...' came the chant.

There's definitely something in a name, Liam thought.

By the time they got to the ground, everybody's mood had improved even more and, before changing, they had a kick-about on the pitch. Mad Al and Tony had brought their rubber doll with them but the locals didn't look too impressed.

Rob was right; the pitch was made for The White Horse's style of play. Earlier in the season, the owners of The Golden Lion had sold their massive pitches to property developers, and moved to this tiny pitch which meant that the pub team was prevented from playing their normal passing game and it would also mean that The White Horse boys could 'get at 'em' throughout the game.

Everybody sat quietly in the Community Hall but, as Rob began his team talk, they were interrupted by the caretaker. 'Gents, sorry that we haven't got any changing rooms for you, but you can get changed here and I'll show you where you can get a shower and change afterwards.'

'No problem, mate.' Rob waited until the guy was out of sight before he continued. 'Lads, this is our big chance. Before I name the team, I want to tell you that I've been up all night and been through every formation possible trying to fit everybody in. You know the score – I can only pick 11 players to start the game, but I can also only pick five subs, which still means two missing out.'

'I'm not bothered about a shirt, Rob.' Browny was the first to volunteer.

'Thank fuck for that because you weren't getting one anyway. So...' Rob paused, hoping that Knobhead, who had turned up every week but had hardly ever got a game because he was crap, would also volunteer himself to be a spectator.

However, he was busy doing up the laces of his £120 Adidas boots that he had been out to buy the previous day, so it was conceivable that he didn't hear Rob when he said, 'I am sorry, Knobhead...' or he was simply ignoring it. Rob tried again. 'Knobhead, I am sorry... you're going to have to miss out today.'

He'd definitely heard that one, as Liam saw his bottom lip go straight away. Knobhead tried to look genuinely shocked, giving Rob his best 'How can you leave one of your top players out?' stare.

'Doesn't matter, boss,' he said stoically, 'whatever's best for the team. I'll go and give Steve a hand with the water and first aid bag.' Head down, he started to make his way out of the changing room.

Mad Al couldn't resist it. 'Knob?'

Knobhead looked at him, begging for some support with tears welling in his puppy-dog eyes. 'Yeah, Al?'

'Can I borrow your boots?'

'Yeah... er... yeah, no problem. See if they fit you.'

A few shakes of the head and an 'I was only joking' from Al soon stopped as Rob named the team. The manager then pulled out all the stops to wind the players up – about how they had been written off by everybody and they had nothing to lose. The lads didn't really need a team talk and, apart from the motivational chat, the 20-minute lecture could have been replaced by, 'Run your bollocks off, win every tackle and second ball and don't be scared of handing out a few rash challenges as long as they are not in our penalty area.'

Finally, Rob asked the lads to consider something else. 'Just one more thing, lads. I know we didn't know young Gazza that well but, come on, let's do it for him. He didn't have a load of mates to rely on like we have... maybe things would have turned out differently if he had. Come on, lads, work for each other... and seize the day.'

TELL SOMEONE

There must have been 200 people watching, which was 195 more than usual. Everyone from the pub except Bainesy seemed to have made the effort.

As Liam ran past one of The Golden Lion players, he tried to wish him good luck. 'Have a good game, mate.'

'Fuck off, granddad. We're gonna hammer you.'

Liam looked at him and realised he wasn't joking. He just nodded, but underneath he was seething. Liam had been a bit upset at being labelled old at 31, but he would use his age and experience to his advantage. As they warmed up, he had a quick word with Riggers, who started growling as Liam said, 'Riggers, that young lad just called me "granddad", so what must he think of you?'

'We'll see about that, then.'

Liam went round pumping his fist, geeing everybody up. He spoke to everyone and could tell they were all up for it. Giant was completely focused, banging his massive gloves together. Simon just said 'City' as he went past him. Mad Al and his brother Tony were actually shaking hands with each other, promising they wouldn't argue. Wayne was playing to the crowd, raising his arms and winding them up. Liam knew that Spanish Phil was going to have the game of his life; he'd never seen Phil have a bad game.

Liam's midfield partner Paddy winked at him as they stood next to each other. They knew each other's game inside out, having played football together since they were five years old.

Spuggie was already blowing kisses at the centre-half who didn't really know what to make of it all. Wolfman looked at Liam and smiled. He'd seen it all before and was just glad to be playing.

As the game started, the cocky lad received the ball at his feet as Riggers 'tackled' him. Liam heard the scream and winced as The White Horse player somehow came away with the ball. The ref played on but, sportingly, Phil knocked the ball out of play. Riggers and Liam stood over the player, who had only been winded. As he lay gasping for breath, Liam sensed the opposition didn't seem as committed as The White Horse team; none of their players complained and none came over to see how their team-mate was. They didn't look up for the fight as much as the Horse lads, who were congratulating the smiling assassin.

The lads chased everything, got really stuck in, mostly legitimately, and came off at half-time to a massive round of applause, unlucky not to be leading. Liam kicked the rubber doll out of the way in frustration as they walked into the Community Hall. The manager had decided to take the half-time break inside, out of the way.

'What can I say, lads? That was absolutely brilliant. I've never seen anything like it. I know Wayne's on drugs, but the rest of you played like you were as well. We should be five up and they know it. All I can say is, keep going. Paddy, Liam, superb in midfield.'

Spuggie had been having a right ding-dong with the centre-half who had stupidly laughed at him when he had missed an easy chance.

'I'm going to kill him, man. Just watch me in this second half. Shearer... Shearer. Watch Shearer score.'

Liam drank as much water as he could and then pulled the joker out of his bag. Three packets of Jaffa cakes. 'Right, lads, if you want some more energy, get some of these instant carbohydrates down your necks.'

'Me fuckin' favourites.'

Giant started demolishing a packet on his own as everybody piled in. Even the rubber doll was offered one by Simon.

'Come on, lads, we can do this.'

Rob patted every one of them on the back as they made their way out of the hall. As they walked back on to the pitch, Liam distinctly heard Kate's voice. He turned round to see her standing there with his mum. He couldn't believe it. His mum gave him a big smile and shouted, 'Come on, love, you can do it.'

Liam laughed and he couldn't believe how proud he felt. His mum had never seen him play football until now. It was all the motivation he needed.

The second half was similar to the first with The White Horse not allowing their opponents any time at all on the ball. Liam started to become anxious because he could tell everybody was tiring. He didn't fancy extra time, but it looked like it was heading that way. Both teams had gone on to hit the bar and post but, with 90 minutes on the clock, it looked like the score, unheard of for a pub game, was going to be 0–0 at full-time. Spuggie and Wayne had run themselves into the ground. The back four had been magnificent and Phil and Wolfman had rolled back the years.

During a break in play, Liam asked the ref how long before extra time, and sighed when the reply was 'one minute'. A few of the lads were struggling big time, and he knew that, although they had subs, it looked like they were going to miss their chance.

Spuggie, though, the most positive thinker Liam had ever

met, was having none of it. Giant, who had made some outstanding saves, punted a tired-looking kick out of his hands and the ultimate chaser of lost causes started running. He had no right to get near it as the centre-half shepherded the ball out of play. Somehow, though, as it was just about to go out for a goal kick, Spuggie slid from behind the player and managed to keep the ball in as the defender lost his balance. The number 9 then jumped back up and rounded the goalkeeper before slipping the ball into the empty net and running away one arm aloft, Shearer-style, shouting, 'Shearer... Shearer... Shearer.' He wheeled away towards The White Horse contingent. Pandemonium broke out as he was jumped on by everyone, players and supporters alike. The ref blew his whistle furiously in an attempt to make the players return to their own half, but even he had to laugh when Spuggie emerged butt naked.

Thirty seconds later and the game was over. The Golden Lion were gracious in defeat and even the lad who had goaded Liam wished him luck for the final. After having the craic with all the fans that had turned up, Liam hugged his mum and Kate together.

'To win is great, but to have the two most special women in your life here, I can't believe it.'

'You were brilliant, love.'

'Cheers, Mum.'

'You go and enjoy yourself and make sure you look after our house tonight.' Kate was going straight to work after the game.

'OK, love. Mum, I'll pop round for some breakfast in the morning.'

His mum laughed.

Liam made his way back into the hall. As the lads were starting to pick their bags up to make their way to the changing facilities promised by the caretaker, he seized his chance. He ran and jumped on the rubber doll that was next to Phil. Liam quickly whipped his shorts down and starting taking the doll doggy-style, laughing and shouting, 'Come on, you know you want it.'

He expected at least a laugh from the lads, but they had all gone quiet and Paddy was even signalling for him to stop.

'What's going on? We won, you know!' he shouted, but then Giant also started pointing behind him, hands clasped together, begging Liam to turn round. Liam slowly turned to find nearly a hundred mainly women and children looking at him in complete silence. A Brownie jamboree was taking place.

'Ahh, sorry... er... ladies, just celebrating winning.'

Liam picked up his clothes and the rubber doll and quickly made his exit. Spuggie and Tony were nearly crying with laughter in the communal toilet and shower area when Liam eventually found the rest of the lads.

'Liam, you should've seen them lasses' faces when you were going for it, man. It was brilliant.' Tony actually had tears running down his face. 'It was a good job your mum didn't see you... you wouldn't have been her blue-eyed boy then, would you?'

Liam shook his head. Why do daft things always happen to me? he thought. He would leave the incident out when he went round to see his mum. As he began showering, he couldn't stop thinking how brilliant it had been to see her at the game. He couldn't wait to hear what she had to say.

262

29
Your Mum's a Loony
September 1984 – Liam (aged 14)

Liam had never been so excited in his life. He couldn't wait to see his mum to tell her the news, but first he wanted to see Rob because his mate had always helped him with his football. He knocked on the Johnsons' front window and gave his mate the thumbs-up when he turned from watching the television. Liam made his way through the back door and straight into the lounge.

'I've been selected for Lancashire Schoolboys' trials next week.'

Rob was really pleased for Liam. 'Well done, at least one of us from the estate will hopefully end up playing professional football. Do you want a drink?'

Rob jumped up out of the chair and Liam followed him into the kitchen. He poured Liam a glass of Vimto and opened a can of Trophy bitter straight into his pint glass. Liam was in awe of his older friend. It wasn't long ago that they played together on the park, but now Rob was working full-time and had been going down the pub regularly for the last year or two. Liam was quite small for a 14-year-old, but Rob was already 6 foot 1 and had no problem getting in the pubs.

Liam drank his Vimto as fast as he could. 'I am going home to tell me mum... she'll be well pleased.'

'OK, mate. I'll give our Paddy and Giant the good news when they get in.'

As Liam made his way across the road, he felt special. He couldn't stop grinning and couldn't wait to see his mum.

'Your mum's a fuckin' loony.'

Stringy was a right bastard and always picked on Liam when nobody was about. He was 18 but it hadn't stopped Liam having a number of fights with him as they grew up. He always got beaten, but it was getting closer and Liam had vowed to himself that one day he would get his revenge.

'She should be in a loony bin, you little shit.'

For once, Liam didn't know what to do because he could see a group of people gathered near the side entry passage and knew something must have happened.

'You better be careful, love. Your mum's got an axe.' Mrs Beatty was a nosy bitch and always gossiping, but for once she was telling the truth and Liam knew it. His mum had recently found a small pick-axe in the garden shed and had started to keep it next to her in bed at night. He could hear the back windows smashing as he made his way down the passage.

'You can piss off and if you don't get back in your house I'll hit you with this next.' His mum was shouting at Mrs Lund, the next-door neighbour, who was only trying to calm her down.

Liam peered through the slits in the gate for a few seconds as his mum put another one of the small windows through. Mrs Lund was a lovely lady who had always tried to help his mum.

'Please, Mary, you'll hurt yourself.'

'Get back in the house, you silly old bitch.'

Liam's mum turned towards her and raised the pick-axe as if she was going to hit her. Liam could see that it wasn't really his mum shouting. Apart from the arguments with his dad, she never swore or even raised her voice, but her face was contorted now and she looked like she was possessed.

'Mum, what are you doing?' Liam opened the latch on the gate. 'Give me the pick-axe before you do any more damage.'

It was as if a switch had been triggered as she was now back in mum mode. 'I'm sorry, love, but they told me to do it... I'm going back upstairs.'

She passed Liam the pick-axe and then walked in through the back door. Mrs Lund, on seeing the coast was clear, reopened her back window.

'Are you all right, Liam? I've told Mrs Beatty not to call the police.'

'Thanks, Mrs Lund.'

'Your dad's got a lot to answer for.'

Mrs Lund had lived next door to the family all Liam's life and must have heard everything that went on.

Liam sat on the back step and began to cry. Not for too long, though, in case his mum came back down. He didn't want her to think she had upset him.

Fiona was home within ten minutes and called the

council out to come and replace the windows. She had been doing everything in the house for the last three or four months since their mum had started staying in her room all the time. She did the cooking, cleaning and ironing every day after school as Jean had started shift work at the local weaving mill and was always working. Their dad had started sleeping in the spare room at the weekend when he was home from long-distance haulage and also insisted on going to the pub.

Liam would get himself up every morning for school along with Fiona, who would always make sure he looked smart. They both knew their mum wouldn't be around to help them, as she was always awake throughout the night watching television, smoking and making herself cups of tea. Liam would hear her every night coming past his room, the floorboards creaking and her hand gently scraping along the wall to guide her along in the darkness. She wouldn't have the television on loud but everything echoed in the night. Liam could hear the kettle set off on its journey to boiling point. He could hear the spoon being left on the kitchen worktop and then the telly being put on. He could also hear his mum talking, carrying on conversations with herself, usually nonsense sentences with no meaning. He would often sit halfway down the stairs listening to her.

Sometimes, he or his sisters would get up and try to tell her to go back to bed, but she would just be sitting there in a chair staring at the television – talking to it. She would always say she'd be 'up in a minute', but never was. Their dad never said anything when he arrived home for the weekend. On the odd occasion he did venture upstairs, but he was always shouted at by Liam's mum, and was even threatened with the pick-axe once, so he sought sanctuary in the pub.

Every morning before school, Liam and his sister would go into their mum's room to show her they had got ready for school and say goodbye. She always seemed to be sat up by then and would give them a lovely smile. There was always a promise to have a wash and get changed when they had gone to school. Liam knew she didn't most days because when he arrived home from school he would check the bathroom to see if the towel and soap had been used. It usually hadn't. Their mum would only leave the house if she was really desperate – if Fiona had forgotten to buy her cigarettes or if she had smoked them all. That was when Stringy, who was unemployed, would see her and she would walk past him like 'a fuckin' zombie freak'.

Liam wanted to kill him for what he said, but even his friends had told him they had seen her and said hello, but she didn't seem to recognise them. She had been put on tablets for 'depression', but Liam knew she wasn't taking them, even though he or Fiona would go to her room with the tablets and water. His mum would throw the packet in the outside bin in the middle of the night and refuse to take them. Liam or Fiona would then have to search through the rubbish and find them and plead with her to take them again.

She was supposed to take four a day, but Liam and his sister couldn't be there every time she was meant to take them. He wished his brother James hadn't moved away but he probably wouldn't have been able to help anyway. She hadn't listened to his other brother Mick when he had come round and tried to talk to her. Nobody seemed to be able to help her. None of his mum's family had been to see her for ages since his dad had refused to let them in, and his mum said she didn't want to see anyone anyway.

'We'll be all right, Liam. Mum'll be better soon; I'll put the tea on. Why don't you go out for a game of football?' Fiona always tried to put on a brave face, but, sometimes, not even she was strong enough.

For once, Liam didn't feel like playing football. Fiona didn't tell their dad about the windows. She paid for them herself at the council offices using the housekeeping money she was now in charge of, but their dad probably found out about it in the pub in any case.

Liam didn't tell his mum or dad about the football trials and didn't bother going; he didn't feel up to it. He just wished his mum would get better.

30
Nothing Like a Lazy Bitch
Monday, 15 April 2002

Liam didn't bother having a shower in his new house. He was well hungover after the celebrations and couldn't wait to see his mum and find out what she thought of the game.

As he climbed out of his car outside her house, he could hear the bellowing voice of his dad. He still took his time as he walked the short 10 yards up the front garden path trying to comprehend what was going on. The voice was definitely his father's. Liam slowly opened the front door.

'I fuckin' told you to do it last night, you lazy bitch... you're fuckin' useless.'

The shouting was coming from the kitchen, but, with the noise he was making and with the kitchen door half-closed, his dad hadn't heard or seen Liam's arrival.

'I am sorry, Jim... I just forgot.'

Liam's heart jumped as he heard his mum's pleading voice.

'Fuckin' forgot my arse... you're just a lazy bitch.'

'No, don't, Jim, I'm sorry.'

Liam opened the kitchen door just in time to see a plate smashing at his mother's feet as she cowered against the kitchen sink. His dad had luckily changed his mind about throwing the plate at her head. Jim's face changed from one of sheer anger and hatred for his wife to shock and fear as he looked at Liam.

Liam stood for probably a few seconds, but it seemed like for ever. His dad was 64 years old but he could have been 34 as the memories just came flooding back.

'Liam, what are you doing here so early?'

His dad spoke as if nothing had happened. Liam didn't give him an answer, but went for his dad, grabbing him by the throat. He nearly lifted him off his feet as he banged him into the cooker.

'You fuckin' wanker... bullying me mum like that.'

His dad was trying to say something but Liam wasn't listening. He was now trying with both his hands to prise Liam's hand from his throat, but he had no chance as Liam charged him backwards through the kitchen door and into the living room in one rapid movement before throwing him down on to the settee. He could see the fear in his dad's bulging eyes as he pinned him down by his throat, but he didn't feel any sympathy at this point, just hatred. 'You ever speak to me mum like that again and I'll fuckin' kill you.'

'Liam, Liam... no... no.'

He could hear his mum behind him, her scared voice, but he couldn't stop himself. 'Do you understand? Do you fuckin' well understand me?' he continued, pointing with his free hand at his father's face.

His dad's eyes were nearly popping out as his arms thrashed about, still attempting to escape from his son. Liam had a sudden flashback to the holiday when he was six years old. For a few seconds, he wanted to kill his dad, but he could now hear his mum's voice again.

'No, Liam... no Liam, don't, love... don't, love.'

Liam released the grip and his dad started coughing uncontrollably. He looked round to his mum. 'Mum, get your coat, you're coming with me.'

His mum went straight to the kitchen to the coat cupboard.

'I am sorry... I am sorry.' A hoarse, rasping, pathetic voice came from the living room.

Liam didn't look back as he opened the front door and ushered his mum into his car. As he drove away, he looked at her. She was staring ahead in a state of shock. Liam spoke softly. 'Are you all right, Mum?'

'Yeah, love, I am just a bit shook up, that's all.'

'He's nothing but a bastard, Mum, nothing but a bastard.'

'I know, love, I know.'

As they drove towards his new home, his mum told Liam that the offence she had committed was to forget to put some frozen peas in a bowl to soak. Liam had come in as his dad had walked into the kitchen to find his wife making a cup of tea. He had gone crazy when he had seen an empty plate where the peas should have been.

When they arrived at Liam's, he started to make his mum a cup of tea while she went and sat on the settee.

'How many sugars do you want?'

'Two, love... but don't you want me to make it?'

'No, no, don't be daft, you're in my house now.' He

passed his mum her brew. 'Mum, I wish that bastard would die and leave you in peace.'

Liam had had plenty of conversations with his mum in the past, and had asked on several occasions why she had stayed with him, but he knew now she would never leave him, not after 45 years. He'd also thought his dad had changed and that they had been getting on really well.

'There's no chance of him dying, Liam. I've got at least another 15 years of him to put up with.' She gave her son a smile. 'He's all right normally... it's just sometimes he gets up in a bad mood. Really, love, that's the worst he's been for a while.'

'I tell you, Mum, I've had it with him now. How long has he been like that with you when there's nobody around?'

Liam didn't wait for his mum's reply; she wouldn't tell him the truth anyway. 'Why don't you move in here with me, at least until after the wedding? Or let's ask our Fiona or Jean to let you stay with one of them?'

'No, you're all right, love, your dad wouldn't know what to do without me... I don't think he's ever switched the cooker on.'

'Mum, you don't deserve to be treated like a piece of shit... nobody deserves that.'

She took a sip of her tea. 'I know, love, but I am happy as I am. I can walk round to Margaret's from our house and she'd miss me if I moved. Anyway, I don't want to burden anybody, and you and our Fiona wouldn't let me smoke in your houses. Anyway, you've just scared the living daylights out of your dad. I don't think he'll be doing anything like that again.'

'No. He bloody won't... I am going to tell everybody

how he treats you, including Jimmy and Bert in the pub.'

'No, don't, love... don't tell anybody.'

'Mum, 45 years you've been putting up with him...'

His mum didn't wait for Liam to finish. 'I know, love, I should have left him years ago, but I didn't and that's that. I'm not bothered about myself. I just wanted all me children to do well and you all have. When you have children with Kate, you'll realise what I mean. I did love your dad once, but when you lot came along there was no competition. The love you have for your kids is the greatest love you'll ever know. I've wanted to leave him a thousand times, Liam. I've wanted to kill him a thousand times, too.' She laughed as she carried on. 'Well, you wouldn't believe how many times I've felt like doing away with your father, but I always knew, if I did, I wouldn't be able to see you lot grow up. Wouldn't see you turn out into lovely kids and good adults. I wouldn't have seen Mick and Jean's children and I wouldn't be seeing you get married.'

Liam had never heard his mum be so forthcoming. 'No, you may not think that I've had a good life, but I have, Liam, and I can handle your dad now. If you hadn't come in, I'd have thrown something back at him. He's an old man now. I'm a lot stronger than he is, the lanky streak of piss!'

They both laughed out loud.

'I am sorry I grabbed him like that, Mum. I just lost it.'

'Don't be sorry, love. He deserved it but, to be honest, I am worried about him... he's lost a lot of weight and he's coughing more and more but he won't go to the doctor's again.'

'Mum, you'd be better off if he popped his clogs anyway; you'd have the house to yourself.'

'I know, love, but I remember when you lot had all left home and the house was empty with your dad on long distance. I didn't like it then, I was too lonely. You've all got your own lives to live now and I don't want to be a bother to you.'

Liam knew he hadn't looked after his mum as well as he could have done and the guilt had started to play more and more on his mind. 'Mum, I'm sorry I've not helped you more in the past. Sorry I've been a tosser sometimes, telling you to do this, do that, get me this, get me that.'

'Oh, don't worry about it, love, you've given me something to do in the house. I don't mind doing anything for any of you... it keeps me busy.'

But, before she could carry on any further, she burst into uncontrollable sobs.

'Mum, Mum, what's wrong, love? Please stop crying... Mum, please, what's wrong?'

'I am so sorry, love. I should have told you before but I've never had the courage. I've never told anyone. Oh I am so sorry, love.'

'Mum, it can't be that bad, can it? Come on, tell me; you'll feel better for telling somebody.'

He passed his mum some tissues, but the way she was going, he'd need another boxful.

'I am sorry, love, I can't tell you. I can't...'

'You can, Mum, don't worry. It won't matter, honestly.'

Minutes passed before Liam could get any sense out of her. He was starting to get seriously worried as he had never seen his mum in such a state. 'Come on, Mum, please... I'm sure you'll feel better if you tell me what's on your mind.'

Eventually, she managed to regain some composure as Liam rubbed her back.

'Liam... it's your dad.'

'Yeah?'

'He's not... your dad... he's not your dad, love.'

'What?'

'I am so sorry... I am so sorry.'

'What, Mum?' Liam couldn't take it in. 'Say it again, Mum... what did you say?' His voice faltered, as he was stunned at what she had said.

For the next hour or so, Liam sat unmoving, numb, as his mother explained herself. 'After our Fiona was born, for some reason I felt really low, Liam. Call it the baby blues... but your father, well, he didn't want to know, didn't understand.'

'Yeah, it's OK, Mum... carry on.'

'Because of the money situation at the time, I had to more or less go straight back to working at the bingo hall. There was a temporary manager, Liam, and he was so nice to me, so different.' She placed both hands over her mouth and nose as her whole body began to shake.

'Shhh, it's OK, Mum. It's all right, I promise.'

'We would talk every night when the club closed. Your dad was working away all the time and, when he was home, he was just going to the pub. Our James would look after your other brother and sisters and I only started quite late anyway. I was feeling so low, Liam... and then it just happened.'

'Mum... Mum, how can you be sure?'

People had always said that Liam and his brother Mick looked more like they were from his mother's side of the family, but could his mum be really certain?

'Liam, your dad would get that drunk that he wouldn't remember if we'd done anything in bed or not.' His mum went quiet and Liam could sense her embarrassment but she wanted to carry on. 'I am sorry, love. It only went on for about three months and nobody ever found out.' Tears started trickling down her cheeks. 'He got transferred to London and, although we said we would keep in touch, we never did. I only realised I was pregnant after he had gone. I never told him. I am so sorry, love, so sorry, but I was feeling so low. It was for the best that I never saw him again, because I could never have split the family up and it would have brought us so much shame. I hope you can forgive me. I've wanted to tell you before but, when you said you were getting married, I was so happy for you I didn't want to spoil anything.'

'Mum, Mum, don't worry, eh? I mean it.'

Liam hugged his mum and he did mean it. She had been through so much in her life, in a weird way, Liam didn't begrudge her three months of happiness. He still felt shocked at the news, though.

'Listen, Mum... this is our secret. Nobody needs to know. Let's talk about it again after the wedding, eh? That's if you want to. If you don't, we don't have to mention it ever again.' Liam wanted to protect his mum and wanted her to know how he felt. 'Anyway, I've still got the best mum in the world.'

Neither was able to say anything for a while after that,

and Liam was glad his mum made the next move. 'Will you take me home, love? I best see how he is.'

He couldn't believe his mum was still worried about his dad.

She broke the silence on the car journey back to her house as Liam was still too dazed to say a word. He had hundreds of questions he really wanted to ask his mum, but now wasn't the time.

'Is everything going OK with the wedding plans, love? Is Kate all right with everything?' As usual, she didn't give him time to answer. 'I can tell Kate's different from your other girlfriends. I've never seen you looking so happy. I know you'll look after her; you've definitely got the Lee caring genes from my side. Did I tell you I wanted to be a nurse once?'

'Only about a million times, Mum.'

They both laughed. And, as he did, Liam wondered at just how selfless she had been, and how she would have made a wonderful nurse.

As she got out of the car, Liam winked at his mum. 'Don't worry, Mum, don't worry yourself... everything will be fine.'

He then made his way back to his house. He slumped into his chair trying to take in what his mum had said, and various thoughts vied for space in his head. He'd had many repeated conversations with his mum, especially when she'd had a few beers, and she'd always talked sense. She was fond of her mottos and sayings, and a recent one in particular stuck in his head. She had seen it on a board outside a church, and it read, 'Be kind. Everyone you meet is fighting a battle.'

Liam knew exactly why that sentiment had appealed to his mum, and why it meant so much to him. With his mum's help, and Kate's, he had won his battle. He would make sure in the future that she felt no guilt at what she had done.

He was really glad that she had unburdened herself of her dark secret. If anyone could understand what it meant to bottle up hurtful memories, and choose to share them with no one, then it was Liam. He now hoped his mum would feel as relieved, as free, as he now was, having shared his deepest, darkest secrets with someone he loved.

31
Don't Be Dead, Dad
Sunday, 21 April 2002

Apart from Liam losing the keys to the house, the night had been absolutely brilliant. He and Kate had made their way instead to Kate's mum's and his fiancée was now asleep next to him. He only hoped Kate hadn't minded when he had secretly stripped naked in the bay window behind the curtains at Rob's before opening them as if he was on stage. His friends laughed as he revealed his meagre assets to everybody yet again. Anna had told him, laughing, that he should seek help for his addiction. Kate had cringed at the time as he spent the whole Kylie Minogue song dancing in his birthday suit, pointing to her. It was a pity he could only remember the '*I just can't get you out of my head*' refrain.

Even though he had been hoping to lure his bride back to their house for a night of passion, he didn't mind what had happened. He would find the keys at Rob's; anyway, he loved being in Kate's single bed, as he could be even closer to her. He leaned up and reached for the pint of water she had brought up for him the previous night. It reminded him that, when they had eventually made it to bed, Kate had said she would go back downstairs and fetch something for him to drink. He would feel better in the morning if he drank it, she had said. He must have fallen asleep before she even came back to bed, and he cursed himself at being such a useless sod.

Leaning over her, he caught a glimpse of himself in the dressing-table mirror. God, he looked rough. Kate, on the other hand, still looked every bit the Egyptian goddess in her usual prone position. Her hair was still immaculate, her face looked stunning and she didn't snore like Natalie; it was more of a quiet purr. In fact, Liam could hear her brother snoring much more loudly on the other side of the bedroom wall. These big modern houses did have their downside, he thought.

He started thinking about the conversation he had had with his mum. It had been really weird sat there being told that the bloke you had always thought was your father wasn't.

A movement from Kate dragged him back from his reverie. He drank the pint of water in one and the rehydration seemed to kick in; he felt better, anyway. He checked his watch; it was only 8.00am so he could get away with another hour's sleep and be more relaxed about playing the Caribbean Club. He did think about getting himself back to sleep really quickly with a brisk ham shank, but he had a double reason not to. First, he didn't think Kate would appreciate it and, second, he never did the business on match-day mornings to conserve his energy. He knew he shouldn't have drunk so much because he had broken his self-imposed 48-hour alcohol ban, but Paddy and Simon had kept buying him pints before they headed back to Rob's. Anyway, big matches never seemed to get in the way of Rob's parties.

Liam started to drift off picturing the tackles, headers and passes he was going to make in the game – the usual stuff he visualised. The game would be the championship decider and Liam was confident they could get revenge for the 6–0 thrashing in the first game of the season. It had been amazing how poor the rest of the teams in the division had been. Luckily, the Caribbean Club had been deducted three points for playing an unsigned player, so a victory would more or less confirm part one of the double.

For a moment, he thought Kate's alarm was ringing before he realised it was the phone downstairs. Bloody hell, three minutes after eight on a Sunday morning and somebody was calling. If he were Kate's mum, he'd give the caller a right bollocking for disturbing them so early. A cough on the stairs confirmed it was her mum heading downstairs to answer the phone.

Liam tapped Kate on the shoulder and she obligingly turned on her side, allowing him to snuggle into her body from behind. He felt so safe and warm melting into her curves as she slept. It felt so natural, knees bent, following the contours of her entire body, his stomach pressing against her back and a protective arm across her slim hips drawing her into him. How was it that he was the one protecting them both, yet he felt such a sense of safety and security? He didn't know, but it felt good.

A quiet tap on the door and a whisper of 'Liam'

brought him back to reality. He nearly blurted out, 'Make us a brew, Mum,' but, realising where he was, he woke Kate up, embarrassed about answering. He still felt awkward sleeping in Kate's bed at her mum's house. Kate called out a muffled reply to her mum, but it was definitely Liam that she wanted to speak to.

'Liam, I'm sorry to bother you, but it's your sister Fiona on the phone and she says she needs to speak to you urgently.'

Liam remembered he was supposed to ring his sister to tell her if he and Kate were going round for Sunday roast. She couldn't be ringing to confirm that so early, could she? And how did she know they were here?

No, something was wrong – something was definitely wrong. His dad had been complaining more and more about feeling unwell in the last few days and, even after what had happened over his outburst, Liam knew he was still his dad, only in name perhaps, but he couldn't change the fact that he had been the 'dad' for all his formative years, that he had brought him up.

As he passed Roslyn on the stairs, her look of surprise made him realise he had forgotten to put his boxer shorts on, but he had been too preoccupied to think about covering up.

He picked up the receiver. 'Fiona, what's wrong... is it me dad?'

'I think you better just come home, bruv... we'll tell you then.'

'I'm on me way.'

He raced back upstairs, nearly barging Roslyn out of the way.

'Are you all right, Liam... do you want me to run you home?'

Kate's mum was absolutely brilliant, but he knew she would take ten minutes to get ready and then another ten minutes to take him home. The way he felt, he'd be home in two minutes. He kissed Kate on the forehead and whispered that he'd call her later. Oblivious to what was going on as she slowly brought herself to consciousness, she looked sad with her big brown eyes peering at Liam.

'I'll call you later – something's up at home.'

'Liam...'

He was dressed and out of the house in no time. It was so quiet in the well-kept cul-de-sac; he could hear his feet pounding the pavement as he started the mile or so run round to his parents' house. The running and the surroundings made him think back to his childhood when he and the lads would play knock-a-door-run, the Grand National over people's hedges and go apple raiding in these posh parts. Then he focused again on the present. What was it his sis had said? 'We'll tell you then.' Who the hell's 'we'? It can't be me dad, it can't be, please don't let it be me dad. His thoughts tumbled one after the other. 'Oh no... me dad's dead... me dad can't be dead, can he? The selfish bastard will miss the wedding... don't be dead, Dad, please. I forgive you for being a bastard to Mum and treating us like shit. It doesn't matter... please don't be dead.'

As he entered the council estate, a dog started barking and chased after him. Liam wasn't in the mood and turned and ran after the mongrel, screaming abuse at it. This only caused the other stray dogs to start barking, but he soon charged off towards his parents' home.

He rounded the corner and, immediately, he saw something was obviously seriously awry. Everybody's cars were there – Fiona's, Jean's, Mick's and he even reckoned his mum's brother's car was there; Brian must have arrived to console his sister. Liam leaped the front gate as usual, forgetting he was still semi-pissed, so, as he caught his foot on the top, he did a half-forward roll, completing it in one motion. Adrenalin took him through the front and hallway door and into the living room in an instant.

He was greeted with a cloud of smoke being generated by the occupants of the room. Jesus Christ, this was what had probably killed his dad, but these bastards were laying into the fags like there was no tomorrow. He looked round but couldn't take anything in. It was like being a boxer in the ring, dazed and disorientated, with the corner men trying to give the fighter instructions, the crowd shouting, but Liam's mind was racing so fast he couldn't take anything in.

Hang on... he looked at his dad's chair and he was sat there. There were tears in his eyes, but he was sitting there nonetheless. Liam then thought it had to be one of his relations – what the hell was going on?

'Jesus, Dad, I thought you'd popped your clogs, you old sod... what's happened? Is it someone from across the water?'

Fiona put her arm on his shoulder. 'Sit down, Liam – sit down.'

'What's wrong, sis?' He knew his sisters were much closer to his aunts and uncles in Ireland.

'No, sit down, will you? It's me mum.'

'Your mum? Me mum? What's wrong?' He looked

round the room and the realisation hit him like a sledge-hammer. She wasn't there.

'It's mum... she's died. She's passed away in the night.'

'No, not Mum, please, not me mum... oh God.' Liam slumped in a chair and put his hands over his face.

Fiona explained that his dad had got up to go to the toilet in the middle of the night and his mum had complained about having indigestion. When he had awoken again for his usual 20 minutes in the toilet, their mum had not said anything when he had got back in bed, which was very unusual. The doctor had already been and said she'd probably had a heart-attack and died in her sleep. 'I've been trying to ring you at home for the last hour or so, thinking you were asleep.'

Liam surveyed the sad faces of everyone looking at him but he still couldn't really take anything in.

'Mum's still upstairs if you want to go and see her. She looks really peaceful.'

'I would, Liam... go and say your goodbyes while she's still in the house.'

Jean was only trying to help, but Liam didn't have the energy or the bottle to go – how could he? How could he now tell her that he loved her so much? How could he now thank her for giving him such a wonderful childhood, and loving and caring for him so well? How could he now pay for her to go on holiday and treat her like a queen for all she'd done for him? He wanted to tell her that he never meant anything he had ever called her – right from being a boy of five when he swore at her until the day before when he had jokingly called her for having some food marks on her cardigan.

People were talking to him, but he was still in his own small world. He looked over to his now frail, elderly-looking dad and felt sorry for him. He never, ever thought his mum would go before his dad. He knew how badly his dad had treated her but they had been a team for 45 years. His mum had given everything to her husband and five kids and now she was gone. She was the most loving, gentle, caring woman you could ever want to meet.

How could death be so final? You should be given five minutes with each person you are close to so you could tell them what you thought of them. Then you'd be able to tell each other how you were going to miss one another. Liam knew he'd made his mum proud, but he also admitted to himself that he had let her down. He had given too much to other people because he wanted to be liked, but not enough to his mum because, basically, she was his mum and had always loved him, unconditionally. This woman loved all her children and now she was dead. How could she be? She was his mum.

She's always been there for us, and she always would be, Liam had thought. She had another ten years in her at least, ten years in which he was going to repay her for all the love and support she had given him. Ten years to come good on all the promises he had made to her as he'd grown up. No, she didn't have any time left. She wouldn't even see him get married and she wouldn't eventually see her baby son's first child.

After talking to his brothers for a few minutes, Liam made an excuse of going to the toilet and hauled himself out of the chair. He was heading towards the door just as the phone started ringing in the hallway. It was Rob.

'I've been trying to ring you at your house for the last 20 minutes. Are you back at Mummy's for some breakfast, you little-dicked fat boy?'

Liam could hardly muster a reply. His mate was devastated when he managed to mumble what had happened. Rob said he'd let everybody know and finished by telling Liam that, if his family needed anything, he was only a phone call away.

As Liam trudged upstairs, his legs were getting heavier and heavier as he neared the top. Go left and he would be in his mum and dad's room. He could say his goodbyes to his mum there and then, but he didn't feel strong enough. He took the easier option of his own bedroom for a lie-down and to think. Nothing had changed. His mum had left his bedroom as if he still lived there. He climbed under his quilt to hide from the events surrounding him for a while. Could he have done anything to help her if he had been at home?

He hadn't been under the quilt for long before he seemed to be in another place. In a semi-dream state, he could hear wailing, incessant sobbing and groaning; it took a while for Liam to realise that it was the sound of his own grief, crying and curling himself up into a tight ball – he didn't feel 31 now.

32
Love Her as in Childhood…
Thursday, 25 April 2002

Love her as in childhood
Though feeble, old and grey
For you'll never miss a mother's love
'Til she's buried beneath the clay.

When he had read Frank McCourt's book *Angela's Ashes* a year before, Liam had copied the poem out in the front of his day-to-day diary. He remembered being upset when he read the poem, thinking what a wasted life his mum had had.

Now, on the morning of her funeral, this was all Liam could think about. He took out of his drawer a beautiful picture of his mum when she was 19 years old, a time when she should have had the world at her feet and, most likely, entertained the dreams that all teenagers would have dreamed. The only problem was that the colour of her dress was white, and the photograph was taken on her wedding day.

At least she had managed one of her childhood ambitions of getting married. The dress, however, concealed the early stages of pregnancy and the start of a career in motherhood. She had always told Liam that none of her children had been any trouble, but Liam knew how his friends and their wives had struggled with one or two children, never mind five. There should even have been six, as his mum had told him years ago, ever so matter-of-factly, that she had had a stillborn baby between James and Mick, another son she was going to call Anthony. She had told Liam out of the blue one evening.

'I had Anthony for a boy and Jean for a girl. He was beautiful, Liam. Your dad didn't see him but they let me hold him for a few minutes,' she had said.

Liam remembered thinking at the time how strong his mum must have had to be to cope. He just hoped that she had felt better for telling him the secret she had carried alone for over 30 years. It was as if she had wanted to tell him before she died and Liam respected her so much for that.

'Liam, are you coming downstairs? Everybody's getting ready to go.'

Fiona could have opened the bedroom door if she'd wanted, but 20 minutes earlier Liam had told her that he wanted to be alone and have some time to think about his mum before they went to church.

'OK, Fiona… I'll be down in a minute.'

He placed his hands over his eyes and started to allow the memories of her to wash over him again. Different occasions danced in his mind's eye, happy and sad – his mum taking him to infant school on the first day. He remembered kissing her and running into the schoolyard, before turning round and running back and hugging her legs before having to be coaxed back. He laughed to himself at the memory, then immediately felt a pang of guilt when he remembered his mum, who was only trying her best, buying him a bike that was too small for him one Christmas. Santa Claus had also brought him an Everton kit when he, like most Northern kids in the Seventies, was in love with Liverpool.

He clenched his teeth and shook his head as he thought about the only money his mum had ever had, having been left some in an aunt's will. She had spent it all on her children. Liam had picked the most expensive ten-speed racer in the bike shop and his mum never flinched. His dad, whom she shared the money with, never bought the kids anything. Jim would rather buy his 'mates' a pint in the pub and turn his back on his wife's struggle to put food on the table for his children.

'He's a great bloke, your dad, Liam...' and 'Such a decent fella, yer dad...' Liam had heard it all before and always shook his head in disbelief. Recently, when he had let his guard down and told a couple of mates how bad his dad had treated his mum behind closed doors, they had sort of accepted it as if it was par for the course. 'Well, that's how it was in those days,' they'd shrug. But *those* days had become *these* days, and, anyway, it didn't make it right, did it? Even now, his dad had been treating her like dirt, right up to her death. Then again, was Liam any better the way he had let her look after him like he was still a child? He could hear himself saying over and over, 'Sorry, Mum... sorry, Mum'.

He thought back to the seven wasted years his mum had spent fighting depression and felt anger at how her doctor just kept giving him and his sisters repeat prescriptions to treat her mental illness. Seven years she spent up in her room sometimes for months on end before Liam and his sisters had been old enough to understand, decided enough was enough and had confronted her doctor. That same doctor who had never paid her a visit in seven years, despite knowing her condition. Within weeks of the family's threats, her tablets had been changed and she was down to one tablet and leading a more normal life again.

Liam had carried the guilt of her missing years as if it was his fault. How can you let somebody miss seven years of their life like he and the rest of the family had?

He hadn't heard anyone enter his room and was surprised to feel an arm rest on his shoulder. He pushed it away on realising that it was his dad making a clumsy attempt at consoling him.

'I am sorry, son... I... I know I let your mum down. I know I've been a bastard to her.' His dad began to sob. 'I'm so sorry I let you all down. I wish I could bring her back and tell her Liam, I do, I do.'

'Don't worry, Dad, we all let her down. Come on... let's go and give her a good send-off.'

Liam felt numb towards his father... neither pity, nor hatred.

They made their way downstairs to join the rest of the family. Liam knew it would be a day of self-control as he'd make sure he didn't get involved in any arguments while his emotions were in turmoil. He would try to keep his mouth shut as his fellow mourners made trivial comments about his mum. Her 'close' friends and family members, who hadn't seen her for years, would all tell him how lovely she was. People would feel desperately sorry for his dad, while his friends from the pub would only ever see him through their rose-tinted spectacles.

'Saint in the pub, sinner in the house... that's your dad.' The saying his mum had once told him now kept running through Liam's head as he climbed into the car behind his mum's coffin. His brothers were already there and he smiled at them both.

In their different ways, all three had been close to their mum. Liam couldn't help having a joke with Mick about when he had rung his mum and she had said, 'Who is it?' and Mick had replied, 'It's me... your favourite son.'

'Oh, is it you, James?' she had answered.

They all laughed as the car made its way to the church. The brothers talked about the good times they had had – they were hard times, too, when they were younger – but they were good times with their mum. Although Liam never really showed it or felt close to his brothers since they had grown up, he felt nothing but love for them now.

As the cars turned the corner into the churchyard, Liam took a deep breath. He was going to be strong for his mum. He was still struggling to accept that he was at his own mum's funeral. He had been telling her for a long time that, if she carried on drinking and smoking, it would be the death of her, but the reality of it all was now hitting him. He was at his own mum's funeral; inevitable it would happen one day, but no one had realised just how soon it would be. His legs felt weak as he clambered out of the car.

He managed to keep his composure as he shook hands with a number of people. His sisters stood stiffly with his dad and Liam left them to it. They had always been on better terms with their dad than the lads were, although this didn't mean they liked how he had treated their mum. Liam wasn't angry with his sisters for helping their father through the day. In his own way, he knew that his dad must have loved his mum, but he could not forgive him.

He looked round as somebody tugged at his sleeve. Liam turned to find Kate standing behind him. He hugged her before realising that her mum was next to her.

'Hello, Roslyn ... thanks for coming.'

Roslyn spoke very softly. 'Liam, I know I didn't really know your mum, but Kate's told me she was a great woman. I hope you don't mind me coming along and paying my respects.'

'A great woman'. Liam smiled and felt a sense of pride. In an instant, he realised how close he had grown to Kate and her family and in such a short time.

'We'll see you inside,' Roslyn said and, before he could answer, Kate and her mum had disappeared into the church.

Liam looked at the coffin on the bier; his mum was inside that box. He stared as the undertakers started pushing it into the church and down the aisle. He was mesmerised by the word 'MUM' set out in flowers and placed on the lid of the coffin. He hadn't been to many funerals, but, when he had been, he'd always felt for the families as they followed their loved one behind the coffin. It didn't feel real now and, as they slowly made their way along the aisle, he looked around and saw friends and family all glancing round, looking at him and his father, brothers and sisters.

The Johnsons, O'Sheas and other friends and family from the old estate were all there. As Liam sat down, he looked behind and smiled at Mrs Johnson and the lads. He may have been heartbroken, but he also felt a deep sense of pride and love for his circle of friends and family. He was still amazed at what Rob had told him about the reaction of the entire football team when they'd been told about Liam's mum's death on the previous Sunday. They had gone out and beaten the Caribbean Club 2–0 with the manager saying it was the most determined he had ever seen a group of lads play and it was all done for Liam and his mum.

The priest said some wonderful words that had been written by his sisters. Jean and Fiona had also made up a lovely poem simply called 'Our Mum'. Every beautiful word summed up what Liam had been thinking. By the time Fiona had left the pulpit, people had been laughing and crying at the same time.

The service passed by very quickly before everybody made their way down to the cemetery. As the coffin was lowered into the ground, the prearranged music swept around the mourners. Liam shook his head and allowed himself a big smile. He remembered the many times his mum had played the record when she'd had a few drinks, singing along to Louis Armstrong's 'What a Wonderful World'.

'Make sure they play it at me funeral, Liam,' she would say laughing, before repeating, 'No, I mean it, love, please get it played for me.'

Everybody shook hands and hugged. Liam made a bee-line for Mrs Mitchell. She was struggling to control herself, tears flowing down her rosy-red cheeks. 'Come here, love,' she sighed. Liam hugged her as if she was his own mum. 'I'm going to miss your mum so much, Liam... the talks, the fun, the laughter we had.'

'I know... I know.'

As everybody started to make their way to the social club, Liam and his brothers held back. He gave Kate a kiss and told her he wouldn't be too long. They then waited until most of the mourners had gone. Harry the gravedigger, whom Liam and Mick had both played football with for years, then took three spades from out of the back of his van and passed them to the brothers.

'Love you, Mum,' they all said before they began filling in the grave. 'Love her as in childhood, though feeble old and grey, for you'll never miss a mother's love 'til she's buried beneath the clay.'

Liam was missing his mum already.

33
End of an Era
Sunday, 12 May 2002

'You've heard what's happened, haven't you?' Liam hadn't but knew something was definitely amiss from the tone of Rob's voice. And 8.30am on the morning of the Cup Final wasn't a good time to be told that you've lost one of your star players and, more importantly, possibly the chance of a cracking drink after the game if the team won. That is what Liam was now being told by the manager on what he had hoped to be his finest footballing achievement for years. Spanish Phil, along with Liam's brother Mick and Jack the landlord, had been arrested at different locations in early-morning raids by the police. Steve had rung Rob to tell him the news.

'They've fucked it up, you know, Liam. It was all right when your Mick was doing his trips to France and even flying to Spain but, in the last few months, him, Jack and Phil have been kicking the arse out of it.' Rob then went on to explain to Liam some recent business transactions.

They had been doing an unbelievable roaring trade with the fags, booze and God knows what else.

'Tell me it's not drugs, though?' asked Liam, concerned.

'No, don't think so.'

Liam knew his brother enjoyed a toot and Spanish Phil usually started the day with a spliff. He and Liam still laughed about the time Liam was working at the local leisure centre as an instructor and Phil had come in for an induction. He had laughed as he started filling in a fitness questionnaire.

'Eh, Liam... what's this question number two – '*Have you got any joint problems?*' That's a bit personal, innit? What am I supposed to put? No, I really enjoy them all?'

Liam now hoped that, if Phil and Mick had been mad enough to start importing cannabis, they were only doing it for their own personal use and not for the rest of Chorley's pot-heads.

'Turns out that Jack's been helping to distribute the fags all over for your Mick and Phil with all his contacts in the pub trade in Manchester. Steve reckons they've been grassed up, no pun intended, by some Manchester gang who were into the same scam.'

Liam didn't have to ask Rob how he knew all this with Jack being an ex-copper. He was usually one step ahead.

'Steve told me that Jack got a phone call first thing from one of his mates telling him he was going to be busted, so, you never know, they might be all right yet. See you at half-nine at the Horse.'

Liam wasn't so sure that his brother would be all right. What had started as a decent money-earner had recently got completely out of hand. Mick had started making money hand over fist. Liam had been worried for his brother, but had not wanted to make him feel bad about his newfound wealth. Mick had taken the death of their mum more to heart than Liam in some ways and, although a month had passed, he was still visiting her grave most days. He had also spent a week in Liam's spare room before finding a flat. His marriage was more or less officially over, although he told Liam that he knew he was making a terrible mistake. Liam didn't want to cause his brother any more unnecessary grief and, since their spat in the pub and the death of their mum, he had definitely become closer to him. Their dad had done enough to make both of them feel like failures anyway, so Liam didn't feel that he had to add to Mick's woes by telling him to be careful. He only hoped at this point that he had been.

When he arrived at the Horse, Liam knew that Jack was definitely in trouble as all the lads were standing around outside or sitting on the wall as police investigators made their way in and out of the 'crime scene'.

'He's fucked it now.' Kenny was shaking his head as Liam started to get the kit out of the back of his car. 'I've been here 15 minutes and they've been taking out boxloads of fags and booze. I don't think he'll get away with personal consumption with this one, not even Jack.'

Liam could tell that Kenny wasn't joking, as they knew that, even if he managed to keep himself out of prison, Jack would be losing his licence. Looking round at the lads, Liam could tell that nobody's mind was on the game. Everybody had heard about the arrests and they were worried for Jack and the two lads.

Knobhead, at least, put Liam's mind at rest. 'No, definitely no drugs involved, solely fags, booze and perfume – bloody good perfume, though.'

As they arrived at Victory Park, the home of Chorley FC, Liam was trying his best to motivate the lads, but he could tell that nobody really seemed up for the game.

'It's a bit of a shit-hole, innit?'

Giant was right. Some years ago, Chorley were once a very strong non-league outfit playing in the Vauxhall Conference and had a ground to be proud of, but now it was looking as tired as old Stan's face.

In the dressing room, Rob tried his best with the motivational stuff but somehow Liam knew it was a game too far. Chorley Under-18s shouldn't have really been in a Sunday pub league for a start, and most of them played in the first team on a Saturday. The Unibond First Division might not appear to offer a particularly good standard of football, but Liam knew that the young lads would be super-fit. The intimidatory tactics wouldn't really work either, because they played against tough blokes week in, week out. They had not lost or even drawn all season. Not only that, but Riggers, who would usually be up for giving them a kick or two, was buzzing because his son was playing against him. 'Everton are looking at him, you know, so make him look good, will you?'

Riggers also helped out with the training for the Chorley team. Not exactly the usual fighting talk but, in the end, the young lads didn't need any help.

Liam shook hands with some of them as they went to collect their trophy and winners' medals. Riggers was as proud as punch as his son as captain picked up the trophy. The 4–0 result had been more than fair and Liam knew that the opposition had shown some respect by taking it easy in the last 20 minutes.

Rob was the first to catch up with Liam at the end of the game and gave him a big hug. 'Thanks for a great season, skipper... I've thoroughly enjoyed it.'

He then opened the two big cooler boxes he and Steve had lugged out of the changing room. They were full to the brim with Boddington's and Stella and, within minutes, the champagne was being popped and sprayed everywhere.

'Don't worry, mate, we all knew we'd get hammered today... our Cup Final was against The Golden Lion.'

Back in the changing room, the banter had started to flow. 'Eh, Giant, you missed a good game today. Liam, that lad in centre-mid was only about 14 but he still took the piss out of you. What about that nutmeg?'

Nothing seemed to be able to shut Wayne up, but Liam was soon on the offensive. 'Spuggie still looked faster than you today, Wayne. I think I'll have £50 on him. Who's holding the bets?'

'No chance, man.'

Wayne looked at Spuggie but, for once, he was looking very subdued. He was nearly as bad as Liam for the sulks when they had been beaten. Mind you, he had travelled all night from Southampton after watching Newcastle getting thumped 3–1. Wayne was just about to say something else when Spuggie jumped up with an almost-full bottle of champagne he had just been passed. 'We are Champions League... say we are Champions League.'

He sprayed Wayne and then everybody else as he jumped around manically like only he could.

'Can I just have some quiet please? Come on… come on. Two minutes.' Rob was trying his best to regain order but he was covered in champagne, tops, shorts and socks from all different directions. 'No, no… sit down, everybody.' As usual, everybody eventually did what Rob said. 'I just want to thank you all for a great season.'

'It'll be even better next season because you're sacked.' Knobhead jumped in at the wrong moment, as usual.

'No, seriously… I just want to thank everybody for a brilliant year.'

Liam could see Rob was getting emotional.

'You lot mean more to me than you can ever imagine and to win the First Division and get to the Final of the Cup has meant everything to me.'

Cheers rang out.

'It wouldn't have mattered if we'd got hammered week in, week out; just to be with you lads for the season, not forgetting Mick and Spanish Phil, has been an honour.'

'Stop it, Rob, you're going to get me all upset.' Kenny was trying to make light of the situation, but underneath he was probably feeling a bit emotional, too.

'No, most of us have grown up together, and getting the chance of being back like this for one last chance has been fantastic.'

Liam knew what was coming next.

'I hope somebody wants to carry on next season. I would if I could, but I'll be working away a lot more… but I'd just like to thank you all once again for turning out all season – thank you.' Rob then ran out of the changing room before anybody could think of anything nasty they could do to him.

Liam was surprised to get a phone call as he left the changing room. 'The Chorley Three have been released on bail.'

Steve had already made his way to the pub and found Jack, Phil and Mick sitting at the bar. Once the beers started flowing and his brother assured him that Jack had pulled some strings and called in a few favours, hopefully to ensure that they wouldn't be facing prison sentences, Liam started to relax. He sat down next to the landlord and gave him a hug.

'You all right, Jack?'

'Aye, no problems, lad. Well... just one. I'll be losing me licence.' Jack winked at Liam. 'The good thing is, between me and you, I've already sold the pub to the Poole chain.'

Liam nearly spilled his beer. Graham Poole was a local businessman who owned a large number of the wine bars in the North-West. Unfortunately, Liam didn't think he would be taking over The White Horse to keep it as a drinking man's pub and he didn't think the back room would be able to stay as a recreational drugs den.

'I know, son. He's on about turning it into a wine bar. It'll be an end of an era with The White Horse and he might even want to change the name.'

Liam didn't blame Jack at all for selling up. A number of other local pubs had closed down and The White Horse had been really quiet recently. Sunday for the karaoke seemed the only decent takings night the pub had. Liam had been in the pub on a Friday and Saturday night when there had been seven or eight people in, maximum. The pub was a bit like a standard packet of Jack's crisps – past its sell-by-date – and, with Rob and most of the lads going back into retirement, it was going to be the end of an era. No pub and no football team. Liam was just glad they'd had one more season.

34
The Jolly Boys' Outing
Saturday, 18 May 2002

Liam's choice of the stag venue hadn't gone down well with everybody. Some of the lads had been trying to persuade him to go to the sunnier climate of the Costa del Sol again. Others had mentioned the usual – Newcastle, Dublin, Edinburgh and even the trendier venue of Prague. Of course, Kenny wanted to go to Amsterdam for the hundredth time to see if he could beat his record of nine ladies of the night in 24 hours.

Spanish Phil, Wayne and Nicky had also pushed for Amsterdam simply for the recreational drugs, but Liam was having none of it. He wanted to make sure that every man and his dog who wanted to go on his stag do would be able to go. With the help of Rob and Paddy, they had decided that because it was such short notice they would reinstate the old Jolly Boys' Outing.

Recently, the lads had been more adventurous with their choices of location, getting away with anything from two- to five-day trips from Manchester to Marbella. These had all been superb, but with the financial implications it had meant fewer and fewer of the lads being able to go. Liam wanted anybody who fancied an all-dayer to put their name down. When the poster went up on the notice board, it was met with a uniform 'You're taking the piss, aren't you?'

Liam's Stag Do – Jolly Boys' Outing: All-Dayer to Blackpool
Saturday, 18 May 2002

8.30am –   Full English breakfast and a Free Pint

10.30am – Coach trip to Pilling, Blackpool
(No piss stops allowed on way)

11.30am – Arrive at Royal Oak. Commencement of Bowls,
Pool, Darts, Dominos Competition and Card School

1.30pm –   Running Buffet

3.00pm –   Presentation of Trophies

3.15pm –   Coach Trip to Blackpool dropping off at
Tower Lounge

9.30pm –   Coach return picking up at Wine Lodge and
back to White Horse

10.30pm – 'til late – Liam's Karaoke Special Last Night
(Possible Strippers)

Please note coach departure times are prompt.
No straddlers please – you will be left.
Approx price for Taxi Blackpool – Chorley £40 (Ask Kenny)
Total Cost £15 all in.

Some had threatened to boycott the stag do when they heard that Kate and, inevitably, their wives and girlfriends, were going to London for a long weekend and they had ended up with a day trip to the seaside.

However, once the moaning had died down, the 44-seater had been filled within two days. Everybody – including old Stan and Harry – had booked on it and a few who hadn't seen the poster or had missed out on a seat had arranged to go by train. It seemed as if the whole pub was up for having a bender.

On the Saturday morning of the stag do, when Liam walked into a packed, buzzing pub at 8.20am, he knew he had made the right decision. He was given his free pint by a smiling Jack who had the usual pound signs in his eyes, knowing he'd make the money back within the next two hours.

Liam looked round and felt a shiver go down his spine and the goose pimples came up on his arms. He couldn't believe how many people had turned out. He knew a few of the locals were booked on the outing just for a good drink, but he also knew that everyone of his 'proper' mates were all there, too. From his brother Mick to his 'other' brothers, the Johnsons, right through to Spuggie and Harty, the only out-of-towners on the trip. He could tell by everyone's faces they were up for a good time. He had tried to persuade his teetotal brother James to come along, but wasn't too displeased when he declined. James may not have appreciated some of the antics that would be taking place.

Kenny was first to shake Liam's hand. 'Great laugh this already. Just a pity that Jack is making some money from us again.' Always subtle, Kenny.

Wolfman was next over with the trademark back-crunching bear hug. 'First one in the pub, skipper, and I've already had three pints.'

Two hours later and a number of the lads were already tipsy. Jack had made a small fortune with his final 'private party' arranged with his ex-police officer mates.

As they started trooping on to the coach, the driver started bollocking Rob for taking a can of beer with him. Everybody else had hidden their beer in bags and under their T-shirts. 'You've no chance. It's more than me job's worth to let you drink on the coach.'

The driver was a stocky fellow with his sleeves rolled up ready for action. Liam was behind Rob and noticed the Royal Corps of Transport tattoo on his forearm. The stag wanted to avoid any potential trouble this early in the day. 'All right, mate... what if we give you a quid a person? Would that help you turn a blind eye? A few of us are ex-forces and we respect you've got a job to do.'

'Err... err... all right, no problem, lads. I want to have a laugh as much as the next person. Go on then, you've got a deal. Just stick all the empties in these bags as we go along.'

Jack was the last one on the coach. The locals couldn't believe he was going to spend his money in other people's pubs, but he still got a cheer when he announced that the first beer back in The White Horse at 10.30pm would be on him.

Within only 50 yards on the clock, some wise guy shouted out, 'Are we nearly there yet, driver?' and another joker shouted, 'I want the toilet, Daddy.'

Liam thought it would be best to try and keep the driver sweet. 'Sorry about the lads, mate. Just a bit of banter, that's all.'

'No problem, lad. I can handle it. It's alreet as long as I get me money.'

The first part of the coach journey took them straight through Chorley town centre.

'Moony time... moony time.'

It was only a few at the back at first, but by the time the coach was at the main set of traffic lights in the town centre, there must have been at least 40 bottoms pressed against the windows. It was amazing what an early-morning beer did to normally sensible people. The town centre was packed with shoppers and Liam rose from touching his toes to survey the scene. He spotted Simon's mum at the Royal Bank of Scotland cashpoint along with a group of others. They stood, mouths agape, looking up at the bottoms of men aged from 17 to nearly 70. Simon spied his mum from between his legs and ducked down as quickly as he could.

'Me mum'll recognise my arse and I'll be in trouble with Jane. Th'old dear tells her everything.'

By the time they had reached the motorway, most of the high jinks had settled down. However, Spuggie wasn't entirely finished. While all the lads had been pulling moonies, he had put a red clown nose on the end of his willy and had been unveiling it to motorists from the back seats. Most of them surprisingly had been flashing their lights in approval, enjoying some fun on a Saturday morning. Others just shook their heads and must have wondered what the hell was going on.

'Oy, man. Whatsupweya? Divent ya know how to have a good time, or wha'?' Spuggie had now made his way down to the front to have a word or two with the driver.

'Eh, I've already said, I don't mind having a laugh, me. I can mix it with the best of them, I can.'

'Come on then, man, be a sport and put this red nose on for the lads.'

'No problem... owt for a bit of fun.'

The driver attached the red nose that had previously been hanging off the end of Spuggie's todger on to the end of his bulbous nose. He then put his hand up to acknowledge the instant rapturous applause he received.

The singing started shortly after and, by the time they had reached Pilling, they had sung through a selection of songs by The Drifters, Tom Jones and others at full volume.

When the coach pulled in, Liam gave the driver the agreed 'beer tax'.

'I'll see you lot at about quarter-past-three then. What a great laugh that was.'

Liam struggled to keep a straight face, as he imagined the driver having to breathe in the lingering smell from Spuggie's well-used cock.

'Right, lads... before we get goin', I just want to tell you that Mr and Mrs Millington think we are St George's Bowling Club on our annual outing, so best behaviour from the start.' Rob was a genius with his strategy of allowing pubs to accept large groups of lads.

'Come on, get goin'... I'm dying for a piss.' Knobhead was already drunk.

The lads swamped the main bar of the quaint country pub, which had one of the best bowling greens in the North-West at the side.

Mr Millington looked absolutely horrified at the

number of people in front of him. 'Er, er... Just a minute, young man.'

He was struggling to remember Giant's round of seven lagers, three Guinnesses and a bitter. He recognised Rob as the organiser who had come to see him.

'Excuse me, young man, are you sure you're a bowls club?'

'Yes, course we are... we have already organised the competition.'

'Well, where's everybody's bowls then?'

This was a good question and it stumped Rob for a second or two. 'Well, it's our club do, but we were only going to have a leisurely game and spend a fortune behind your bar drinking all the finest ales we've been told you have. Have you any spare bowls by the way?'

'Yes, of course we have, no problem. Edith will get you some.'

It seemed that all landlords were the same when it came to making money and Mr. Millington must have thought all his Christmases had come at once.

However, some three-and-a-half hours later, after threatening to call the police, he was glad to see the back of St George's Bowling Club, whom he had banned for life from visiting his establishment. It wasn't the swearing in the lounge that did it or the fracas that broke out during the card school when someone was called a cheat. It wasn't the mess the lads had made eating the buffet. It wasn't even when Edith had decided to collect some glasses from round the bowling green and found that the burst of brilliant sunshine had encouraged some of the lads to remove their tops, which wasn't allowed. No, it was only when she realised that at least ten of the lads on the bowling green were, when she glanced round again, playing bowls stark bollock naked. She had screamed, but not in pleasure. Not in 40 years of having the pub had she witnessed anything like it.

Jack, Rob and Paddy managed to dissuade the couple from calling the police, insisting that some of the boys had done it for a dare. Liam hoped that, when the couple had finally calmed down and counted how much was in their coffers, they wouldn't be too upset. He didn't envisage being welcomed back, unless they changed names again, but they hadn't caused any real trouble.

The antics resumed as soon as the coach set off again for Blackpool. The singing was deafening. '*The White Horse Rambling Club, we ramble on from pub to pub to pub...*' Liam looked round the coach and saw everybody was laughing and joking and generally enjoying the day out. He was sat next to Spuggie whose Geordie accent was becoming even more unintelligible.

'Liam, man, I luv the ban'er. Ya and the lads, man, ya should be Geordies. Ya would be able to come and watch the Toon. Na, being serious, Liam, these are the best lads in the wooorld.'

'One Geordie bastard... there's only one Geordie bastard... one Geordie bastard...'

Spuggie rose to the ovation and, as usual, tried to outsing 40 lads. 'With an N, and an E, and a W C...'

Liam moved down the coach, supping his can, and joined in different conversations as they continued on the short journey to Blackpool.

'Liam, have you heard this? Harty reckons I have the devil inside me.'

Mad Al and Harty had somehow ended up sitting next to each other and Harty, whom Liam had noticed had been very quiet all along, had started with more of the God Squad stuff.

Recently, Liam had been bored witless with an argument he'd witnessed between Harty and his boss Ian about religion. It had been a rather strange 'my God's better than your God' type of argument. Liam knew that this wasn't the time or place for a former top shagger to start preaching about his newfound faith, but it was too late.

'How's your knee now, Liam, since Harty healed it?'

Liam had instantly wished he hadn't told Paddy that his ex-army mate, on hearing that he had damaged his knee ligaments playing in the final, had got down on his knees and prayed to it.

'Just remember, if it starts healing straight away, it's not me who's done it, it's God's work,' Harty had said, clasping the knee with both hands. Two weeks later and Liam was still limping badly.

Paddy was always joking with Harty and usually he would be answered back with a humorous put-down, but Liam could tell that this time Harty wasn't interested. Harty turned round to face Giant, thinking he might indulge in a more intelligent conversation.

'You couldn't do anything with me cock, could you, like make it the same size as me feet?' Giant put both his size-14 feet up in the air, but Harty wasn't having any of it.

'You've all changed, you lot. Satan has got hold of you all.' He then sat back down next to Al but turned to look out of the window.

But Paddy couldn't let him off the hook quite so easily. 'Oooooh,' he burst out, eyes popping, 'driver, don't take us to the pub, take us to the nearest church and drop his holiness there.'

Liam and Rob exchanged glances, shaking their heads. One thing Liam was trying his best not to do was change. Yes, there were many things in his life that had moved on – settling down with Kate, the house and the wedding – but underneath Liam was essentially the same as he'd always been. Now he had managed to tell Kate about everything, he had never been happier. He knew Harty had been searching for something in his life from their army days. If getting into religion made him happy, fair enough, he had thought. He just didn't want his friend ramming it down everybody else's throats.

'What's wrong with you? Anybody would think you were getting married or something?' Tony had caught Liam deep in thought. 'Come on, let's go and get stuck in.'

Liam hadn't noticed that the coach was coming to a stop near the Tower Lounge.

'Right, lads, have a good few hours and I'll see you back on here for nine-thirty prompt.' The coach driver had jumped up at the front of the coach still wearing his red nose. 'I've never met a better bunch of lads. Have a great day.'

'Fuck me, what's happened to him?' Liam couldn't believe the transformation.

'He's been on the wacky backy with Knobhead and

Phil. They've got him well stoned,' replied Kenny with the telltale smile that he'd had some, too.

'Come on, skipper, let's go and make it special.' Tony, like Liam, loved Blackpool for its tackiness – stag dos, hen parties galore and the anything-goes atmosphere. The Tower Lounge was absolutely buzzing as they all made their way to the bar.

'This is absolute madness.'

Liam's brother Mick passed him a beer after negotiating his way round 20 leering policewomen.

'One of them just offered to handcuff me and give me a good spanking. It's only four o'clock in the afternoon... this is fantastic.'

It may not have been everyone's cup of tea, but Liam loved Blackpool and especially the Tower Lounge. People who were usually quite reserved could be seen gradually losing all their inhibitions and having a great laugh.

The lads, to some extent, looked out of place because the majority of stag dos and hen parties were wearing fancy dress, but it didn't matter. Having everybody together and sharing the craic was all Liam cared about. Even old Stan and Harold had made the trip. Stan at 76 must have been one of the oldest revellers ever to get a slap on the face after pinching a dancer's bottom.

Some of the fancy-dress outfits were brilliant. Liam burst out laughing in the toilets as he found himself in the central urinal with Spiderman to his left and a Ninja Turtle to his right. Everybody was having such a good laugh that, after a vote, it was decided that they'd get a bite to eat somewhere, and then stay in the Tower Lounge until the coach picked them up.

TELL SOMEONE

The five hours flashed by and the night just got better and better as the beer flowed. Liam was getting steadily pissed, but he was making sure he was keeping it under control. To the mock disgust of Spuggie, he turned down a second cocktail of shorts. He'd learned a harsh lesson the last time he had woken up from a blackout and he intended to remember everything the next day this time.

Instead, he stood back and watched all the lads having an unbelievable time. Everybody was finding different ways to amuse themselves: Spuggie and Wayne never left the dance floor; Wolfman and Giant only left the bar to go to the toilet, while Rory and Nicky must have chatted to everybody from Wonder Woman to Miss Whiplash. Liam couldn't believe it when Paddy, as the Best Man should, rounded everybody up telling them it was 9.30pm and that the coach was waiting.

As they made their way to the pick-up point, Liam could see Nicky, Paddy, Spuggie and Giant planning something and he feared he was about to be stripped naked and left to fend for himself.

Luckily, it was Wayne they had been plotting against.

'Come on, Wayne, it's time for the sprint challenge against Spuggie.'

'Place your bets, please.' Kenny was in on it as well.

'No problem man, let's do 100 yards and I'll give you 20 yards start, Spuggie.' Wayne was worse for wear and fell straight into their trap.

'OK, 20 yards start it is then. You go there, Spuggie, and you start at that lamppost, Wayne. But, for the craic, we want you both to run just in your boxer shorts. One hundred quid says Spuggie will beat you.' Kenny knew the money would lure Wayne into the trap.

'No problem man. I'll run naked if you want me to.'

Wayne was now bouncing up and down and manically shadow boxing with Mad Al. Within seconds, he was stood next to the lamppost dressed only in boxer shorts and shoes. Liam couldn't help thinking how fit he looked; he never did any exercise but still had the physique of a middleweight boxer.

'Are you ready... get set...'

Just before Kenny said go, Wayne was grabbed from behind and, within seconds, he was being cellophane-wrapped to the lamppost. Before he could comprehend what was happening, Browny had also ripped Wayne's boxer shorts clean off.

'What you doin'? What you doin', man?'

Wayne didn't have a chance to struggle as the operation had been carried out so quickly. In a matter of seconds, he had been fully cellophane-wrapped to the lamppost with only his head and his impressive manhood being left exposed.

As the coach pulled away, a crowd of women were gathering around him and a number of girls had already had a grab of his todger, believing it to be fake.

'He'll be all right. I put 40 quid in one of his shoes and told him I left his pants with one of the bouncers.' Rob always had contingency plans ready for any given situation.

The coach driver, sensing the chance of making some more money, had put his red nose back on and was telling everybody they were free to have a beer on the way home.

By the end of the night, Liam had lost his voice from singing and his face was aching from having laughed so much.

Jack had been true to his word and put on a superb spread of food and Karaoke Dave had put on a free show. A succession of lads strutted their stuff, singing anything from Elvis to 'Nelly the Elephant' and Liam wasn't even bothered when the strippers failed to materialise. In fact, there were hardly any women in the pub but it didn't matter because it added to the camaraderie of the lads. Liam was given a massive round of applause when he was eventually coaxed up to sing. He was just finishing what everybody said later was a fantastic rendition of 'It's Not Unusual' when Wayne returned to even more applause. He had a massive grin on his face.

'You bastards!'

That's what Liam loved about the lads. Nobody took anything too seriously and everything was usually taken in the right spirit. The fact that Wayne, as he explained afterwards, had chatted up and then scored with one of the sexy policewomen who was impressed with the size of his truncheon helped, but he would have taken it all in good heart anyway.

Liam made sure he was the last man out of the pub and shook hands with everybody there.

Jack grabbed his hand as they stood in the doorway of the pub. Liam knew that not everybody would be sad to see Jack leave, but he certainly would be.

'That's the best day out I've had in years, Liam… all the lads have enjoyed it. I'll miss this place when I move back to Manchester.'

'Cheers for a brilliant night, Jack. We'll miss you as well, you know.'

After a brief drunken hug with the landlord, Liam and Spuggie, who was staying at his house, stumbled out of the pub.

'We are Champions League... Shearer and Bobby Robson's black-and-white army...' were all Liam heard from his mate on their walk home.

'Kate?' He couldn't resist giving her a call when he got in. 'Sorry for calling, but I've had a brilliant day and a wonderful night. I can't wait for the wedding day now. It's going to be the best day of our lives. Love you!' he shouted into her answer phone.

'Liam, man... you're well in love, aren't you? Now you know how I feel about Newcastle.'

Within minutes, Spuggie was asleep on the settee. What a day, Liam thought. It was up there with the best of the Jolly Boys' outings.

35
Life Really Can Get Better
Friday, 7 June 2002

The next three weeks went fantastically well. Kate spent more and more time with her mum ensuring every detail for the upcoming wedding would be perfect. Liam had never realised how much went into the planning and was glad that Kate and her mum seemed to have everything under control.

Without any fuss, Kate had managed to change the ceremony time from 1.00pm to 3.00pm so that everybody could watch England v Argentina. This gesture had won all the lads over.

'Proper woman that, Liam,' Mad Al had said on hearing of the change of times. 'Best way to get started, that. She knows which side her bread is buttered on,' he'd continued, sounding like he really knew how to treat a lady.

On the morning of the wedding, Liam woke up and gently eased himself over to Kate, spooning himself snugly around her silky smooth body. He managed to manoeuvre one of his arms underneath her body and the other encircled her stomach and waist as he settled into their favoured, slowly waking-up position. Without opening his eyes, he edged closer and kissed the back of her neck, whispering 'I love you', and waited to hear her usual purred response.

'Fuck off, you queer bastard...' screamed Browny as he leaped out of the double bed. 'You can forget about coming out of the closet on your wedding day – there's no turning back now, you arse bandit!'

Browny then left the room mumbling about making the coffees.

Liam looked at the clock... 6.55am. They'd only slept for about four hours, but for some reason Liam felt as fresh as a daisy. This was it, he thought, the start of the best day of his life. He couldn't believe how quickly the wedding day and the game had come round. If England could beat Argentina it would be fantastic, but underneath, without telling the lads of course, he didn't really care. Marrying Kate was all he really wanted.

In the last couple of months, Kate had helped Liam enormously in overcoming the grief over losing his mum. Liam, in turn, had had a chance to sort things out in his mind over everything that had happened, and the disclosure she'd made about his dad. Liam knew that his dad was oblivious to what had gone on and also knew that his mum must have been having a terrible time to seek the love of another man. He truly wasn't upset at what she had done. He had actually started looking at it from another angle – if she hadn't fooled around, he may never have been born. He still felt weird about what she had told him but somehow he had managed to deal with it, and file it away somewhere in the deeper recesses of his mind – at least until after the honeymoon. For now, his dad would be his dad and that was that. Of course, he'd been devastated over the death of his mum, but he knew he'd done enough crying to last a lifetime. It was time to move on.

'Are you lot getting up or what? The brews are ready.' Browny didn't wait for a reply but, instead, started humming the theme tune to *The Great Escape*. Before long, Liam had made his way downstairs and they were soon joined by Giant and Paddy from the spare room. 'In-ger-land... In-ger-land...' soon followed. Along with his Best Man and two of his eight ushers, he was going to make the most of his wedding day, starting early.

He knew it was ridiculous having so many ushers, but he'd had a team talk with the chosen ones and they'd all agreed to chip in for their outfits. It had saved Liam from any hard decisions and Kate thought it was hilarious.

The banter started as soon as the lads had their coffees, which Browny had left on the table. When Browny eventually came out of the toilet, Liam took one look at him and choked, desperately tried to stifle a laugh, spraying coffee over everything in his path. Browny's face had been shoe-polished black, but he hadn't realised. Luckily, the new mirror had not been fitted in the bathroom yet. Liam remembered that the night before Wayne had been telling Browny that, because of the generous size of his tool, he could have been one of his brothers. It appeared that the other lads must have taken some action to make his transition more convincing once Liam had gone to bed.

TELL SOMEONE

After they had pulled Liam's leg for the thousandth time about his last night of freedom, Paddy decided it was time to get things moving. 'Reet then, let's get off to Morrison's for a full English...'

As they queued up to order their food, Liam gave the lady serving a wink and put his finger to his lips to warn her not to say anything. She still couldn't resist a chuckle as Browny made his way towards her.

'You look happy, love,' he laughed.

'Always happy to see people like you lot with shiny, smiley faces so early in the morning.'

Browny gave her a wink. As he sat down, he was his usual humble self. 'I am sure she fancied me, then. Did you see the way she was looking at me – mad for it, she was.'

The four friends tucked into their breakfasts. Liam still felt superb, and was amazed that he had no traces of a hangover. The talk was now about England and the chances of them beating Argentina. 'We better beat those Argie bastards. I couldn't stand it to see those gloating twats if they beat us again.'

The pain of '98 still hurt everybody, but Giant had found it particularly upsetting at the time. Liam remembered him blubbering outside on The White Horse's steps shouting about Beckham letting the country down.

Liam was enjoying the various conversations between the lads but he was also daydreaming. As Paddy was lamenting about how poor England had played in the first game of the competition when they had only managed a draw against Sweden, Liam was thinking about Kate. He was actually wondering what style of dress she would be wearing.

'What do you reckon, Liam?'

He didn't have a clue what Giant was on about, and he just about stopped himself from saying, 'Well, I hope she wears a tight-fitting number to show off her stunning figure...' so he just nodded and the others carried on the conversation.

'You bastards! This will never come off.'

Browny had been to the Gents and had spotted that he now looked like a black-and-white minstrel. Liam checked his watch; it was already 9.00am, only three-and-a-half hours to the big game. Rob and his brother Mick, another two of the ushers, made their way towards them with Rob looking rather pale. 'I've already puked about five times. I must have had a bad pint,' he moaned as he sat down.

Liam couldn't help but laugh. Rob had drunk several bad pints, but what do you expect when you lie across one of the pub tables like Paul Gascoigne doing his 'dentist chair' goal celebration, and demand that everybody pours beer down your throat. Liam had spotted a few people picking up dregs and pouring them down his mate's gullet, but Rob had been oblivious to it all.

'Good laugh, eh, little brother?'

'What a night, eh, Mick?' Mick had been unable to stay the night at his younger brother's after convincing his wife to give their marriage one last chance, a curfew being part of the deal.

'Bloody mad night... I thought them coppers were going to lock you two up. Anyway, here's your wallet.'

After a lull in the chatting due to everyone finishing

their breakfasts, Giant let rip with one of his famous farts. Within seconds, the smell had spread everywhere and Browny started to heave. Liam usually wasn't bothered too much by normal farts, least of all his own, but Giant's were different. It was as if his guts had come out of his backside and you could almost taste the warm smell instantly. To the obvious relief of the other early-morning diners, the lads left the restaurant with Browny still looking like he was going to hurl at any moment.

By 11.00am, they had opened a bottle of champagne and Giant and Paddy had opened some cans of Boddington's. Mad Al, Tony and Wayne then arrived to join in the pre-football/wedding get-together. As Liam passed Wayne his suit, Al was quick to get in a quick dig. 'When was the last time you wore a suit, Wayne? When you were in court?'

'Yeah, yeah...'

Tom Jones started blasting 'What's New, Pussycat?' out of the stereo as the lads reminisced about previous stag dos and weddings. They remembered how Rob had stood at the front of the coach starkers for a good half-hour when they were on his stag do to Blackpool – he conducted his orchestra very professionally that day, and waved happily to all the passers-by when they stood in traffic. Paddy was still embarrassed about the 'woman police officer' he was convinced was going to arrest him until she stripped, pulled his pants down and gave him a good spanking at breakfast on his stag do in Newcastle.

Fantastic times, thought Liam, and now it was his turn to come from the subs bench and join the married team.

'Great night! You lot must be rough as a dog.' Big Rory

and Tony had turned up to join in the warm-up before they all headed to The White Horse. Strangely, Liam still felt fantastic after having had such a manic night.

'Anyway, who slept with Liam last night and did you have to wear your wet suit?' Tony wouldn't let Liam forget his bedwetting escapade with Natalie.

'Come on, let's get going.' Rob was already getting the pre-match jitters as they scrambled into the cars loaded with suits on coat hangers. Paddy was making sure everybody had gathered everything together when Browny came out of the toilet – his face bright red from scrubbing the shoe polish away.

'You tossers... I'll get you back for this.'

'Shoes?'

'Yes.'

'Flowers?'

Paddy was definitely in Best Man mode.

'Yes, come on, Paddy, let's go.'

It was 12.20pm when the lads walked into The White Horse to a large cheer. The place was packed to the rafters with St George's Crosses draped everywhere – everywhere except for over the bar where there was a 'Congratulations Liam and Kate' banner. Liam received a number of pats on his back as he made his way over to Simon and Spuggie and the rest of the lads.

'Eh, bonnie lad, are you ready for a great day? It'll be like winning two World Cup Finals for you today when England win and you marry Kate, you jammy bastard.'

Liam could just about make out half of the machine-gun delivery of his Geordie mate. He just nodded and smiled, which he got away with most of the time, and gave Spuggie's girlfriend Heidi a hug and a kiss before whispering, 'How do you put up with him?'

As Spuggie made his way to the bar, Heidi told Liam how made up Malcolm was to be an usher. 'Bloody hell, Heidi,' Liam replied, 'I'd forgot he was called Malcolm... I've got to tell the lads.'

Spuggie had told Liam at freshers' week how his dad had named him after the great Newcastle centre-forward Malcolm Macdonald, which was possibly a wonderful tribute at the time, but he'd suffered from it since.

'Anyway, Heidi, I had to make him an usher because he was threatening to wear his Newcastle top.'

As the big screen showed the teams coming out, a massive roar reverberated around the pub and the usual shout went up, 'In-ger-land... In-ger-land... In-ger-land...'

The first thing that Liam noticed about the game was how many England fans were in the stadium. It was his dream one day to follow England in a World Cup, although he thought it was somewhat premature to ask Kate about the chances of him going to Germany 2006.

There was the usual booing of the Argentinean team and cheering of the England players as they were announced. 'We won the war...' was started by some bright spark, but Liam wasn't interested in all that jingoistic stuff. He only wanted England to win to wipe out the memory of the 'Hand of God', and he could still see Batistuta nodding his head in agreement to Beckham's sending-off in 1998. This still did his head in every time it was replayed on television. Yes, he wanted revenge, but only in footballing terms.

However, on seeing the England line-up, he wasn't too

sure that England could put one over one of their fiercest rivals. Nicky Butt was starting his first game for nearly six weeks and Paul Scholes was playing out of position down the left-hand side.

'What do you think, Liam? We better win or it'll be a shit weddin', even though it's sunny.' Simon never meant to offend and he never did, but Liam did start to think to himself that the day could go one way or the other – win and the wedding would be a fairytale, lose and it could go pear-shaped... except for him and Kate.

As the match started, he still wasn't convinced. Paddy turned to him. 'Look at that sun outside, man. Your mum's looking down on you – don't worry, this will be your day, I promise.'

'You fuckin' dirty Argie bastard.'

The game had started at a really fast pace and the Argentineans were attempting to rough up the England players. Batistuta, especially, was leaving his foot in. Liam loved the ref Collina, the bald-headed, startle-eyed Italian who would have looked quite at home in the Wine Lodge on a Friday dinnertime. A massive cheer went up when he booked Batistuta for a late lunge on Ashley Cole.

Liam still didn't like the shape of the England team with Scholes out on the left, and he was beginning to get seriously worried. Luckily, the problem was solved when Owen and Hargreaves decided to collide with each other, resulting in an injury to Hargreaves. He was subsequently replaced by Sinclair.

'I can't believe Sinclair is coming on... he's shit.'

Browny didn't really know that much about football, but even Liam was confused with Eriksson bringing

Sinclair on. He was fielding an inexperienced player in a crunch match, who was deemed not good enough to be in his original squad.

However, it proved to be a masterstroke. All of a sudden, England began to take control. Liam didn't like to say it, especially with the O'Shea brothers standing next to him, but Nicky Butt was having a stormer. In fact, everybody was, including Emile Heskey who was coming back and winning the ball time after time. When Michael Owen hit the post, the roof nearly came off the pub. Liam looked round at all his mates pushing and shoving each other, fists pumping, as if to say, 'Come on, we can do this.'

One of the biggest cheers of the first half was when Beckham 'accidentally' caught Gonzales with a stray elbow. Liam thought it was strange when you considered what made people laugh with delight. The sight of blood pouring down an Argentinean's face brought the whole pub to a cheering frenzy.

Then, as half-time approached and Liam looked at the clock to think about going to the loo, Beckham took a dive on the edge of the box. This brought a sigh from some of the lads but, all of a sudden, the ball squirted out to Owen on the left and, as he cut inside, a defender seemed to touch him...

'Penalty!'

It was as if England had already scored. People were jumping up and down, grabbing hold of each other. The pub was in absolute uproar. Liam just wanted to see who was taking the penalty and hold on to the contents of his bladder for a little longer. His heart sank when he saw

Beckham stepping up, not because he didn't like him, but it seemed a fairytale too far. Could Beckham really score against Argentina after everything that had gone on?

'Get away from him, you Argie wanker.'

Giant had noticed Simeone trying to shake hands with Beckham as he was waiting to take the spot kick. Liam could hardly breathe as Beckham took a deep gulp of air, ran up and smashed the ball down the middle.

'Yeees...'

There was a simultaneous explosion, with everybody jumping up and down and screaming in delight. Liam could hear glasses smashing as a table went over; everybody was going ballistic as Beckham ran over to the England fans kissing his badge. Some bottle, Liam thought, some bloody bottle.

As the celebrations continued, Liam headed for the toilets. He glanced at himself in the mirror. He had started to look tired, but the sunbed had done its job as he was at least looking vaguely tanned. He smiled at the mirror, clenched his fist and signalled a 'Come on, this is it' to his reflection. He thought about Kate and wondered how she would be feeling with less than two hours before their wedding.

'What you looking at, you ugly sod?' Knobhead pushed Liam into the mirror as he made his way to the urinals.

'It'll be a good night tonight if the score stays the same.'

'Thanks for inviting us all day today... the missus was made up,' he continued.

Liam was really pleased to hear Knobhead's words. He wished he could have invited even more of the lads to the daytime, but he had already sacrificed a number of relations he hadn't seen for years so he could invite the majority of the lads all day.

'Eh, do us a favour will you, Knobhead?'

'Anything, mate.'

'Don't take the piss out of the United boys today, will you?'

'No, no, will I 'eck. Still can't believe Arsenal did the double meself.'

Liam knew the O'Shea brothers were still in mourning about United not winning anything and only finishing third in the Premiership. Simon had also stoked the fires by rubbing in City's return to the top division and talking about them being good enough to qualify for Europe.

By the time he returned to the bar, the half-time whistle had gone. Mad Al grabbed him by the balls. 'We're going to do it. Are you nervous or what? She might not turn up yet, especially if she finds out how much wanking you do.'

Liam didn't really know how to reply to that one, and just laughed.

'Can everybody please shut up a minute...'

Liam was aware of Jack trying to get some semblance of order as everybody had become a half-time expert, offering opinions about what would happen in the second half and what Sven's strategy would be.

'As you all know, young Liam gets married this afternoon and, on behalf of all the bar staff and regulars, we want to wish him well.' A large cheer went up as Jack battled on.

'Order, order...' shouted Rob who must have known what was coming.

'We would just like to... shut up, will you... present you with a gift so that you will remember the best day of your life even more. Everybody in the pub has put a bit in so we hope you like it.'

Liam couldn't believe it. It was a beautiful watch with the inscription on the back 'Liam & Kate 7/06/02'. For once, he didn't know what to say and ignored pleas for a speech.

'Thanks, everybody,' was all he could muster.

The second half began and England started to take control of the game. Liam couldn't believe what he was seeing. An England team was actually passing the ball around. He was still worried when he saw that Veron had been replaced by Aimar, the young Maradona lookalike, but England were playing brilliantly.

Owen's early second-half chance as he burst through was met with a massive collective gasp as it flew past the post and there was near pandemonium when an 'unfit' Beckham ran half the length of the pitch and poked the ball just wide of the goal.

All the lads were pumped up by now and the England chant was going round the pub. Liam was upset when Heskey was substituted as he thought he had played brilliantly. Everybody then thought they were in dreamland as England put what seemed a million passes together before Sheringham smashed a volley from the edge of the box, which the keeper parried. Spuggie started to jump all over Liam in his normal hyperactive, overexcited way, but it had started to get more tense as England decided to sit back. When Michael Owen was substituted for Wayne Bridge, the pub went quiet.

'Are you taking the piss, Eriksson? What you trying to do, give us a heart-attack?'

Liam could see the sweat pouring from Giant's forehead as he screamed at the screen. The pub was now like a sauna. Liam looked at his new watch; two minutes to go. The Argies were now all over England.

'Please God... please God... please God... '

At special times like this, Liam always tried his best to see if there really was a main man and to see if he was listening. Right to the final whistle, the Argentineans were pouring forward, but, as Liam closed his eyes to try and visualise Beckham picking up the World Cup, the pub exploded. All the boys hugged each other in one central scrum as they jumped up and down. Paddy jumped towards Liam. 'Fuckin' hell, look, Liam.'

As they continued to bounce up and down, Paddy pointed towards Fat Bainesy who had spun round on his bar seat and was actually smiling.

'Jesus, even he's happy!'

'Come on, Liam... we better start getting ready.' Paddy then brought Liam back to reality as he presented him with his suit holder and, along with another 14 of the lads, they headed towards the beer garden to get changed.

The banter by now was flying as Liam checked the time. 2.20pm. Still 25 minutes to go to beat the bride to the venue.

'Do you write your own scripts? It doesn't get any better than this.' Rob jabbed Liam in the ribs and put his other arm round his shoulder. Liam couldn't help but laugh as he looked round to see all the lads in various states of undress trying to get their suits on.

'Who wants to borrow me instant shower?' Browny threw his deodorant on to a table.

Liam knew as he opened up his suit holder he was going to be in for some fierce stick.

'You're fuckin' joking, aren't you?'

Only Paddy had been allowed in on the secret that Liam was wearing a different jacket to the rest of them and the cheers and laughter that started when Liam whipped his gold jacket out proved that it had served its purpose.

'You bloody poof! You can't wear that!'

Tony ruffled Liam's hair, as he looked him and his jacket up and down.

'Suits you, sir,' shouted Simon and Rory added, 'Trust Liam to try and upstage the bride.'

He was only joking; he didn't know that it was Kate's idea and that she'd even chosen the jacket.

'Car's here. Come on ushers, do your job. Get these idiots to the church.'

Liam and the ushers were met with a massive round of applause as they made their way back through the pub. A few whistles broke out and old Stan joined in with the 'What the fuckin' hell is that?' chant.

Liam was loving it as he climbed into the car with Paddy. 'This is it, boss. Get your serious head on for an hour or two and show Kate how much you love her. Remember, this is her day.'

Liam knew exactly what Paddy meant. He had a habit of taking over occasions even if he didn't mean to, but he realised this was Kate's moment, and he knew it was time to be serious – for the time being anyway. That's what Liam loved about Paddy and the rest of the lads. They knew when to have a laugh, but most of the time they also knew when to behave themselves and keep each other in line.

Liam closed his eyes for a few minutes and allowed himself to think of his mum, and look back on some of his happiest times with her, moments that had them both creased up with laughter. The good times far outweighed the bad and he knew that this was the day that would help to banish all his demons completely.

'Liam, we're here, mate.'

Paddy touched Liam's shoulder and gave him a broad smile as the groom opened his eyes.

'I don't know what you were thinking about then, but keep that big daft grin on your face for the rest of the day. Come on.., your public awaits.'

36
Thank You
Saturday, 8 June 2002

L iam looked at his beautiful sleeping bride. What a day... what a night. He couldn't believe how fantastic everything had been. England beating Argentina and marrying the girl of his dreams... life could not get any better. England going on to win the World Cup would just about top it off.

He laughed as he remembered telling Mad Al and Spuggie that, if England reached the World Cup Final, he would fly back from his honeymoon to watch it with the lads. He now started to have a panic attack. What would he do if England *did* get to the final? He hadn't really thought about it and he would have to cross that bridge if it happened. Would they be able to change their flights? Would Kate agree to fly back? He didn't fancy watching England win the World Cup in some hotel in St Lucia, no matter how beautiful it sounded.

He started to think back over the previous day to put

that possibility out of his mind. Everything had gone perfectly, from the moment he arrived at the church and everybody had a laugh with him for wearing the gold jacket, right until the end when he managed to perform his marriage duties at the end of a magical day.

The speeches had been brilliantly received with Liam nearly managing to outdo his Best Man with what Rob described as a 27-minute world record attempt for the longest groom's speech. He hadn't gone over the top about his mum not being there, but a number of people had come up to him afterwards to tell him she would have loved his story about her being the best mum in the world. His poem about her had also received a massive cheer. His Uncle Brian had hugged him, crying, telling him that the poem said everything about his mum and finished by saying that she'd be watching over Liam at the wedding, proud as punch.

Paddy hadn't been too hard on Liam, with the Best Man's speech concentrating on his good points. However, he made sure he got in the 'wetting the bed' story by presenting Kate with a double bed–sized safety sheet, much to the bemusement of her mum and dad.

Kate's dad's speech was also fantastic and, after some beautiful words about his daughter, he finished by thanking Liam for making his daughter very happy. He also said how very proud he and his wife were now they had acquired another son, which made Liam feel a little choked up for a while.

When they had the first dance to Dido's 'Thank You', Liam and Kate had clung to each other and kissed all the way through it, but she had laughed as soon as the song had finished and the music exploded into 'Everybody Needs Somebody' by the Blues Brothers.

Along with the Best Man and ushers, Liam had donned the trademark black trilby hat and dark sunglasses and they had danced their practised routine. Throughout the celebration, the dance floor was filled with laughing, whirling, gyrating friends and family.

Overall, the night had been fantastic with even the DJ commenting that he'd never seen so many people up dancing – or, at least, attempting to dance. The England result had helped because the majority of guests arriving for the evening do were a little worse for wear, but in a mood to party. When the DJ started playing 'Three Lions' and the theme tune to *The Great Escape*, which he had thoughtfully added to his collection, the place went mad. Later, when Wolfman did his strip to 'Thriller', the place had erupted again and nobody seemed that perturbed at the sight of him walking around 15 minutes later still semi-naked trying to find his pants. Browny eventually gave him his trousers back after Kate's nana had nearly had a heart-attack as he passed by her table. This was not before Mad Al, 'for a laugh', had attempted to set Wolfman's hairy back on fire.

Thinking back, Liam couldn't remember anything going wrong. He couldn't think of anyone they'd invited not being able to be there, and he was also surprised how much fun Kate's family, relations and friends had been. His own sisters had cried as Liam and Kate had emerged after the wedding, and he'd managed to have a good chat with them at the reception. James wouldn't break his alcohol ban even to toast the happy couple, but he had tried to dance. Liam's dad looked like he had enjoyed a great day as he was carried out of the venue by a number of his sisters over from Ireland. No family arguments at all, which was great.

The exploits on the dance floor were also eye-popping. One of Kate's nurse friends Rachel had even topped Spuggie's dancing exploits near the end by walking across the dance floor on her hands while wearing a short skirt. Liam laughed to himself as he remembered Paddy getting slapped on the back of his head by Anna for getting too close to the action.

Liam now looked at the bedside clock – 6.45am. Their early-morning breakfast would be arriving in 15 minutes' time as they had to be at the airport by 8.30am. He tried to remember what time he and Kate had made it to bed and laughed as he recalled Simon forming a guard of honour in the Residents' Bar before getting everybody to sing 'All You Need Is Love' as they went to bed.

It had been a struggle to find a seductive way of peeling off Kate's beautiful dress after about 15 bottles of Budweiser. However, the sex they had then hadn't just been for the sake of it, although it was a bonus. Liam had still managed to make love to Kate because he had somehow sobered up the minute the honeymoon-suite door had closed. They had then been alone for the first time that day. Well, he had felt like he had sobered up; Kate would probably have a different perspective when she woke up. Liam made a mental note to thank Mad Al for the Viagra tablet he'd slipped him an hour or so before the happy couple had retired to bed.

Remembering the energy they had managed to

summon up and the way they had managed to share an earth-shattering climax together started to make Liam feel quite horny again. He looked at his new wife and then had a peek under the quilt. The king-size bed made it easy for him to slide to the edge. She would never know, he thought, and he didn't want to wake her yet. He wrapped his fist around his todger just as there was a knock on the door. Shit – breakfast in bed. Another knock woke Kate and she turned to look at Liam.

'Liam, thanks for giving me the best day of my life.'

Liam smiled at his new wife.

'No, thank you... I love you.'

They cuddled in close to each other. Liam hoped that, once they'd eaten breakfast, Kate would finish what he had just started.